"Set in a beautiful and exotic country besieged by political and religious struggles, *Loveswept* is a compelling story of a young Turkish woman's romantic encounters that transcend deep cultural differences. A must read. Once you start, you won't be able to put it down."

Helen S. Astin
Distinguished Professor Emeritus, UCLA
Co-author of *Women of Influence, Women of Vision*

Loveswept beautifully portrays how the political and cultural transformation of a country deeply impacts personal lives. Standing at the crossroads between traditional values and a modern life, Neri must battle societal expectations on women as well as overcome her fears. Her journey is a journey of reclaiming one's own identity.

Almila Ozdek, Ph.D. English
The George Washington University
Washington, DC

www.parkgatepress.com

Loveswept

www.dionysusbooks.com

In memory of my parents

Loveswept

A Cross-Cultural Romance of 1950s Turkey

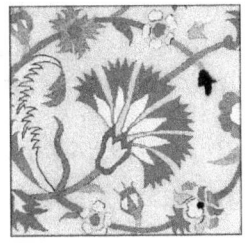

by

Engin Inel Holmstrom

Dionysus Books / Parkgate Press

Publishers Online!

For updates and more resources, visit
Dionysus Books and Parkgate Press online at

www.dionysusbooks.com
www.parkgatepress.com

Cover design by Yüksel İnel and Dionysus Books
Cover image from a painting by Engin Inel Holmstrom

ISBN-13: 978-1-937056-50-6

Library of Congress Control Number: 2011940194
Library of Congress Subject Headings:

Fiction.
Fiction in English.
Fiction (Istanbul, Turkey)
Fiction--Political aspects--United States.
Fiction--Psychological aspects.
Fiction romance.
Fiction--Social aspects.
Fiction--Women authors.

First Edition November 2011
[Parkgate Press: Dionysus Books reference number: 005]

Loveswept

Part I

What is deep, as love is deep, I'll have
Deeply. What is good, as love is good,
I'll have well. Then if time and space
Have any purpose, I shall belong to it.
If not, if all is a pretty fiction
To distract the cherubim and seraphim
Who so continually do cry, the least
I can do is to fill the curled shell of the world
With human deep-sea sound, and hold it to
The ear of God, until he has appetite
To taste our salt sorrow on his lips."

Christopher Fry
(From The Lady's Not for Burning)

1

He could not get rid of the image of corpulent pashas lounging on silk cushions, leering at near-naked dancing harem girls. The ship was approaching the Dardanelles and he had never been to Turkey before. He knew almost nothing about it except what he had seen in Hollywood movies. He remembered a line from an encyclopedia: the Ottoman Empire collapsed and was replaced by a secular republic in 1923, only twenty seven years ago. He had read in school about the battle the British had fought with the Turks and lost at Gallipoli. He had not been born then and his knowledge of history was limited. The ancient Roman walls near his Northumberland home had always interested him more than his own country's wars.

He peered into the darkness. He could see a wedge of light appearing beyond the mass of the Anatolian plain. On the left, the sliver of land jutting into the Aegean Sea was shrouded by mist. He loved working the late shift. The stars, the silence of the night interrupted only by the pulsing machinery and the soothing sound the ship made cutting through the inky sea heightened his senses, making him feel at rest with the world.

The pilot-room door opened and the captain walked in.

"Good morning, sir, couldn't you sleep?"

"Slept like a dog. Didn't want to miss the strait." Reilly—the captain—liked Bill, his young second officer whose interest in foreign lands reminded Reilly of when he too was young and full of wide-eyed enthusiasm for unfamiliar sights. That old feeling was still there although years of roaming the seas had somewhat dulled its urgency. He always suspected that the dissatisfaction with the known was why generation after generation of men went out to sea and endured its hardships and loneliness.

"We are approaching a very ancient land, Bill. You know what's just behind that hill where the sun is rising? Troy. Helen of Troy and her old story of lust, jealousy, and destruction."

Bill smiled, amused. "We are probably going over the skeletons of the thousand ships that her face is said to have launched, once upon a time." They both stared at the sea which was just beginning to come alive with the golden light of dawn.

Captain Reilly walked over and studied the open chart, then pointed towards the Gallipoli shore. "And just over there on a beach, thanks to British arrogance, my father died in 1915 with thousands of other Irishmen."

This was news to Bill. "In Gallipoli?" He regretted the doubt in his voice. "I mean, I thought it was mostly Anzacs who fought there."

The question lingered and was broken by the appearance of Mr. Basu, an Indian passenger, aboard on business. Mr. Basu had a clipped British accent: "No, thousands of Indians, mostly Gurkhas, also died in Gallipoli. I believe the overall death toll for British and Dominion soldiers was over forty thousand."

"That many?" Bill raised an eyebrow. "I had no idea."

"Churchill's folly," said Reilly, "and all for nothing."

"Why did we lose? Weren't the Ottomans called the Sick Man of Europe?" Bill, though not cynical in nature, always felt skeptical of reasons justifying war.

Reilly shrugged his shoulders, staring at the hill where he hoped his father's remains were buried in the English cemetery.

"Maybe not everyone can be conquered and colonized," said Mr. Basu, a knowing edge to his voice.

The awkward moment that followed was broken by the first rays of sun hitting the windows on the Gallipoli side of the strait. As they watched in silence, one by one each window was lit, the colorless glow revealing soft waves breaking on a sandy shore. Then a sweet sound rose from the village, the muezzin's first call to prayer, just as another voice joined in from the Anatolian side. They had all heard the Muslim call to prayer before but there was something mystical in its call, the harmony of its voice echoing between the shores. In this unfamiliar land, Bill thought, people were waking up to pay homage to their God and pray for His blessings. A shudder went through his body. A new day was dawning and he felt a mixture of anticipation and uncertainty in his breast.

2

It was still dark when her aunt's maid woke her up. Neri was groggy, having not slept well. She was too excited about going home for the spring break from school.

She washed quietly, taking care not to wake anyone. Going to a boarding school in İstanbul, Neri spent most of the weekends at her uncle's flat in Maçka, an exclusive section of the city. She and her cousin Alp were close, having grown up together, and her aunt Beria made sure that Alp took her along whenever he and his friends went to the movies or parties during the weekends she stayed with them. The boys treated her as a member of their tight-knit group. However, they were overly protective, glaring at any young man who dared to approach her. No doubt considering it inappropriate to flirt with the close relative of one of their own, they were making sure that no one else would either. Still, Neri enjoyed going out with the boys even though she sensed that her presence sometimes interfered with their romantic escapades. If they ever complained, it was always behind her back.

Her aunt Beria was like a second mother to her, loving and supportive. Neri did not feel hurt that no one had bothered to wake up and see her off. On the contrary, she felt proud, interpreting it as proof of their trust in her. In contrast to other people, her uncle and aunt agreed with her parents that it was perfectly all right for a young Turkish girl to travel alone. She cherished her family's confidence in her. It made her feel independent. They always treated her the same way they treated her cousin. She had never heard the word 'no' simply because she was a girl.

She finished her cup of tea and her breakfast of sourdough bread, quince jam, cheese and olives, kissed the maid goodbye and went out, closing the door quietly behind her. She walked down five floors with her small suitcase and opened the heavy iron-and-glass art deco gate of the apartment building. Its elongated tulip design never ceased to fascinate her. The air was cool and a little damp. The cobblestones shone under the street lamps.

The street was almost deserted. Most of the apartment buildings were still dark with only a few windows lit. She walked up to the corner where the grocer was opening his shop. Wafts of freshly-baked bread made her mouth water. On the opposite corner vegetable stands were being organized into fine arrays of colored shapes where purple eggplants, green peppers, red tomatoes, and yellow lemons competed for attention even in the dark.

She rounded the corner just as the tram to the Sirkeci train station came to a stop. She got into the first-class car with its red cushioned seats. The inside already had its usual smell of slightly wet wool and human bodies. There were three older men who glanced at Neri with surprise and a young male student who looked at her with interest. She was used to being stared at. One saying Turks liked to utter was that gazing at a beautiful woman was not rudeness but a blessing—a saying Neri suspected was coined ages ago by some dirty old men. God knows she had heard it enough. She put her nose to the window and vacantly observed the outside—a good tactic not to catch anyone's eye, particularly the young student who would interpret it as encouragement. She did not want any hassles.

She loved going home but she also loved her school. It was a private American-run institution with a large campus perched on a forested hill overlooking the Bosphorus. The strait's mesmerizing

19

colors visible through the sweet-smelling wisteria in the spring were a constant distraction to the young girls in class, "with their heads in clouds and hearts only God knows where" as her exasperated English Lit teacher once complained.

Classes were taught in English by native speakers. Many of them were old spinsters from England who had been teaching in Turkey for years. The crop of younger teachers was mostly American. They had two or three-year contracts and were themselves only a few years older than their students. She preferred the older teachers who were more patient and more invested in their students. The others still bore the stamp of distraction, the self-centeredness of youth. She detected a touch of sadness in the older ones. Her fertile imagination fed by the novels she was reading attributed their sadness to broken hearts, to beaux lost in wars or romantic tragedies fit for the golden age of Hollywood.

There were more people in the tram now, more students, mid-level bureaucrats who had to be in their offices before their bosses, and shop keepers on their way to start a new business day. Every seat was taken. Many passengers were standing, knuckles white on the straps. No one was talking. Everyone was still sleepy or had too much on their minds. Neri tried to imagine what bothered them: money or love problems? She opted for love. At age eighteen, she was a hopeful romantic.

Now they were going over the Galata Bridge that separated the Golden Horn from the Sea of Marmara. Hundreds of brightly-colored fishing boats bobbed up and down in the wake of ferryboats, themselves puffing up ugly tufts of dark smoke out of their stacks as if to signal the displeasure of their captains. Why no boat ever capsized in the busy harbor was one of the mysteries of life in İstanbul.

Finally, they were at the Sirkeci train station. She got her ticket, boarded the train and settled into a first-class compartment. It was a six-hour journey but one that passed quickly. She loved reading and today there was no one else to interfere. Being an only child, books and later the movies had become her major source of entertainment and means of escape from the loneliness she now and then felt. They filled her imagination with make-believe sights, tastes and sensations, enriching her psychological world and sometimes feeling just as real.

Soon enough Neri was at her destination. She closed her book and got her suitcase. When the train door opened, she flew into her father's arms. He kissed her on both cheeks and scrutinized her face.

"Neri my rosy-cheek girl, you look wonderful, not tired at all. Did you have a good trip?"

"Yes, I did, father."

"Did anyone bother you for traveling alone?"

"No, father, no one did. I was alone in the compartment anyway."

"I better get you home quickly. Your mother is waiting for lunch. She told Yusuf to prepare a feast with all your favorites."

Moments later they climbed into his red convertible which her mother always mocked as too flashy and too "teen-agey". It was an hour's drive but time passed quickly once they started talking. Neri was eager to tell him about a young man she had met from Robert College, another American-run school in nearby Bebek. The two schools shared social occasions all year long which fostered serious romances, often leading to summer marriages after graduation.

"So far he's invited me to two parties at Robert College, and I'm thinking of inviting him to one at our school." Neri explained.

"You like him?"

"Yes, I do."

"Why?"

"I don't know... He's nice...and listens to me." Metin laughed.

"That's how I caught your mother. You better be careful Neri, you know your mother wouldn't allow you to get serious with anyone before you graduate."

"*Babacığım*," Neri replied, using the word of endearment for 'father'. "I'm just going to ask him to a party, not marriage!" Metin stared at his daughter, detecting a trace of uneasiness in her light tone that shouldn't have been there.

"What's wrong, Neri? Having boyfriend troubles?"

She shook her head, too quickly Metin thought. "No, nothing's wrong. It's only that sometimes I think I'm different from most other girls. My aunt says I'm too outspoken."

"Does she? And what's wrong with being outspoken?"

"Nothing, I guess, unless you're *too* outspoken, which according to my aunt, I am."

"Your aunt is a very reserved, quiet person, Neri. Don't try to be like her or anybody else but yourself. We love you just the way you are, my dear."

Neri already felt much better and tried to forget the unease she sometimes felt with the boys she met...that they expected less challenge and more submission from her. Why can't they be like her father? It was so easy to talk to him. No wonder her friends who came to their summer house in İstanbul liked him so much. He was relatively young and not at all stern or distant like her friends' fathers.

Quite simply, Neri loved her father because he was involved in her upbringing from day one. He had read her stories, challenged her in games and puzzles and taught her to swim, sail, ride horses and play tennis. Like her mother, but more so, he was not judgmental and listened with patience and understanding. And he was always on her side.

Neri remembered how their first year in Tekirdağ, someone had objected to the sight of her bicycling to school, despite the fact that she looked like a nun in her black uniform with its white starched collar and heavy black stockings. Furious, Metin had marched into the principal's office and told him what he thought of this stupid objection of "moral conventioneers"—he called them—of all small towns who believe it their God-given right to monitor the behavior of everyone, always behind closed curtains. The principal had wisely agreed that he didn't like these people either who always remain anonymous, relying on vicious gossip as their method of influence. "No wonder most of us fear slander more than anything else," he'd said, promising he would not bother Metin again with such trivia. They'd shaken hands and parted as friends.

However the moral conventioneers' objections to Neri and her family's ways did not end with the bicycle incident. They objected to her mother too, particularly to her habit of riding her horse alone. Then the next summer, they were shocked to see Neri, then a mere girl of twelve, swimming out in the open sea rather than inside the women's bathing *hamam*, an ugly walled wooden platform built on stilts just a few feet from the shore. Eventually the town came to accept her family's "modern" ways mostly because of the business her father had brought to town and because of her mother's generous charitable activities. The next year, the mysterious disappearance of the women's bathing *hamam* was attributed to her parents but probably the new governor who was rumored to be progressive had something to do with it. Still the sight of half-naked women frolicking openly in the sea was said to remain a sour subject for the town's elders even though increasing numbers of old men seemed to have developed a sudden interest in walking along the coastal road which offered a full view of the beach.

But the differences between her family and the small town did not bother Neri at all. She was convinced that her world was the right one and that eventually everyone else would catch up with the new vision of Turkey as a modern and enlightened country, free of religious restrictions and superstitions. And she liked the pretty little town, particularly the way it came into view right after ascending the last hill. She clapped her hands like a child and held her breath as they rounded the top of the hill, and there it was set against the shimmering Sea of Marmara with its houses of dark wood, red-tiled roofs, and mosques with white minarets.

The sight of a large ship on the horizon slowly making its way toward the town was unexpected, however. Rarely did any ship of considerable size ever stop in Tekirdağ other than the weekly boat from İstanbul. They lost sight of the ship as they descended into town and thought little of its arrival.

Going through the main street Neri noticed some new stores, including a record shop, but her father said the selection was very bad. They passed her old middle-school, the public park and the row of old houses known for their intricate lattice work and arrived at the unpaved coastal road with its full view of the sea and the beaches. Eager to get home, her father did not slow down but maneuvered expertly around numerous potholes. The ship now loomed larger, having already docked. They could see the flag clearly and read its name, S.S. Clintonia.

"It's a British merchant ship," Metin said, "I wonder what it's doing here." Suddenly Neri's heart filled with sweet anticipation as if she'd just opened a new book with its promise of unknown experiences, sensations and adventure.

3

After docking and securing the ship, Bill took his binoculars to view the small town. Crowded neatly around a gentle hill, Tekirdağ looked peaceful. Doves cooed in the distance and now and then the quiet was interrupted with the shrieks of children playing soccer in a nearby clearing. A tree-lined street went straight up from the pier and disappeared. There was little traffic. It surprised Bill to see women in European clothes, not covered at all but exposing an elbow here, a knee there. A few were wearing loosely-tied kerchiefs.

Most unusual for a Muslim country, he thought as the familiar sight of men playing backgammon in front of coffeehouses caught his eye. Bill and Captain Reilly had bought a backgammon board in Bombay and were trying to learn the game but it was not easy. Near the harbor, nestled among plane trees was a remarkable small mosque with a single squinch dome and a slender minaret. Its proportions looked exquisite.

"That's an incredibly beautiful mosque," remarked Captain Reilly echoing his thoughts. Bill pointed to a row of wooden buildings by the sea.

"They look interesting too, don't they?" The houses all had ornate carved panels and latticed balconies. Some were painted white and shone bright in the midday sun. Others were left to the mercy of the elements and darkened to a rich sheen of almost pure black. They attested to the town's rich past. Before Bill and Reilly could turn their heads, a red American-made convertible with the top down came out of the street behind the houses and sped away on a bumpy dirt road. It was an incongruous sight. They heard a chuckle behind them.

"Nice looking town, full of surprises," added Mr. Basu surveying the scene. "That's a very interesting mosque."

"How old do you think it is?" asked Bill, "I'd like to know. Do you think we can go inside?"

"Well, we could ask the Turkish customs official. I saw one coming up the plank," said Reilly. "That is, assuming he speaks English."

The official did speak English and not badly either. A thin man with a sallow face all lost in a too-large jacket, it appeared he had gone through some terrible ordeal and lost weight. Coughing, he explained he had "good news and bad news," a phrase he'd picked up from American movies and was eager to use. "The bad news is that there is a problem with your import papers. We had to send them to the main office in İstanbul before we can allow you to unload your cargo."

Reilly was not pleased. "And how long will that take?"

"Oh, maybe a week, maybe more." This was indeed bad news because an idle ship's crew usually got into trouble after a few days.

"As you see," said the Turkish official, "our town is small and lacking amenities. There is a movie house but they usually show old American movies, sometimes dubbed into Turkish. There is only one restaurant in town and, of course, no bar."

"And the good news?" Bill asked.

"The good news is that we have a very modern wine factory here, and I'm sure the owner would be happy to show you around. Shall I call him and arrange for a visit? Many of his wines have already won medals in international wine festivals."

A wine factory in a Muslim country was a total surprise—one that also offered an intriguing diversion. They were happy to accept the offer and asked whether he would accompany them to the factory, but the customs official apologized saying he needed to stay in bed and get well. Then he gave them the necessary permits to go ashore and pointed the way to the factory. It was on top of another hill a couple of miles from the town. With their binoculars they could make out its gate.

The road to the factory looked paved and snaked up along neat rows of grape vines extending as far as the eye could see. A thick grove of trees crested the hill before a house with a wide terrace facing the sea. A large factory building painted white with a tall chimney stood nearby. A rail system connected the factory with a private pier. All in all, it looked like an impressive and modern enterprise.

"Before you go, can you tell us something about that small mosque?" Bill asked. "Would there be any objection to our visiting it?"

The customs official brightened. He liked showing his knowledge to foreigners. He told them that it was built in 1553 by the famous Ottoman architect Sinan whose mosques were usually monumental. "This one is one of the few small mosques he built and is considered unique. It's also famous for its 'faience' decorations and beautiful rugs." He took out a piece of paper and wrote something on it. "You can visit the mosque anytime as long as it's not during these prayer hours," he added, pleased with himself.

4

Neri took her parents for granted. The sun rose in the east, the stars came out at night—well, most nights anyway—and she had wonderful parents. That was that, an irrefutable fact of her life. So what was she supposed to do? Face East and Praise Be to Allah? She didn't always appreciate her friends' repeated reminders of how lucky she was. More importantly, she sometimes resented the pressure of having such loving and wonderful parents placed on her. The fear of disappointing them was as familiar as breathing in and breathing out.

Neri not only loved but idolized her mother, the star of the family, or more accurately the sun—however erratic—around which she and her father orbited. In a totally patriarchal culture, her family was indeed strange, particularly her mother Nermin who was uncharacteristically outspoken and aggressive. In mixed company, Nermin was less reserved than most other Turkish women and had no qualms about contradicting or challenging men, including Neri's uncle, who was the head of the entire Ersoy family. Even Neri's father would not dare question his brother who was eight years his senior. Most Turkish women behaved like Neri's aunt Beria who when agitated simply kept quiet, tilting her head to one side and smiling her enigmatic disapproving smile. Tradition dictated that one showed respect to elders expressed by decorous behavior and obedience. Defiance was not tolerated. Circumlocution was an art taught to and practiced with incredible focus by most young Turks, except Neri who was unconsciously adopting her mother's independent and headstrong character. Strangely enough it was her mother who more than once had reprimanded her for not holding her "witty tongue." Each time Neri had shrugged off the reprimand but this morning what her mother said bothered her. It had come out of the blue when they were listening to Neri's new jazz records. In the middle of Neri's account of her busy life at school, the movies she'd seen, the parties she'd attended, and the new boy in whom she "might or might not" be interested, Neri noticed her mother's face saddening inexplicably. Leaning over, Nermin had taken hold of her daughter's hand in a tight grip.

"Try to be more like your quiet proper aunt Beria, Neri," she'd said. "You don't have to show your brilliance all the time. Sometimes it's better to remain in the shadows. Much safer that way."

This enigmatic message troubled Neri. What did her mother mean? Weren't women as good as men? Maybe even better since they had the responsibility of bearing and educating the future generations. At least that's what Atatürk had said when he convinced the Turkish parliament to give women voting rights and full equality with men in 1934. So Neri kept on wondering why it was so important to appear submissive when women were supposed to be just as good as men.

Besides, Neri had seen how people lived in other countries. When she was a small child, they had spent a year in Paris where her father attended the Institute Pasteur for his degree in oenology. They'd taken the Orient Express from İstanbul to Paris journeying through Bulgaria, Greece, Yugoslavia, Italy, Switzerland and finally France. Her excitement had soared every time they crossed a new border and entered a new country. She was fascinated with languages she did not understand and the sights of unfamiliar towns with their peculiar houses, dark peaked roofs, and church spires much taller than the ones in İstanbul.

In Paris they went to museums, the theater and the opera, exposing Neri to art and the magic of make-believe. Her eager mind fed on these new experiences. Long after they were forced to return home because of the start of World War II, she could close her eyes and imagine herself in the paintings she'd seen or in the stories she'd witnessed on stage. Paris enlarged both her actual and fantasy worlds but left a lingering hunger in her for truth.

The world was no longer uniform but a complex mask of national and individual lifestyles. People varied greatly and what made sense in her country could be totally nonsensical elsewhere, lessening the sanctity with which all her country's moral conventions were presented as absolutes.

These rules of propriety, the endless list of *dos and don'ts,* were serious thorns in Neri's otherwise rosy life. She never forgot the day her uncle let her enter a room ahead of him, saying now that she had turned sixteen, she'd become a young lady and ladies always entered first. Neri had felt like a princess until her aunt reminded her that being a lady meant paying attention to decorum and doing what was expected of her. So despite her parents' permissiveness, expectations of others weighed heavily on her. She found them near suffocating. She accepted the fact that she had to please her parents and her family, but everyone else too? Why did she have to worry what the neighbors would say? Sometimes she really envied the life of American teenagers depicted in the movies. They seemed to be so free and happy. Always dancing and singing—at the drop of a hat. In comparison her life was more like those Victorian women in British movies with their buttoned-up morality. Still, Neri knew she should not complain. She enjoyed freedoms most other youngsters in villages or small towns could not even dream of. She had a good life.

Neri surreptitiously touched the little blue bead her mother had pinned inside her bra to ward off the Evil Eye. For good measure, she knocked on wood three times and muttered *Maşallah,* asking God's protection for her blessings.

Inconsistencies in her personality didn't bother Neri. It was a price one paid for living in a patriarchal authoritarian culture. Like most Turks, she knew she was fatalistic. Unlike many others, however, she was also an optimist. Deep down on an intellectual level, she had serious reservations about the existence of God, yet she constantly prayed to Him for help and protection. She was afraid of the Evil Eye; she said *Maşallah* and *İnşallah* as often as anybody else despite the fact that she had been raised to believe in herself, to trust her judgment and ability to shape her own destiny.

These inconsistencies, instead of paralyzing or handicapping her, seemed to function in a way that gave her strength, each contradiction helping her to push further away the restricting barriers imposed on her by her culture, thereby enlarging her own personal space and sense of freedom. On those rare occasions when she was gripped by claustrophobia which she suspected was induced by the constant cultural expectations of others, she made herself feel better by literally visualizing herself lifting its oppressive weight with her two, sometimes strong, sometimes not so strong, arms. While Islam helped define the identity of most Turks, defying its confining strictures and the authoritarian nature of Turkish culture provided her with a sharper definition of her self...a characteristic she knew she'd inherited from her mother whom she adored.

Upstairs in her old room, she put on her tennis outfit and glanced at herself absent-mindedly in the mirror. She was looking forward to her tennis match with Emre, the young man who was interning with her father to become a winemaker. But she was worried too. The academic pressures of her school did not allow much time for tennis. She and her roommate Leyla often spent their free time walking beyond the tree-covered campus to a clearing called The Plateau that overlooked the Bosphorus. The view was magical, a constant display of shifting colors and movement. Neri also loved watching the big merchant ships go by, trailing the horizon to foreign locations. They reminded her of the wider world and its teasing mystery—one day, she would think, one day. Neri was happy here but also yearned for something more. She wanted to travel to faraway places and meet exotic, unknowable people. She was restless, an "overeducated chick" as Leyla called her, whose hatching time had come.

Before leaving her room, Neri gazed at the merchant ship moored at dock. She was curious. Rarely did any ship of that size settle into port for so long, especially without unloading cargo. The vessel was waiting for something or someone, and fancifully Neri's mind told her heart it had come for her. This raised her spirits for the effort of the afternoon. She went out, determined to win her match.

The wooden benches surrounding the court were already crowded with the wives and children of the factory's managerial staff, many of whom lived on the premises. These matches provided a source of much needed distraction and entertainment. They applauded her as she approached the court.

Neri was surprised to see her father's accountant was there with his elderly mother. She would never have imagined the old woman to be a tennis enthusiast. She went and kissed her hand and placed it on her forehead—a sign of respect.

"Neri, how are you my beautiful girl?" asked the old woman. "We are all counting on you to win today."

Neri laughed. "I'll do my best but don't tell me you've a bet going on?"

"Only with my son," she answered.

"You mean you bet against me?" Neri asked the accountant.

"Only because I've seen Emre practice every day," he said with an apologetic smile.

"Well, we'll see what good it'll do him today," Neri smiled and moved to greet Emre who had finally arrived.

"Hello, Neri," he said, kissing her on both cheeks. Since last year, they'd become good friends after discovering their love for books and tennis. "You heard about the bets?"

"Yes, I also heard that you've been practicing every day. That's cheating, isn't it?"

"Not if your practice partner is your father!" They both laughed out loud. Neri's father had a unique style on the court, rarely moving but forcing his opponent to do all the running. She remembered the humiliating losses she had suffered at his hands.

She would not wish them on anyone, including Emre himself! Neri started playing cautiously but just as she was getting her game back, her mother called her, sounding urgent.

"Neri, your father wants you in his office immediately."

"Mother, we just started playing. Please call and tell father I'll be there as soon I finish teaching Emre a lesson!"

"Neri, I'm not kidding. You have to go now. Your father needs you."

However Neri pleaded, Nermin would not listen: Neri had to go and see her father. She was being summoned! Not comfortable receiving such blunt orders from her father, Neri apologized to Emre, promised a rematch soon, made a swift curtsy to her audience and started running.

5

It had been an easy walk to the factory. The afternoon sun was pleasantly warm and the calm sea, flat as a sheet, mirrored the deep blue of the sky. Only the sound of gentle waves lapping disturbed their thoughts. They had no problem at the gate. A young man in clean overalls was waiting to escort them to the factory. The hill was steeper than it looked from a distance but the climb felt good after the ship's cramped cabins.

As they neared the top, a little breeze stirred the blossom-scented air, infusing it with something sweet and intoxicating.

"What's that smell?" asked Bill.

"It's cognac," said the captain, inhaling sharply. He looked pleased. "Obviously they produce cognac too. I'd love to have a bottle or two." Bill smiled, knowing Reilly's affinity for drinking.

A man in his mid-forties greeted them in front of the factory and took them to a large well-furnished office. He had light-brown hair, hazel eyes and a friendly face. He was not swarthy, did not have a big belly or mustache and was dressed in gray slacks, white shirt and a tweed jacket, looking very much like an English country squire. 'So much for my Ottoman stereotypes,' thought Bill. The man had a strong handshake and said something in Turkish which no one understood. Then he tried French, asking the whereabouts of their English-speaking customs official? Mr. Basu explained in his limited French that the poor official was sick with flu. The man introduced himself as Metin Ersoy and he would be happy to show them around. It quickly became apparent, however, that without an English translator the conversation would become very cumbersome. Nevertheless, their host smiled and told them to sit and relax.

"The cavalry is coming," he said and went to his desk to make a phone call.

After a few minutes the door opened with a bang and a young girl appeared, dressed in pristine white shorts and halter-top. She was clutching a towel and a tennis racket. Her face was flushed, with chestnut-colored strands of hair sticking to her wet forehead, and she had big almond shaped hazel eyes with long lashes. She was breathing hard, and when she saw the visitors she stopped short, surprised.

All three men stood up, just as startled by her appearance as she was of them. There was a quick exchange of words between the girl and the proprietor. She nodded and faced the visitors.

"I apologize for the way I look. My father told me that you need a translator. If you'll excuse me for fifteen minutes or so, I'll go and put on something more appropriate." With that, she flashed a big smile at her father and left. They all sat down again except Bill who was still standing staring at the closed door.

"Hey Bill," said the captain, "you can sit down now." Metin smiled. This was not the first time he had seen men's reactions to his daughter.

6

Neri did not remember how she got home. She did not remember what she told her mother. She did not remember how she took her shower and dressed. Her heart was beating wildly. All she remembered was a pair of blue eyes, blond hair and a tall lean body. He might not have been the handsomest man she had ever seen, yet when their eyes had connected, she had felt a jolt in her heart she had never experienced before. She ran back to the office on feet that seemed not to touch the ground.

This time she took care to enter the room demurely. She was now changed into a navy blue skirt and white shirt. She had flat shoes on, carried a lightweight sweater, wore no makeup or jewelry, and she looked like a student but no less alluring or exotic than before. Her father introduced her as "Neri, short for Neriman." It was obvious he was proud of her. Neri shook hands with the men, avoiding the second officer's eyes.

"Your English is very good. Where did you learn it?" asked Captain Reilly.

"I go to an English-speaking private school in İstanbul."

"You speak with a slight British accent. Are your teachers British?"

"Some of them, yes."

"Are you here on holiday?"

"Yes, it's spring break."

"Well, it's our good fortune then, isn't it, Bill?" Reilly clicked his fingers, trying to snap Bill out of his trance, but Bill could only manage a nod, his eyes still locked on the girl. To break the mood, the girl's father decided to start the tour of the factory which turned out to be larger than they expected. It was very modern and clean. Workers in rubber outfits and boots were washing down the white-tiled walls and the floors. The large copper distillers had been rubbed down to a bright sheen. The place was strangely deserted and quiet. Metin explained that their busy time started in late summer when grapes were brought in by land and sea and the long months of wine-making began.

In addition to wine, the factory was also producing brandy, the first of its kind in Turkey, named "*Kanyak.*" Metin told them that the French Cognac industry had taken him to court in Paris, protesting that he had stolen their trademark. However when he'd explained to the French judge that *Kanyak* literally meant "burn the blood" in Turkish, an apt name for brandy, the judge had appreciated the play on words and had ruled in Metin's favor. He now offered a little brandy to his guests and they all wholeheartedly concurred that it was appropriately named.

It took them nearly an hour to go through the factory. Then they went down to a large underground cave where wine was kept for aging. The place was stacked with all sizes of oak barrels, some taller than ten feet. Before Metin let his guests taste his wines, he personally demonstrated how to appreciate them. He poured wine into a glass and tapped it with his nail.

"Always hold the glass between your forefinger and thumb, like this. Then hold it up to the light and examine its color and clarity. Before you smell it, swirl the wine round and round in the glass to release its odor, then take a big mouthful, not a sip, and slowly chew the wine in your mouth which allows you to taste all its complex flavors. Finally, you spit it", and he did so into a copper bowl on the concrete floor, adding with a twinkle in his eyes "the last step is not mandatory."

It didn't take long before they started feeling good. No one seemed inclined to make use of the spit bowl. Captain Reilly in particular was in his element. He was telling jokes that Mr. Basu found hard to translate into French. Most of the humor was derived from listening to the Irish brogue but Neri was able to make her father understand. Meanwhile, Bill remained unusually quiet.

Just as they were returning to the office, a truck passed them, full of men in football outfits, cheering and waving flags. Metin went to congratulate them while Neri explained that the factory's soccer team, The Grape Crushers, had just won another victory in a nearby town. Captain Reilly and Bill glanced at each other. This was certainly good news. Most of the sailors played soccer and it would boost their morale if they could play against the factory team. It was decided that there would be a match after the sailors had a practice run or two. They all walked down the hill to the soccer field which was just off the coastal road.

To Neri's delight, Metin suggested that they should accompany their guests back to town. They could see if her mother, visiting a friend there, would be ready to leave. They started walking, Neri and Bill falling back and for the first time beginning to speak to each other. He found her warm and easy to talk to but what fascinated him most was her transparent face that belied her cool and proper demeanor. Every time she looked at Bill, a deep pink crept over her high cheek bones, and her eyes flashed warm with feeling. She is just as bewildered as I am, he thought. The intensity of her physical pull was overwhelming and he had already stopped resisting. Trying to appear calm and collected, he found himself asking her inconsequential questions.

"Tell me something about these old houses we're approaching. I noticed them when we docked. They're beautiful."

"Forgive me," Neri answered, "I don't know if you're familiar with the plight of the Spanish Jews called the Sephardim?" Bill shook his head.

"Well, it's a fascinating story. After the fall of Granada to the Christians in the 1490s, the Spanish Inquisition went after their

Moorish and Jewish populations. The Ottoman Sultan Beyazid offered the Jews of Spain asylum and settled them in provincial centers all around the Empire, including here in Tekirdağ. They all did very well but one particular Sephardic family prospered both financially and politically. About two hundred years ago, Sultan Osman III gave the family these beautiful houses, one for each son, in appreciation of their services. Over the years, most of their descendants immigrated to İstanbul or to other countries but one branch stayed here until last year when they moved to Israel, including my mother's best friend, Rachel. However, the whole family returned a few days ago, and my mother went to welcome them back."

"Why did they come back?"

"I don't know the details, but my mother said Rachel complained about the prominence of the German-speaking Ashkenazim Jews in Israel. I guess they did not make the Sephardic Jews feel welcome. Mother said Rachel was happy to be back home."

"You definitely have an interesting history here."

"Oh, we have all sorts of interesting stories. See that white house up on the hill over there? It's a museum now, but it once belonged to a Hungarian prince and his family who also sought asylum in the Ottoman Empire. If you are staying long enough, I can show it to you." She looked at him hopefully.

She wants me to stay repeated a little voice inside Bill's head. He tried to control his excitement. "I don't know how long we'll be here. We're waiting for official documents from İstanbul before we can unload our cargo."

Neri had no idea of the effect she had on him. She was too occupied trying to conceal her thoughts and feelings. She felt light-headed just because she was near him. The unknown sensations surging inside her were clouding her reason. It was as if she had opened her eyes to a lost wonder of the world in human shape for the first time—a beautiful but intimidating experience. As much as she wanted to, she could not bring herself to look at Bill. Those two soft lines on each side of his mouth that gave his young face a slightly sad and vulnerable look were irresistible to her. She wanted to reach up and smooth them. Instead, with all the admonishments about 'how a good girl should behave' ringing in her ears, she found it absolutely essential to keep her eyes on the back of the three men walking ahead. Now and then, she pulled her sweater tighter around her chest. She did not want Bill to hear her loudly beating heart.

Metin led them to a shortcut to the harbor—a narrow lane by the sea at the back of the old wooden houses. For a split second Neri's and Bill's hands touched and electricity went between both of them. They jumped apart and looked at each other, laughing nervously. Neri noticed that the tip of his blond eyelashes glittered in the sun like gold dust. She missed a step and he swiftly grabbed her arm to steady her. His hand was cool but it burned her skin.

Just about the same time, as Neri's mother was enjoying a cup of tea at Rachel's living room, one of the women looked out the window and gasped. "Nermin, you better come here," she exclaimed over her shoulder. "Your daughter is walking hand in hand with one of those English officers from the ship."

Nermin rushed to the window just in time to see Neri lift her face and beam a full smile at a tall, handsome man who was beaming back. Nermin could feel the heat of his smile all the way up to where she was. With a mother's instinct, and remembering her own courting days for a moment, she knew exactly what it meant.

"Excuse me a second," she said, turning toward Rachel: "May I use your back door?" and without waiting for an answer, she ran down two flights of stairs and burst out, startling everyone.

Immediately Metin introduced his wife, trying not to laugh at her sudden appearance. She was a good looking woman in her early forties with bright brown eyes, a dazzling smile, and a shapely body. She was wearing a fashionable silk print dress. Her hair was darker than her daughter's and cut to perfection. The girl had inherited the good features of both parents, Captain Reilly thought. Are all Turkish women going to be so striking and why do they have this stormy way of bursting through doors? Is this something weird about their culture that I've never heard before?

"I hope my husband offered you a taste of some of his fabulous wines," Nermin began in flawless English. Then with an apology, she took her husband aside and asked him why their daughter was walking side by side with "a strange young man?" Nermin sounded agitated and added that everyone inside Rachel's house was talking about them. She omitted telling her husband why she was so upset: the electricity between Neri and the young man was detectable all the way down from the second-story window.

"What are you doing, Metin?" she whispered in annoyance. "You know how this town likes to gossip. They'll be talking about this one for weeks."

"Let them talk, for God's sake," Metin replied. "That's what people here do all the time, right? They'll be leaving in a day or two. I'm just trying to be hospitable."

Nermin glanced at her daughter and the young man. The way they were trying to appear normal while, Nermin imagined, they were experiencing a tidal wave of emotions nevertheless touched her heart. Taking Metin's arm, she turned back towards the three men and invited them to dinner for the next day. She whispered to Metin she had to go back to her friend's house: "I'll be home soon, but right now I have a lot of damage control to do," she said, pointing to a bunch of women grinning from the upstairs window, beckoning her back inside.

Returning to the ship, Bill remained on the deck a long time, watching the receding figures of father and daughter on the dirt road. They were hard to see silhouetted against the orange sun setting beyond the hills. Captain Reilly came out looking for his shipmate. Bill's reaction to the girl had not escaped his attention and he was getting concerned.

"Bill, how are you doing? Are you alright?"

"Of course I am. Why do you ask?"

"Since you saw that girl, you look as if you've been smitten."

"Smitten?" Repeated Bill and coughed. "That's an odd word, isn't it? I don't know if I am smitten or not."

"I do." Reilly stared at him, his face blank. Bill felt obliged to continue.

"I really don't know how I feel. Maybe bewildered is a better word. I've never met anyone like Neri. She is very attractive. In fact, the whole family is appealing. They made me feel at ease as if I'm connected to them. Does that make sense?"

"Sure but you better watch out, my boy, this is no place to get involved. We are in a Muslim country and you've heard the stories about Muslim parents, haven't you?" He looked up as the sun touched the horizon. "Besides, don't you already have a girl back in Newcastle?"

"Yes," Bill said, with a sigh more like regret than admission just as the sun disappeared.

7

The next day felt like torture to Bill. He knew there was no chance of seeing Neri until the evening and he was restless and uncharacteristically short tempered. Everyone on the ship tried to avoid him.

In the afternoon, the ship's football team walked to the field and started practice. Half way through, Bill saw Neri turning the corner on her bicycle. His heart pounding, he approached her. But before he could say anything, the sailors, startled by the sight of a gorgeous girl in shorts, began to cheer and whistle, infuriating Bill. Neri, blushing, answered their cheers with a smile and half wave and then quickly took a bag of oranges from her basket. Since he was closest, she handed the bag to Bill and left without looking up and pedaling fast. Bill turned and faced his teammates. No one dared meet his eye.

Finally the long day waned and it was time to go to dinner. Already Bill was quiet and deep in thought while the captain and Mr. Basu kept a steady stream of conversation going, speculating what kind of food they could expect and who was going to win tomorrow's soccer match.

They were met at the door by Neri and escorted to a large rectangular room on the first floor that served as dining and living room combined. The dining section had a round table, already set for dinner, and an antique buffet displaying a well-executed oil-painting of still life overhead. The living room had big comfortable chairs in soft shades, lots of books, an upright piano, a British-made radio-gramophone set, more oil paintings on the walls, and fresh flowers in vases. It was a discreet and welcoming room, more Western than Oriental, and not at all what Mr.Basu told them to expect. The view of the sea from the terrace was beautiful—a complete panorama if not for the ship in the harbor.

The food was delicious: a mixture of lamb and vegetables, served with rice, followed by Çoban Salatası—shepherd's salad, they were told—of thinly sliced tomatoes, green peppers, onions, parsley and mint in a lemony vinaigrette dressing, and börek—a dish of delicate flaky pastry filled with white cheese. Instead of dessert, a fruit and cheese plate was wheeled in with a good bottle of rosé wine. Finally they settled in the living room and were served Turkish coffee in tiny porcelain cups. The conversation turned to winemaking again, and with Nermin translating, Neri moved near Bill who was inspecting her family's book collection.

"Have you read all these books?" He asked.

"Yes, I have."

"You must love reading."

"If you're an only child, reading becomes your only source of entertainment." Bill glanced at her. Was there a tint of regret in her voice?

"Next to listening to music," she added.

"For a young person, you seemed to have read an awful lot of books . . . . I'm impressed."

Was he making fun of her, Neri wondered? But no, he seemed sincere, almost eager to please her.

"I started very early," she said. "Actually, it's a funny story."

"Tell me, please."

"Well, I was in first grade and was just beginning to learn to read. We were visiting a friend who had a cottage up on the Black Sea coast. They had set up a cot for me in his library. I couldn't

44

sleep so I took a book down, opened a page and tried to read it. It wasn't easy. But I persisted and was finally able to make sense of most of the page."

"Do you remember the name of the book?"

"No I don't, but it was about a woman and a man. They were standing in front of a garden gate...I remember the gate was white, and they were saying goodbye." All of a sudden Neri's face flushed. She hesitated.

"And..." he prodded.

"This is embarrassing... Anyway what I read was that while the man was holding the woman tight, she moved her hips causing the man to groan." Her face was red now. How charming, Bill thought: she's shy.

"Remember I was about six then and had no idea what was happening." I don't, not even now, Neri thought. "So the next morning I told my mother how I'd tried to read a book and asked her about the sentence I didn't understand. I still remember the look she gave my father, trying to hide her amusement."

"Did she explain?" Now Bill was really curious.

"Of course not! But they told me that if I studied hard, I'd one day be able to read all these books. I think this is when I realized that there was a mysterious world of grownups out there waiting for me to discover. So I became an avid reader."

"This is a wonderful story," Bill said sincerely.

"It was one of those 'Aha!' moments for me," Neri replied, glancing at him quickly. Why was it so difficult to look at him? She felt that if she stared longer than a split second, she'd never be able to take her eyes away.

Just then Neri heard her mother calling her. "Neri, Captain Reilly wants to hear some of your records."

Neri had a large collection of American jazz and dance records. Captain Reilly chose Glenn Miller's *Moonlight Serenade*, one of Neri's favorites, and asked Nermin to dance. Seeing Bill approach her, Neri's heart missed a couple of beats but once she settled in his arms, it felt natural as if she had never left them. Dancing was the only legitimate way for most Turkish boys and girls to get physically close without disapproval. It was a running joke among the students that all it required for romance to kindle in Turkey was a plain dance floor and not moonlight.

Neri liked going to dances; she was a normal girl with normal appetites but at eighteen she had never been kissed let alone made love. She had enjoyed dancing with some boys more than others. Still, like most of her friends, she was an innocent when it came to sex. Human sexuality was a taboo subject among parents who assumed their daughters would quell such feelings and wait for the right man and marriage. Although some girls back at school were rumored to have 'necked,' maybe even gone all the way, it had taken Neri and her roommate Leyla a biology class in their sophomore year before they had absolutely realized what came after all the kissing and necking they had seen in American movies. The confusion of trains going through tunnels and fireplaces suddenly flaring up was beginning to make sense. Still, however much the girls pretended to be sophisticated when it came to sex, none of them had any idea what havoc a strong chemistry between a man and a woman could cause.

Only now, Neri had begun to learn it fast and furious in Bill's arms.

As for Bill, he liked the feel of his hand on her back covering nearly all her small waist. Neri's head came just under his chin and her hair smelled vaguely of lemon blossoms. Whenever she glanced at him through those long eyelashes, he could feel a sensuous shudder going through his body. Trying to compensate for the rush of strong emotions, he found himself chatting like a clumsy teenager.

"Do you go to dances a lot back in school?"

"I don't know what you mean by 'a lot' but yes, we have a couple of parties each year with the boys from Robert College, a school nearby."

"So you already have a boyfriend?" He'd been dying to ask that. Neri seemed pleased with his question.

"I don't have any steady boyfriend yet," she answered. The emphasis on 'steady' and 'yet' did not escape Bill's attention.

"Good," he said shamelessly and laughed so hard that her mother Nermin, still dancing with Captain Reilly, turned and looked at him sharply. Bill had a feeling that he was making a spectacle of himself, that everyone was beginning to suspect his feelings.

But what was he feeling? He did not know how to describe it. It was crystal clear, however, that every time he thought about leaving Neri, the pain he felt deep inside alarmed him. He wanted to explore why he felt so helpless and confused. He knew he had sailed into uncharted waters. The irony of the expression was too much: nice place for a navigator to be! The whole thing was too sudden and too intense. He felt as if he was watching someone about to step off into a deep crevice with no idea how to prevent it.

When finally Reilly mentioned it was time to leave, Bill thought the night ended much too quickly. He wasn't ready to figure things out yet—just wanted to stay with this mysterious, untouchable Neri a little longer.

8

The soccer match the next day turned out to be a disaster for the ship's crew. They were fit but out of practice. During the first half, the factory team scored eight times, embarrassing both the winning and losing sides. Even the workers and their watching wives began cheering the ship's crew and gave Bill a big hand when he scored a goal. During the second half, the Grape Crushers slowed down their game, scoring only three more times before the game came to a merciful end at eleven-one. The crestfallen sailors cheered up, however, when they were presented with two cases of wine.

Before leaving, Bill told Neri of the group's interest in the mosque and she agreed to meet them there an hour before evening prayers. At the appointed hour, Bill was not surprised to see Metin standing with his daughter in front of the mosque. He was beginning to realize that they were not going to be left alone. He remembered what Captain Reilly had said about Muslim parents.

Although small, the interior of the mosque looked spacious with sunlight streaming through stained-glass windows adorned with geometric flower designs. With the exception of Mr. Basu who had been to İstanbul, the sailors had never seen such motifs before.

The brilliant reds, turquoises, and blues of the windows were repeated in the richly-colored tiles on the walls and the intricate carpets. Reilly thought the overall impression was a celebration of life, unlike the gloomy feeling he sometimes got in the dark churches of his country. When he expressed his admiration, Metin muttered that the mosque was built four hundred years ago, but for so many centuries now, "religion had done nothing but sucked the life out of people." This was an odd statement, Reilly thought, but maybe the girl had made a mistake in translating. Otherwise it would appear Metin was not a fan of his own country's religious devotion.

After they left the mosque, everyone returned to the ship except Bill who was busy talking to Neri and appeared reluctant to leave. Despite his misgivings, Metin felt obliged to ask the young man over to the house. They drove home in silence. Nermin was gracious in her welcome when she opened the door but directed a discreet inquiring look at her husband, who just shrugged his shoulders. After an aperitif, they all sat together in the living room trying to have a conversation, but it wasn't easy. Neri seemed distracted and reluctant to share Bill. So Nermin decided to hurry the evening by telling the cook to prepare dinner early.

While Neri was helping the maid to set the table, Bill started looking over their book collection again, this time more carefully. Many were Turkish translations of European and Russian authors, some of whose names he could recognize but most he had never read. The same was true with the books in English. Bill felt disappointed in himself. Then he saw the chess set. It was the most beautiful and unusual set he had ever seen. The ivory pieces were exquisitely carved and naturally yellowed with age. He picked up a knight and rolled it between his fingers. It felt warm and alive. His reverie was interrupted when he heard Metin say something.

"My father wants to know if you play chess," explained Neri.

"Yes," he answered, a little reluctantly.

"You are not going to humiliate the poor man," Nermin commented in Turkish.

"Nobody plays chess to lose," Metin said, a boast Neri heard each time her father defeated her. "It's the game of life," he would say. He believed that chess was an excellent tool to teach "life strategy", winning by following the rules as well as learning to face the consequences of wrong moves. But Bill was not humiliated, at least not totally. It took him a respectable half hour or so before he acknowledged defeat. He had thoroughly enjoyed the game although he had been continually on the defensive. Metin was a formidable opponent, much better than Captain Reilly.

"How was he?" Nermin was curious.

"Not bad at all," responded Metin in Turkish. "He is skilled, creative, and not at all sneaky. But he lacks killer instinct. He needs challenge. You know what, I really like him."

Me too thought Nermin. They knew very little about the young man but he was likeable. He displayed two qualities highly valued by Turks: he was polite and respectful. All in all, he came across like a decent human being, plus he was charming and good looking. The fact that he was attracted to Neri made him even more appealing to Nermin. Neri sensed the change in her parents. Was Bill growing on them?

After dinner, Neri and Bill settled on the carpet in front of the gramophone and started listening to music. Her parents stood awkwardly at the other end of the room, uncertain what to do.

"Let's go upstairs," Nermin said.

"No, that's not proper or wise." said Metin. "Let's sit here and play bezique."

"This is ridiculous!" Nermin whispered. "We look like those narrow-minded suspicious parents you're always ridiculing. What do you think is going to happen? He's not going to ravage her under our roof. You said you liked him."

"I do, but do you think it's wise to encourage what's brewing?"

Nermin glanced at her daughter and Bill. Two beautiful youngsters, she thought, caught up in a web of mutual attraction, unaware of the heartache waiting for them. She sighed. "We may already be too late. You know, Metin, Neri is eighteen. This is the first time she's been attracted to a man. She can't remain a child forever. Maybe it's time for her to sample what you once called the elixir of first love?"

Metin laughed. "Did I really say that? I probably wanted to impress you with my vocabulary. But in this case, if she gets any more involved, elixir or not, her heart is going to be broken."

"Well, that's life, isn't it? Maybe she'll learn something from it. Besides aren't you the one always saying we should trust our daughter?"

"I trust her, and I'm even willing to trust him. What I don't trust are those feelings they're experiencing. Have you forgotten how we couldn't keep our hands off each other? Don't you remember how you used to pretend that you were Greek whenever we got caught kissing. You felt ashamed, and you thought that your shame would be doubled if they knew you were a Muslim girl. Well, what was improper for a Turkish girl then is still improper for our daughter now."

"Hmmm...you were never this rational when you were making love to me!" She looked at him accusingly but with a glint in her eyes.

"That's my point. Rationality and physical attraction don't go together. There'd be no books at all if people fell in love rationally."

"So you think they are falling in love?"

"Well, if they are, it has to be a record! It's been only three days since they met, for God's sake. How on earth could we have known that they were going to get this serious in such a short time?"

"Well, we did, remember?" The memory made her smile warmly and Metin gave her a long loving look. Maybe the fact that they had themselves experienced such a strong attraction the first time they met explained their reluctance to interfere. They both knew that in no other house in Turkey would a father and mother allow their daughter to sit so close to a young man and then watch the sparks fly. On top of that, they knew very little about Bill other than he was a foreigner.

Oblivious to her parents' worries, on the other side of the room Bill and Neri were discussing the mosque. They seemed to have intuitively come to the conclusion that it was safer to talk about impersonal subjects. They knew that if they started to

51

discuss what they were feeling, at some point they would have to admit the strangeness of their situation. Such an admission could surely destroy the consuming magic of the physical attraction they were enjoying regardless of its hopelessness.

Bill had been fascinated by the mosque but it also bothered him. He did not understand his discomfort totally, but he was beginning to realize the mosque's exotic beauty was a reminder of their different worlds. He did not consider himself religious, but he was still a Christian, and she was a Muslim. It didn't seem to matter right now, but wouldn't it matter if they got serious? Would it be possible for them to develop a serious relationship?

The idea was appealing but hopeless. How could he get a girl like Neri? Her parents would never allow it. Besides what was he going to do, take the girl from her comfortable home and lifestyle, drop her in a little house in Newcastle and leave her alone while he roamed the seas? Was this his plan? What kind of a life was that for a girl like Neri? So what was he doing here, Bill asked himself, dreaming like a love-sick teenager, allowing his emotions to obliterate his rational mind?

But they were such overwhelming, such irresistible emotions. Plus what was the real harm? He knew the answer but he chose to ignore it. He allowed himself to be caught up in the euphoria since he met Neri. He was captivated by her, by her parents' kindness and hospitality, and by Turkey too. He pushed aside all negative thoughts. He opened the floodgates of sensations and let them carry him without knowing where to, but he was certain he had never felt this happy or reckless before.

Suddenly he noticed that Neri's voice was sounding serious now. She was saying something about the War of Independence the Turks had fought against invading armies after World War I, omitting mention of British forces. But in general he had no idea what she was talking about. Frequently he would get so lost watching her face that he could not follow the conversation. Bill mentioned how excited he was when he first saw the shores of Gallipoli. He was about to blurt out where Captain Reilly's father was buried when Neri informed him that her grandfather had died there. Bill's face clouded over. They both bent over to pick a new record to play.

"What on earth are they talking about?" Metin asked his wife. She couldn't tell whether he was exasperated or angry.

"I don't know," she answered. "But Neri seems to be doing all the talking and he seems to be doing all the listening. Actually, I don't know what he is doing. He seems to be in a trance like you used to be."

"I still am, my dear wife." Nermin smiled sardonically, looking for a split second just like her daughter. Bill witnessed the connection between Nermin and Metin, not without a touch of envy.

"Your parents are still in love," he whispered to Neri. "How did they meet?"

"It's a long story," she laughed.

"I like long stories."

Neri frowned at Bill, but he didn't seem to be teasing her. "Well, first I need to tell you something about my grandmother Belkis. She was a remarkable woman. Her family lived in Erzurum, a city in Eastern Turkey that changed hands between the Ottomans and the Russians a couple of times. Despite war, her family managed to survive and prosper. Grandmother Belkis had no siblings and her parents doted on her and when she was only sixteen, she met a dashing cavalry officer and fell in love but her parents were dead set against the marriage."

"But why?" Asked Bill, interested.

"I guess they thought the marriage would end in tragedy since they knew the lifespan of a cavalry officer in the Ottoman army was very short. They tried to tell her how difficult her life would be, the hardships she would have to endure following her husband from one dangerous spot to another . . . . " Neri suddenly stopped, seeing the odd look on Bill's face. Only now the odd parallel between her grandmother's story and her current situation with Bill dawned on Neri. She blushed, avoided looking at him and continued rapidly. "Despite their objections, however, the marriage took place and soon after my grandfather's unit was stationed elsewhere."

"This story is like a movie, isn't it? You should write about it."

Neri smiled. "Who knows, maybe I will one day. Anyway, over the years she had four children, three sons plus my mother who was the second youngest. When my mother was two years old, her father was killed fighting the Russians. Grandmother Belkis could not return home to her parents because it was very dangerous in the hills around Erzurum, fierce fighting was going on with the Russians and against Armenian insurgents. So she gathered her four children, the youngest son newly born, and fled to İstanbul. The conditions in Anatolia were horrible then. There were no trains and the roads were not safe with Kurdish bandits preying on travelers. Yet by herself and with four kids, my grandmother made it safely to İstanbul. She then managed to provide a good education for all her children, including my mother who was, I think, her favorite. I always thought that my grandmother and uncles adored my mother, could never deny her anything and overlooked, if not encouraged, some of her unconventional behavior."

"Is your mother unconventional?"

"Oh yes," Neri laughed, glancing at Nermin with affection, "so very much! The summer after graduating from lycee, my mother got a job teaching Turkish literature at a Greek school while attending English-language classes at the local YMCA. Both very unorthodox activities, so I'm told. A young Turkish woman working was a rarity in those days, particularly at a Greek school. Attending the American-run YMCA which catered mostly to men was totally out of the ordinary, but then, that's my mother!"

You're exceptional too, Bill was quietly thinking.

"Anyway the school was on the other side of the city and she had to take the ferry. She soon noticed that a young good-looking man was following her diligently on the ferry every day. However, the odd thing was that although he would persist in sitting across from her, he would never look at her directly but would bury his face in his newspaper. This continued day after day, which my mother found both interesting and irritating. So one day my mother took matters into her own hands, and when they got up to leave, she tugged at his sleeve and asked why he was following or ignoring her?"

"You're right. She's not only unconventional but has gumption too."

"I know. You can imagine my father's surprise. I once heard him describe how stunned he felt realizing that in the blink of an eye he'd become the prey instead of the hunter!" Neri and Bill smiled nervously, wondering about the roles they were now playing.

"Once they started talking, my father convinced my mother that it was not a lack of interest but 'his concern for propriety' that had kept him from talking to her. He'd thought that it would be insulting to address a nice Turkish girl out in public without a family member or friend. Still, he couldn't help himself. So every day he tried to come up with an excuse to speak to her while watching her through a tiny hole he'd poked in his newspaper! "

"Well, that's an original approach I've never heard, and I thought English reserve was complicated!" Bill laughed but something about the story bothered him. The convoluted way the Turks seemed to handle the most natural boy-meets-girl ritual was puzzling. He wondered whether her parents would consider his behavior improper right now. He glanced at them, worried. They were still talking, seemingly paying little attention to him and Neri.

"So dating was not allowed in your mother's time," he asked.

"Of course not. But they kept seeing each other for nearly six months before their luck ran out. One day they were on a boat going to the Princes' Islands for a picnic, and my mother glanced up and saw her oldest brother sitting down the deck, glaring at her! The next day, my father went to my grandmother's house and formally asked her permission to marry her daughter, and that was that. So how did your parents meet?"

"Oh, nothing this dramatic, I'm afraid. My parents grew up in the same neighborhood and already knew each other. They were expected to get married, and they did."

"What does your father do?"

"Like me, a merchant mariner. I grew up mostly with my mother, sister, and younger brother. My father was always away at sea. My family life is...different from yours."

"It must have been hard on your father to be away from his family. Hard on your mother too." Then as an after-thought she added: "Why did you choose the same career even though you knew about the hardships it would impose on your family?"

"Because it was expected of me, I guess. In some ways, England is more of a traditional country than Turkey. From everything you told me, your country sounds like it's in a state of constant change. Nothing changes in England." A strange thought occurred to him. Neri may be bogged down with centuries-old traditions, but so was he. People in his class were expected to follow in the footsteps of their fathers and never strive for a better or different life. We'll see about that, he promised himself.

"How did you meet your girlfriend?" Neri looked down. "Captain Reilly told me that you had a girlfriend back home." Bill's face flushed.

"Similar story. We grew up in the same neighborhood and our parents have known each other for years. We went to school together and started going out. Whenever I came home on leave, it seemed easier to take her out than to try to meet someone new. It's become sort of expected, I guess." Bill stopped abruptly, realizing how lame, even deplorable, he must have sounded. What was he doing? Was he minimizing his relationship with his girlfriend back home because he thought that's what Neri wanted to hear? Or was he being truthful? Had he ever stopped and analyzed his feelings? Was the girl back home just a convenience? He began to fidget, totally uncomfortable.

Neri was sorry she'd asked such a direct question. Now Bill knew that she cared whether he had a girlfriend. Although a novice in the cat-and-mouse game between men and women, her intuition was shouting that revealing her feelings so early had been a mistake. It was not only the strategic love-mistake that bothered her. It was something more primordial and cultural. Like most Turks she'd been taught to be cagey. Fear of fate caused them not to profess their desires too strongly, even to themselves. You never knew when whoever was up there in charge of your fate would get offended and decide to punish you. Hubris was not tolerated. Better to let fate dole out what she'd already decided.

Walking back to the ship by the moonlit sea, Bill was lost in thought, but if someone had asked him what he was thinking, he would have found it difficult to explain. His head was crowded with images of Neri sitting close to him on the carpet, so close at times he could feel her body heat, or of Neri pointing at the complex design on a wall of mosaics in the mosque, her face lit with the multi-colored rays of sunlight from the stained-glass windows, her hazel eyes almost green now and looking incredibly beautiful. He savored the memory of Neri leaning over him at the table to take away his plate and her firm breast touching his shoulder for a split second sending shudders through his entire body. He pictured her soft lips curling up at the corners every time she smiled. He tried to imagine how they would taste.

Bill was twenty three and had made love to several women, yet he could not remember being so enthralled by anyone like this. He'd already started to make mistakes while working. His concentration was gone. When on duty, he forced himself not to think about Neri but she had a way of edging into his consciousness and quickly blotting out everything else. She had taken over not just the nerves in his body but his thoughts too. He had no memory before Neri, and after Neri, nothing else. She was an obsession he embraced with his body and soul. He was feeling so lightheaded and happy that he almost broke out into song.

Bill wondered what Turks sleeping peacefully in their beds would do if he started singing at the top of his voice. He began laughing and was smiling broadly while walking up the plank to his cabin. He was glad Captain Reilly was nowhere around to see him. Smitten, indeed!

9

That night an April storm struck the town with thunder, lightning and heavy rain. Each time a bolt of lightning flashed, Neri could see the ship, even at a distance, heaving up and down in heavy swells. It was a terrifying sight and with each flash, she became more and more anxious. She never liked thunderstorms. They always reminded her how fragile men were against nature's power.

"Go to bed, Neri," she heard her mother say just outside the door. "Don't you think they have experienced heavier storms than this? Come on dear, go to bed. You'll catch a cold. Besides, your father says it'll be a short storm."

Going to bed did not calm Neri down. She was basically a well-adjusted optimistic person, but somewhere deep inside her there was a seed of fear of nature that could grow into unreasonable terror. Maybe it was because she was living in a land where earthquakes were common. Or maybe it was the authoritarian and controlling Turkish culture that limited individual initiative, leaving everything to forces beyond one's control. For centuries people had toiled under the absolute authority of a strong central government and the heavy hand of religion that had dominated every aspect of their daily lives. That's probably why most Turks, including the so-called 'modern' ones, were so fatalistic, Neri thought. It was ingrained in their nature to expect the worst. Why else would they utter "*İnşallah*" and seek God's approval before starting anything new?

Years ago when she was only three, she'd watched a house burn. The whole Ersoy family was living together then, and everyone gathered on the top floor to silently witness the beautiful old mansion turn into ashes in the distance. Her father held her close in his arms. Her cousin was whimpering that he wanted to go to sleep, but Neri was wide awake. The fire had fascinated her. She was not sure what was happening but she thought the crimson flames shooting into the sky were beautiful. Then she noticed the expression on the faces of the grownups and their hush voices. Here the first seed of fear was planted, making her deadly afraid of the destructive power of man and nature.

The next morning when she woke, the sea looked innocent and calm with a few dark ripples skimming the surface. Turkish fishermen called these dangerously fast-appearing and disappearing gusts "black cats." The town and the distant hills looked uncannily close after having been washed bright and shiny by last night's rains. The air smelled of fresh earth, tinged with a sweet scent of wild flowers. At least the ship was moored, dark and safe at the dock. Neri felt relief and happiness filling her heart and ran down to breakfast.

It had been a tense night on the ship. The men had discussed waiting out the storm away from the coast but Captain Reilly was sure the storm would be brief. Even so, they had lost one mooring cable which had to be replaced in the dark. By the time they went to bed in the early hours, bone-tired and soaking wet, the ship was still heaving and groaning like a sick old woman. After a few hours of sleep, the first place Bill looked outside his cabin's door was up to the factory. In late morning sun the white building shone bright against a dark blue sky. There was not a single cloud to be seen. He stared at her window. Last night, he noticed the light had stayed on longer than usual in Neri's room. Bill was impatient to finish his chores and go to her.

"Off to the factory again?" asked Reilly when they met for lunch. The question made Bill feel uneasy. Deep down, he acknowledged he was in a precarious situation but he felt helpless. The idea of not seeing Neri was simply not acceptable. He excused himself and headed to the wireless room.

It was late in the afternoon before he was able to leave the ship. The air was cool and crisp and the fast walk helped clear his mind. There seemed to be no one at Neri's house which somehow upset him. He could not explain why he'd expected her to be waiting. Then he heard sounds from outside the house close to the tennis court. He walked around just in time to witness a fast-moving game between Neri and a man about his own age. The benches on the other side of the clay court were full of women and children. When they saw him, they motioned him to come and sit by them. By that time Neri had seen him and waved with a flash of smile.

They were friendly, he thought, these Turkish women. An older woman patted his back and said something which made all the others laugh. A young woman settled her baby on his knee, while the others chatted in Turkish, offering him candy and dried apricots. He had never tasted dried apricots before. When Neri turned and glanced at him with the baby still on his knees, she burst out laughing. It was an incongruous sight but he looked perfectly at ease.

He was watching her closely now. She was a good player but obviously distracted. The game was finally over after she faulted her serve twice. She shrugged and shook the young man's hand and introduced him to Bill, explaining that he was interning at the factory.

"One day Emre will become a serious competitor to my father as he will on the tennis court for me."

"I already am Neri," laughed Emre. "Remember, I just beat you!" Bill could tell that they were good friends and used to teasing each other, so he thought nothing of it. After she said goodbye to her audience, Neri and Bill began walking back to the house.

"We're being followed," Bill said, having noticed an old man behind them, scowling disapprovingly.

"Don't worry, that's Yusuf, our cook. He's been with us since my childhood. He's harmless unless you don't like his food." They entered the house through the kitchen and Neri asked Bill to sit in the living room and listen to music. She would be with him after cleaning up. As he moved away, he could hear Turkish spoken in the kitchen.

Yusuf had known Neri since she was five. She was like a daughter to him and he was upset she'd invited the English sailor – he'd almost spit the words – inside while her parents were away.

"How could you do this?" Yusuf asked. "You know it's not proper for you to be alone with a young man, an infidel and God knows what else!"

Neri smiled. "I'm not alone with him; you are in the house just a few feet away in the kitchen."

Yusuf could not be appeased. "Your mother is going to blame me for this," he said crossly.

"My mother already knows Bill's here today." This was the first time Neri had lied to the cook. Years ago he'd taught her to play marbles when she was a child and always prepared her favorite dishes. The lie hurt her. She felt ashamed and angry. She touched Yusuf's arm and asked him to please prepare tea.

When she got back to the living room, she found Bill standing by the terrace door staring at the sea. She could not read his expression. They were both ill at ease. This was the first time they had been left completely alone. Almost on cue, they took seats opposite each other, putting the width of the room safely between them.

Her brain was running at full speed and imagining all sorts of romantic scenarios. She was in his arms, and he was kissing her. She was touching those lines by his mouth. No, no...she was sitting demurely like a good girl, keeping the distance between them. Did she want to behave like a good girl? She couldn't decide.

On the other side of the room, Bill felt paralyzed. He wanted to take her in his arms and kiss her but for the few short days he'd been in Turkey, he'd learned enough about their traditions to know that this would be improper. Besides, he could not betray her parent's trust and hospitality. Suddenly, he got up and took both of her hands in his, standing at a respectful distance. She looked surprised, as if just awaken from a dream.

"I sent a telegraph to our London office this morning asking if there was a position open for me in our branch in İstanbul," he told her.

She was stunned. For a second she had the eerie feeling that she was still daydreaming. "Why?" she heard her voice asking.

"Neri, surely you know how I feel about you. I can't bear the notion that I may never see you again. If I can find work in İstanbul, maybe we could get together and see if this thing is real or not."

"What do you mean 'this thing'?"

He winced. "Neri, I am trying to tell you that I've fallen in love with you and I was hoping you had some feelings for me too. This has happened so quickly that I am totally confused and not thinking straight. Maybe I misread you. Maybe it was all wishful thinking on my side. Please, Neri, say something."

"It's not wishful thinking," Neri replied, throwing caution aside and looking straight at him with her doe-like eyes, making his heart lurch. They gazed each other for a minute before they heard her parents returning. Neither Nermin nor Metin was surprised to find them together. On their way home, they'd talked about it, hoping Bill would not be there; they were not surprised that he was.

After dinner, Neri and Bill settled on the carpet in front of the gramophone again, talking and playing records while her parents started their card game. It felt like an old routine, very natural, but Nermin made sure that all the curtains were open and every light in the house was on so that anyone walking by would see that Neri and Bill were not alone in the room. The mushrooming gossip was beginning to worry them. Bill's daily trips to the factory had been noticed and were the talk of town. In a small town, gossip was a major source of entertainment and Turks were good at it: nothing tarred a girl's reputation more than idle gossip. But more than her reputation they were concerned about how badly Neri was going to get hurt once Bill left. Acting like grim-faced chaperons was a futile gesture but was all they could do right now.

With her parents just a few feet away, Neri could not bring herself to ask Bill what his working in İstanbul would mean for them. The enormity of what she realized was an act of commitment on Bill's part and its overwhelming implications had scared her. She needed time to think but thought was difficult with him so near. Her body ached for him and her defenses were weakening.

Meanwhile Bill felt for the first time that he could read her emotions clearly, and he was beginning to realize that she wanted him just as strongly. This knowledge intensified his desire, making it painful. He felt compelled to get up and move away from Neri, startling her. He stood in front of the terrace door gazing out. The air smelled of lilacs, and the moon was big, glowing like an orange lantern, throwing copper-colored reflections on the dark sea.

"Neri you should see this moon," he exclaimed, more in control now. "It's wonderful!"

Neri's parents joined them and they all went out to the terrace. He noticed Metin had his arm around his wife, and he wished he could do the same to Neri, but this was not his home and Neri was not his girl. He wished otherwise with all his heart. The urge to belong was overwhelming.

"Wow!" said Neri.

"It's your wishing moon Neri," said Nermin.

"You wish on the moon?" asked Bill. "We wish on the first star of the night."

"When Neri was small, I tried to teach her how to wish on a star," Nermin explained. "You know, the whole 'Starlight, star bright, the first star I see tonight' thing, but she wouldn't buy it. She had her own ideas. You see, here in Turkey, we wish on the new moon but Neri always insisted that wishing on the full moon was a better idea because the full moon was much bigger, so more powerful as a wish-bestower than the new moon or any star."

"That sounds logical to me," Bill said, laughing. "Does it work?"

"I wouldn't know," Neri confessed. "When I was small, I was afraid to anger the moon with frivolous wishes. Besides I couldn't come up with anything to wish for. I was already a very happy child." She looked at her parents with gratitude. "I did have a wish once though, and it did come true."

"What was your wish?" Bill asked.

"To go to the American college and not the French Lycee my father wanted." She smiled at Metin but didn't translate what she had just said.

"I know," Metin said. "I was outdone by a moon." Bill realized Metin understood English much more than he'd let on.

"Anyway, it's better to keep your wish a secret, they say."

"It looks like a good wishing moon," Bill murmured, glancing at her. Something passed between them and they both gazed at the moon quietly.

This is not good, Nermin thought. They are now communicating without talking like old couples. How could they reach this level of intimacy in such a short time? This is not going to end well, she feared, feeling responsible. She and Metin had let things get out of hand. It had been a mistake to allow Bill to see Neri everyday. She didn't know how they could have stopped him short of being rude, but perhaps at the beginning they could have made him feel less welcome? Bothered and conflicted, Nermin asked if anyone wanted tea and they all went inside.

While waiting for tea, Neri said "Bill," addressing him for the first time with his first name, making him feel that another barrier had come down between them. "Tell me something that you would most like to do. Something you dream about." Bill lowered his eyes. He could not say what had immediately flashed into his mind.

"You would laugh at me but we sailors, we always fantasize about owning our own boat, sailing around the world."

"I guess you all love the sea otherwise you wouldn't be in this profession."

"How about you, Neri? What would you most like to do?"

"I would like to travel and see the world."

"Maybe you can join our little sailing group. I'll teach you how to sail."

She smiled. "You don't need to teach me. I'm already a good sailor." Neri's eyes twinkled as she told him that she'd been sailing since she was thirteen but in another April storm just last year, her boat had crashed onto the pier and broken into pieces. Bill was stunned. He would have never dreamed that one day he would come to a place like Turkey, meet a girl like Neri, fall in love with her, and that she would turn out to be a sailor too. We are meant to be together, he decided, we are 'soul mates', as if that answered all his worries.

"Tell me about your home town. Is Newcastle beautiful?"

"Newcastle beautiful?" Bill laughed. "No, not at all. It's a mining town, mostly coal. Maybe you heard the saying about 'bringing coal to Newcastle?' It's a grimy old town with a history going back to the Norman and Roman times. It takes its name from the castle built 800 years ago."

"We have a 500-year old mosque in İstanbul called the New Mosque."

"I'd like to see İstanbul one day," Bill said with a meaningful look. "Anyway, Newcastle is on the River Tyne and the countryside is beautiful, dotted with old mansions and castles. I wish I could show it to you."

"So do I," she said blushing. "You have a sister, you said. How old is she?"

"Seventeen and she wants to go to university." He didn't add she'd be the first in his family.

"That's good, isn't it?"

"Yes, and I'm going to help her get there. I'm saving money for her," Bill admitted, a little embarrassed.

"What about your brother?"

"He wants to be a merchant mariner, like my father and me." We're all in the same rut, he thought.

"Do you like what you do? It sounds like a lonely life to me."

"It is, but it's the only one I know. Up to this point I've never thought of doing anything else." He looked at Neri, trying to fathom her thoughts.

"And now?"

"Now I'm thinking of seriously changing my life. Neri, even if I can't get a job in İstanbul, I'll find a way to get back here, one way or another."

"Good," she said and they gazed at each other.

Just then Nermin told them that tea was ready. They all sat around the table drinking and talking. Bill asked why women in Turkey were not covered like in other Muslim countries. Neri said it was a hard question to answer.

"Some people argue that it is written in our holy book. But most people cannot read the Koran in Arabic, so they rely on what others say. I think many come up with interpretations that suit their beliefs. My father reads Arabic well enough to know that the only thing the Koran proscribes is modest clothing for both men and women. He says there's nothing in the Koran that explicitly states women should cover themselves from head to toe." Neri was silent for a minute, deep in thought. Bill did not mind. He loved watching her face.

"Over a thousand years ago when Turks were living in Central Asia," she elaborated, "women rode with their men, fought with their men, and ruled with their men. But after we accepted Islam as our religion, our customs started to change, slowly at first then rapidly after we began to rule over the Arab lands and adopt their ways. But you know what? Village women who work in the fields have never covered themselves. The change in the cities, particularly in İstanbul, started with the War of Gallipoli."

Not Gallipoli again, thought Bill.

"It was the demand for nurses that gave women a legitimate reason to throw away the veil. Eventually more work opportunities opened for women, changing the way they dressed. After Atatürk founded the republic, a law was passed banning the practice of coverage. My mother was lucky. She never had to cover herself."

"I can't imagine you in a black *abaya*," Bill said to Nermin.

She laughed. "I can't either."

66

"I personally believe that the tradition of forcing women to cover themselves has nothing to do with Islam but everything to do with the need of men to control and keep women at home, out of the public arena, unequal and dependent on them." Metin bent down and kissed Neri on the cheek, although he claimed to understand not a word she said. She looked beautiful even when angry, her spirits elevated by her convictions.

"You would have made a good suffragette, Neri," Bill said. She beamed, pleased with the compliment. "Your father said something about religion when we were visiting the mosque the other day, remember? What did he mean by it?"

"My father practices Islam in his own way, privately. He believes in God, he gives alms to the poor, he reads the Koran to pray for the souls of his loved ones who have passed away, but he doesn't attend mosque and is a strong secularist. He rejects the Sharia Law. He believes in the separation of state and mosque and disapproves of the intrusion of religion into public life. All of which, of course, makes him a heretic in the eyes of many."

"I'm not familiar with the Sharia Law. What is it?"

"It's God's law, the law of Islam. Mind you, not necessarily what's written in the Koran but what's added over the centuries. Any so-called religious man can come up with his own interpretation of Koranic verses and introduce another 'no-no' to rule our lives. I call it men's law! It's what relegates women to secondary status. It's what allows old men in many other Muslim countries to marry under-age girls, practice polygamy, and treat their daughters like cattle, to be traded off for profit or pleasure."

"Too strong a language, Neri," Nermin chided.

"It's not, mother, and you know it. You had three brothers who treated you like a human being and a mother who valued you. Even today with our secular laws women do not have the same rights as men. For instance, why is it always the fathers who're given the custody of their children and not mothers?"

"Change is a slow process, Neri. Traditions don't die quickly; it requires time...and speaking of time," Nermin looked at Bill apologetically. Bill realized with a start that it was almost midnight, and he got up to leave.

Taking advantage of her parents leaving them alone at the door, Bill held Neri's hand and whispered: "Neri, I do love you with all my heart. Even if I can't get a job in İstanbul, I promise you that I'll find a way for us to be together. This is something I want more than anything else in life and that was my wish earlier on the moon. You do believe me, don't you?" His eyes were pleading.

"I do," she said. "That was my wish too."

After Bill left, Neri said goodnight to her parents and ran up to her room, feeling strangely unsettled. Something had changed inside her. All the time when she was unsure about his feelings, she had been content, enjoying for the first time the overwhelming sensation of loving and desiring a man. But learning that he loved her had sobered her up. She no longer felt like a teenager. She had become a grown woman, in love and loved. For the first time in her life she felt responsible for another person and she was concerned for him.

Daydreaming was over. She could no longer run from reality. A life with Bill was a pipe dream. She knew her parents would never allow her to be with him since he was a foreigner, he did not live in Turkey, and he was 'just a sailor.' How many times she'd heard the saying that if you give too much freedom to a girl, she'd marry a drummer boy or sailor? And here she was, in love with one! Neri sensed they would get hurt but she had no idea how to prevent it. She sat on her bed defeated with tears on her cheeks.

Back in their bedroom, Nermin was trying to shed the strong sense of dread she had felt all evening. It was impossible not to notice the warmth and sexual tension between Neri and Bill. What had she and Metin been thinking about, letting things go this far? Were they allowing themselves to vicariously re-live their own passionate past through their daughter?

"Something has changed between them, hasn't it?" Nermin asked her husband.

"Yes, it's intensified. Maybe Bill told her how he was feeling. I hope she has some sense left to realize that the whole thing is impossible."

"They were acting blind to reason. He'll be leaving soon and it'll all be over. I can't understand how either of them could think this would end well or that we would let her get seriously involved."

"Nermin wake up! They are already involved. We both underestimated the strength of their attraction, and Neri's going to pay for our mistakes. Although I still don't know how we could have prevented it short of tying her down or sending her back to İstanbul."

Nermin sighed. She had never seen Neri act like this before. She'd thought Bill was just a girlish crush for her, one that would fade away after Neri returned to İstanbul, her friends and busy school work. Nermin now knew she was wrong. The young man's feelings seemed just as strong as Neri's, and her mother did not know what to do next.

10

While Neri was in the throes of despair, Bill was firmly formulating a path to secure his future with her. Learning that Neri returned his feelings had empowered him. He felt invincible. He knew there were many social and cultural obstacles to overcome, but he felt he was up to the challenge. He was beginning to question the wisdom of getting a job in his company's İstanbul office. It was a lowly job and might serve as a first step but offered no long-term solutions. He needed to change his whole life to be with her and to give her the life she deserved.

He was beginning to realize that his life had never been totally satisfactory. He had always felt restless and in search of something. Maybe that was why he had become a sailor, but adventures at sea had not given him what he was looking for. Now he knew what he wanted. But he also knew that his love for her and his dissatisfaction with his life were inextricably linked: to fulfill one he had to undo the other. Bill was convinced that if he concentrated on trying to be with her, he would find a way to escape his own life. She was his beacon, showing the way.

The things he had learned about Turkey had changed him, giving him direction. If a whole country can transform itself completely in such a short time, surely he could too. He had read somewhere that after World War I, the class barriers in England had been shaken. Maybe World War II had had the same effect and it would be easier for him to escape his lot in life. It was up to him, and instead of blaming others, he vowed that he'd try to do something about his own future.

There was something wonderfully attractive about Turkey. He had been to foreign ports and met many people, each with their own history and traditions. He had always been fascinated by the diversity of mankind. But this was the first time he'd lost his sense of being an outsider. It felt as if he belonged, as if he had come to a home he did not even know he had.

He loved his country. He loved his family. Yet here in Turkey this is where he felt he should be. It was his fate. He laughed at the irony: he was already becoming a Turk, talking of fate. What was the saying Neri had once told him that the Turks used when they wished something to happen. Oh, yes, 'İnşallah.' He repeated it to himself three times. He could not remember if you were supposed to say it three times or you were supposed to knock on wood three times. Either way, he was convinced a couple of extra İnşallahs would do no harm.

Bill was almost on the dock when he noticed the intense activity on S.S. Clintonia. His heart skipped a beat. He realized that the dreaded day had come, and they were getting ready to unload their cargo. For a split second he visualized himself turning and disappearing into the dark, but his feet kept dutifully leading him back to the ship. He went up the plank with a heavy heart. Captain Reilly was on the bridge, motioning him to come up.

"We got the papers; we are going to unload tomorrow, right?"

"Exactly," said Reilly. "Come on, I need to talk to you." He led Bill inside down to his private cabin where he poured a shot of Irish whisky for them both. "Have a seat." He took a piece of paper from his pocket and handed it to Bill. It was a telegram from the London office.

"Sorry but I read it accidentally thinking it was official business. Asking our London office for job possibilities in İstanbul, Bill? What are you thinking? It's been evident you were getting attached to the girl, but this is irrational. You want to throw away your career?" He saw Bill's face literally age in front of his eyes as he read the telegram. He felt sorry for the young man but somebody had to shake him back to reality. He let Bill struggle with his emotions for a while, then poured two more shots of whisky.

"Come on, let's talk about this, Bill. I am concerned about you. Let me help you."

Bill was still reading the paper in his hand. "They say there are three positions in the İstanbul office: two junior positions staffed by Turkish men and a Levantine named Scarpello who is in charge. What's a Levantine?"

"I think it refers to Europeans, mostly Italians, who settled in the Ottoman Empire to take care of their trade and business which the Ottomans shunned. Scarpello is probably a descendant of these Levantine families. I believe there are even some English mercantile families who have been living in Turkey for hundreds of years."

"Well then," Bill laughed somewhat bitterly, "maybe I'll become a Levantine too."

"Come on, my boy, this is no laughing matter. Even if there had been a position for you, would you really have left everything and moved to İstanbul?"

"Yes I would."

"But why? You're old enough to know the difference between a crush and a life commitment. And what makes you think living in İstanbul on a low salary as a clerk in a shipping company is going to convince her parents to let you see their daughter?" Bill winced as if he had been punched hard. But why be surprised? Hadn't the same thought occurred to him already?

"I know it looks as if I have acted like a moron recently but believe me I want to spend the rest of my life with her. This I know with a clarity and certainty I've never felt before. I want to change and improve myself too. Meeting Neri and her parents made me realize there is a better way of living. Why is it wrong for me to want it?"

"But they have money, my boy. Some of the things you admire are because they have wealth and status. They belong to another class. I don't know much about Turkey but I know there are class barriers as much here as in England. Here," and he tapped his foot, "you have a good job with a steady income and you're in line for a promotion soon. Marry the girl back in England and be happy. That's what you should do."

Bill did not know how to answer. He wanted to argue that some of the things he wanted did not require much money. He did not want to spend most of his time at sea away from his family. He did not want to come home and spend his days at the corner pub drinking like his father. He did not want ever again to look at a shelf full of books and realize he had not read them. He wanted a steady warm-hearted family life with people who sat around a table and shared their days, concerns and interests, like Neri's parents. And he wanted Neri. He was still young and could go back to school and find a way to get on better in life. He had to try, but how could he explain all this to Reilly when the life he no longer wanted was Reilly's too?

"I'm afraid it may be too late for that," he said vaguely and left, while Reilly stayed in his cabin, feeling defeated. The captain feared it was already too late. Bill had always been a serious and responsible person. He had never seen him act rashly until now but he couldn't really blame Bill. If I had been young, Reilly thought, I would probably have fallen under the spell of Neri himself. She was irresistible. So was her mother. He had also sensed the appeal of the Turkish family. Even the little sleepy town had its charms. This whole area, beset with myths and history, was luring them with its sirens' song. Reilly knew the myth of the sirens with their destructive calling took place somewhere in the Aegean Sea. Were there sirens in the Marmara too? Was Neri one of them? What about Nermin? There was something spellbinding about the place. The quicker we leave this land, he thought, the better for everyone.

11

The first thing Neri noticed the next morning was the increased activity on the dock. She had a premonition that things were going to change. Metin had already heard that the ship was getting ready to leave and had told his wife about it. They had agreed not to say anything to Neri just yet. They knew that Bill couldn't leave without saying goodbye to their daughter and they hoped that a formal parting would finally trigger the healing process, however long it would take.

It was after dinner that Bill showed up, carrying two bottles of single malt Irish whisky compliments of Captain Reilly and the crew for their family's hospitality. Like the first day, Bill was wearing his uniform and looked formal. Metin thanked him and asked him to sit but he "preferred to stand." He had to get back to the ship as there was still a lot to do. He looked at Neri pleadingly, but she kept her eyes diverted, trying to hide her tears. Her anguish was unbearable to him, like a blade in his heart.

Neri's parents were watching them, both feeling their pain. I am glad I'm not this young, Nermin thought. When she had met Metin, there had been times when both of them had questioned the intensity of their feelings for each other. It had been so sudden and consuming. But with each day their love had deepened, and they had enjoyed each other's company knowing that one day they would marry. But their circumstance had been so different. There had been no obstacles like the ones faced by Neri and the young Englishman.

Bill now shook their hands, thanking them again. "We will never forget your kindness," he said, then turned and left without having the courage to look at Neri. Her face crumbled and she was about to start sobbing when Nermin noticed something on the table.

"He forgot his cap," she said surprised. They all looked at it as if it was an alien thing. Metin made a move but Nermin restrained her husband and suggested Neri should go after Bill. They stared at each other for a split second and then Metin handed the cap to Neri.

"Go on, be quick, otherwise you'll never catch him" he said gently.

Neri started running but Bill was nowhere to be seen. He must have turned the corner and was probably halfway down the hill. It was not easy running in the dark but Neri knew the road well. When she came around the corner, she could see his figure moving slowly. She cried his name and came down running. She handed him the cap silently. He took the cap, looking dazed.

"I don't want to go," he said. He was like a small boy who's been badly hurt.

All of a sudden all her reserve left Neri. She swung at his chest with both fists. "I don't want you to go either," she sobbed. Bill bent down, her fists collapsing on his chest, took her into his arms and kissed her. The silence lasted a moment.

"This was my first ever kiss," Neri whispered, still in his arms. He moaned softly and kissed her again, this time a more intense, exploring kiss. Gently her arms crept up around his neck. He was now holding her very close. They could both hear each other's hearts. She reluctantly pulled off looking Bill fully in the eyes, then she reached up and ever so softly caressed the lines by his mouth.

"I have to go," she said simply.

Bill stood a long time staring even after she disappeared in the dark, then he turned and started reluctantly down the road toward town. He had no idea if he'd ever see Tekirdağ again.

Part II

Why did she love him? Curious fool, be still!
Is human love the growth of human will?

Lord Byron

(From *Lara*, Canto II)

12

Neri was washing dishes in a small dark kitchen and sobbing. She was miserable and felt claustrophobic in a bad marriage which was nobody's fault but her own. All her friends and family had warned her about marrying him. She had not listened. She had imagined herself a martyr, rebelling against anyone and everyone who couldn't possibly fathom the feelings she had for Bill. She had been bitter for such a long time and so blind to reason that she forgot that it was not her parents who had prevented her from capturing the only happiness she thought she could ever have. Bill had simply stopped writing. Moreover, he had never even once mentioned marriage. So whom had she rebelled against? She had no answer.

At the beginning of her marriage, Neri had genuinely hoped that she could be happy. All her life, she had been so loved and cherished by her parents and family that she could not imagine others not loving her. Yet Bill had dropped her without warning, and she was no longer sure about her husband's feelings.

Her problem was that she had never stopped dwelling on the past. She was still preoccupied with yesterday. Had she misread Bill's feelings and intentions? Hadn't he reassured her repeatedly that he would find a way to get back to her after the job in İstanbul did not pan out? She used to read his letters over and over again. There was never any hint of his intention to stop writing. In April, exactly a year after they met, she had received a telegram on her birthday, followed by another long loving letter, then nothing. Bill never answered the letters she sent. She did not even know if he was alive. After a while she faced the fact that it was over but needed to know why. Only then could she be expected to put the whole thing behind her and move on with her life.

The experience and the disappointment had changed her, made Neri afraid of commitment and instead led her into a marriage everyone thought would fail. The more her parents and friends tried to convince her that it was a bad idea, the more stubborn she'd become. She wanted to punish her parents for their unrealistic expectations and belief she would never make a single mistake. She could miss someone's character and she had! It hadn't taken her long to realize all the stupid destructive things she did after Bill had stopped writing were nothing but the tantrums of a rich spoiled girl who had never learned to deal with rejection. She was now ashamed of her behavior but it was too late. She was in a 'hell of her own making' and had no one to blame but herself.

The flat Neri and her husband Ismet had rented on the first floor of the apartment building was in a new neighborhood of Ankara, Turkey's capital. The building was at the bottom of a hill, and the kitchen window looked onto a muddy backyard less than twenty feet in width. An ugly tall embankment built against the hill protected the building from mudslides, but it also cut any sunlight to the first and second floor units. The view from the front was good, overlooking a grove of poplars rising up the hill where Atatürk's mausoleum was situated. She liked looking at the stark large building inspired by Hittite architecture. The back view of the house, however, she hated as much as her life.

She now dried her hands, hung the towel on a hook on the wall, and glanced at the back yard. Then she gasped with pleasure and stood there motionless. About a month ago the janitor of the building who brought the newspaper and fresh bread to each unit every morning had planted two small peach trees. One had produced a white blossom pink at the edges. Shining in the narrow wedge of sunlight reflected from an upper window, the blossom was quite beautiful. Glistening and trembling delicately in the breeze, it seemed to challenge the surrounding ugliness with great hope.

Neri kept on staring at the blossom and little by little she could feel the heavy weight of her despair and helplessness begin to lift. There was still beauty in the world, she thought. Maybe one day she'd find it in her life. For the first time in a long while, the resemblance of a smile crossed her face.

13

Neri met her husband Ismet at the annual dance given by St. Joseph, one of the French lycees in İstanbul. It was just before graduation. Neri was in one of her caustic brittle "Eve Arden" moods—aptly named by her friend Leyla—and did not want to go. All through her senior year, Neri had been on a self-destructive path. She had dated indiscriminately and as soon as any young man showed the smallest sign of getting serious, she would ditch him and date someone else. No one, including her parents, had been able to talk sense to her except Leyla. If it hadn't been for her, Neri's reputation could have been seriously damaged. Now Leyla wanted to go to the St. Joseph's party and she wanted Neri to accompany her.

They had been roommates for five years and Neri loved Leyla like a sister. They were an odd pair. Leyla was blond with blue eyes, shorter than Neri and more subdued. Her parents lived in Ankara and her family was well-known and respected in political circles. In contrast to Neri, Leyla had been taught to be "seen and not heard." Her quiet demeanor, however, hid a strong will and certainty about what was her due in life. She could be very persuasive. Neri knew she owed Leyla a lot for her loyal friendship, so at the last minute she had caved in and agreed to go.

St. Joseph was one of the many foreign-language schools that had opened up during the Ottoman Empire to educate the sons of the minorities. Eventually however, Turkish families had started sending their children to such schools too, having realized the economic advantages of multi-lingual education. Neri's American school was one of the few foreign-language institutions for girls.

Tickets to the St. Joseph's annual dance were hard to get. Once a year, the French teachers and administrators shed the school's conservative academic reputation and threw a party that was popular with all private school students. It was always held at a fancy venue in İstanbul. Leyla had been dating a St. Joseph graduate for nearly a year now and she needed to use Neri as an excuse in order to keep the relationship secret from her family, at least until after graduation when her boyfriend was going to ask Leyla's parents for her hand in marriage.

Their party was large, with friends from other tables dropping by all the time. The DJ was playing popular American songs and Neri was constantly on the dance floor, having a good time. There was no alcohol served but the hormone-laden atmosphere was contagious. Neri was determined to have fun and was in one of her recklessly flirtatious moods. Although she was used to being ogled, one particular man's insistent gaze was beginning to annoy her. He looked older than most, was of middle-height and had short-cut brown hair, greenish eyes, and a prominent Ottoman nose that Neri didn't like. He was smartly dressed and was currently ignoring his date who looked like an American.

During a break, Neri was surprised to see the man talking to Orhan, a friend of her cousin Alp. She had not seen Orhan ever since her cousin had gone to the Unites States for graduate studies. They seem to be arguing. Finally Orhan shrugged his shoulders and brought the man to their table and introduced him as Ismet Eloglu. When Ismet asked her to dance, Neri felt she could not refuse because of Orhan. Ismet was a good dancer, which she liked but there was something very possessive in the way he was holding her. It made her feel uncomfortable and curious at the same time.

Orhan claimed the next dance and to her great surprise he warned her bluntly to stay away from Ismet. "He has a bad reputation as an unscrupulous womanizer."

Neri suspected as much but in her rebellious mood these words were all she needed to throw caution to the wind, and she agreed to dance with Ismet again. She was both attracted to his sexual confidence and repelled by it. He wasn't at all like the shy boys she had enjoyed tormenting for the past few months. Neri knew she was being reckless, but 'why not?' she thought. Hadn't she been a good girl too long already?

14

About five months after Bill left, Neri returned to Tekirdağ to attend the Governor's Ball celebrating the 27th anniversary of the founding of the Turkish Republic. This was going to be her first ball. She had a beautiful gown and was excited, leaving Bill and his memory behind for a short while.

As usual, Metin met her at the train station and they chatted comfortably, carefully avoiding the subject of Bill. Then, as they near the town, he told her about the letter he'd recently received from her school's American administrator.

"She complained about your correspondence with Bill. She informed me that the school frowned upon *their girls* receiving letters from sailors, and asked me if they should destroy them."

Neri was astounded. "What did you say?"

"What do you think I said? I told them you were eighteen, knew what you were doing, and it was none of their business."

"Thank you, *babacığım*," Neri said, greatly relieved. She was afraid he would inquire more about Bill, but he did not until much later when Tekirdağ came into view and Neri saw a large ship in the harbor. For a split second her heart missed a beat, thinking Bill had returned but she knew it wasn't so. He was on his way to

Australia, and the last letter she received was from Bombay, India. She knew it would be weeks before she could get another letter. She hated when the ship went long distances without stopping. His letters sustained her, making her believe all their problems would eventually be solved and they'd be together again one day.

If Metin noticed the flittering of hope and disappointment on her face, he didn't show it. "It's another British merchant ship," he said casually. "It came two days ago. I think the governor invited the officers to the ball, but I have no intention of inviting them or anyone else to the factory ever again." He smiled, trying to make it sound like a joke, and Neri didn't respond.

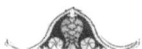

Neri stared at herself in the mirror and wished Bill was there to see her. Her ankle-length ivory-colored ball gown, with its tight sleeveless bodice and full skirt made her look grown-up and elegant. It was a copy of a Christian Dior dress and the dressmaker in İstanbul had outdone herself.

They had been invited to sit at the governor's table. The governor was a tennis enthusiast and had become a good friend of Metin, challenging him on the court whenever his job permitted. Nermin had warmed up to his young shy wife and was constantly encouraging her to be more outgoing, more assertive. Neri felt sorry for the governor. He was an enlightened person with Westernized views, but he probably had no idea of the transformation his quiet little wife was experiencing under Nesrin's tutelage. Many Turkish men paid lip service to modern ideas such as gender equality, but when it came to their wives or daughters they remained stubbornly traditional, preferring them quiet and subservient.

During a break the musicians were taking, the governor pointed to the British officers sitting quietly at a table on the other side of the dance floor. "They look bored, don't they? Nobody is talking to them. Metin, would you mind if I take Neri to their table for a little while so that the poor guys can at least talk to someone?"

Metin hesitated a second before replying, "Of course not."

The officers all stood up as the governor and Neri approached their table. Introductions were made and the governor told the officers that he was "leaving Neri in their care for a little while" to answer any questions they might have. After the usual inquiries about where she learned her English, the captain asked Neri to dance. He was a good dancer and Neri found herself enjoying both the dance and his polite conversation. She had to admit to herself that it wasn't this man's fault if Bill was on the other side of the world and not a member of his crew.

Before she could catch her breath after they returned to the table, another officer asked her to dance. He said his name was Archibald Turner, but his friends called him Archie. He was a young man with dark curly hair and piercing black eyes. She was just getting adjusted to his style of dancing when the fireworks started.

"Shall we go to the balcony to watch the fireworks?" asked Archie. Neri knew most people in the ball would consider their going out alone to the balcony totally inappropriate but she did not want to give the impression to Archie that Turks were too provincial, so she reluctantly agreed. Shortly after they went out, Metin appeared.

"Please apologize to your partner, Neri, but you promised to dance the first tango with me," he said.

After their dance, Metin took his daughter back to their own table, hoping that the incident would go unnoticed. However the next day Nermin heard from her friends that the town's gossip mill which was still dissecting Neri's 'relationship' with Bill had started churning again. Nermin was irritated but there was nothing she could do. She knew defending her daughter's behavior would give unwarranted legitimacy to gossip. So she let them talk but her resentment at the small-minded town grew, and she started pressuring Metin to move to İstanbul permanently.

After Bill stopped writing and Neri became despondent and almost reckless, Metin became convinced that the time had come for them to leave Tekirdağ. There was another reason for the move. Prior to the 1946 general elections, the ruling Republican People's Party had caved in to popular demand and allowed the establishment of a second political party. There was a lot of pressure on Metin from the grape-growers to join the newly-formed Democratic Party and run for election. Most of the vineyards were owned by villagers who were at the mercy of crooked price-fixers and middle men. They wanted someone honest and fair to represent their interests in the Turkish Assembly. Nermin had not been keen on living in Ankara but the idea of her husband playing a role in advancing Turkey's fledgling democracy had quelled her objections.

The elections turned out badly. The Democratic Party suffered a resounding defeat and the papers were full of accusations about stolen ballots and voter intimidation. Some journalists were jailed. The more the ruling party tried to silence its critics, the more dirt they dug up. Finally, President İnönü promised that the government would do everything it could to ensure fair elections "the next time around."

Metin did not run in the 1950 elections but he joined a large cadre of people who worked together to make sure the government kept its promise. He voted for the Democratic Party but remained skeptical about the wisdom of using religion as a tool in the elections. Metin had also witnessed too many discouraging scenes. It was hard to talk of democracy when whole villages voted as a block under the thumb of the local aghas who literally owned the lands and the peasants making a living on them. Although preferable to other forms of government, without a well-educated electorate, Metin thought, any promise of democracy was a sham. He had seen the corruption first-hand and felt ashamed and helpless. Politics was a dirty business and he wanted no part of it. But his friends kept on pressuring him to work for the Democrats at the İstanbul headquarters to fulfill their election promises. It was a tall order. At the same time, Metin couldn't refute the argument that if honest and able people didn't get involved in politics and get their hands dirty, what hope was there? So he eventually hired a manager for the factory and convinced Emre to stay as his winemaker. Then he took his time making the necessary improvements to their summer house in Erenköy to winterize it. Finally, he and Nermin moved to İstanbul at the peak of Neri's rebellion and just before her graduation.

But before they could even try to have an effect on their daughter's behavior, Ismet appeared on the scene. He was polite, respectful and well-mannered, but there was something phony about him like a wooden actor playing a well-rehearsed part. They found it hard to warm up to him. They hoped that once Neri started going to the university, she'd be too busy to bother with him, or better still, she'd find someone more suitable.

But to everyone's shock, Neri, who had always been a top student and graduated with honors from her school, failed the university entrance exams. Leyla blamed it on "one of Neri's Bill attacks" which left Neri "numb and dumb" the morning of the exam so much that she did not even notice the young proctor who lingered around Neri's seat trying to help her with the answers, hoping she would go out with him afterwards.

Neri then tried her hand at finding a job. Her parents supported the idea, hoping that an interesting job would lend some stability to her life until she came to her senses, found a nice husband and settled down like all her friends.

An advertisement in the paper caught Neri's eye one morning. A reputable import-export business was looking for an English-speaking translator. Neri was sure that she'd ace the English exam and went to the address with great confidence. The location was on one of the crooked winding streets behind the New Mosque just off the Galata Bridge in old İstanbul. Her enthusiasm waned when she saw the urine-smelling old building. It was dark and dingy, nothing like the bright modern office she'd imagined. When she entered the room, she felt like a deer caught in the headlights. Everyone stared at her and a short man with brilliantine hair, small eyes, and a fat belly slithered toward her, asking what she wanted. She told him that she was interested in the job and had come to take the test. He escorted her to a large stained table in the middle of the room before she shrunk from his sweaty hand clutching her elbow.

At the table were three men and a woman, apparently getting ready to take the exam. In a corner two sour-faced employees sat dejectedly at old wooden desks. The solitary woman at the test table wore garish makeup, a low-cut blouse and lots of cheap jewelry that jingled every time she moved. She was looking at Neri with open hostility, which Neri could not fathom. Then she began arguing with the fat man about the wisdom of "letting anyone walk in and take the exam, particularly"—and she was almost shouting now—"when it's obvious that the person doesn't even have any work experience."

Neri was becoming more and more uncomfortable as the woman complained to the whole room in a screeching voice that these society girls were trying to get the bread out of the mouth of hard-working people. It was ludicrous and for an excruciatingly embarrassing moment Neri fought hard not to laugh. The scene was straight out of the pages of a popular Turkish novel. It would be hard to imagine a Turkish girl who had not at least once wished she was Feride, the plucky little heroine who after having her heart broken by her cheating fiancé, leaves the comfort and security of her home in İstanbul and dedicates her life to teaching children in remote corners of Anatolia.

Blushing with embarrassment, Neri tried not to listen to the woman. She finished the test quickly, handed it over to the man, and without waiting for him to say anything, ran out. Outside she waited for the bright sunlight to wash away the sour taste and smell. Then she heard someone calling her. It was one of the young men who had taken the test with her.

"I'm sorry to bother you but I want to tell you that this is no place for a girl like you," he said in a soft shy voice.

"Why?" Neri asked. Something about the young man's demeanor was disarming, otherwise she would have ignored him.

"I don't know if you noticed but the owner is *not* a nice man. The whole thing is rigged anyway. They told me that he was going to hire that woman who is also his mistress."

"Thank you for warning me," Neri said with sincerity and shook the man's hand. After a slight hesitation, he asked if he could walk with her. Neri shook her head to mean no and turned away. Sometimes she wished she was more plain-looking if only to be left alone but the thought did not last long.

When she arrived home, Neri told her parents what happened, making fun of the whole episode by acting out the part of the rude woman, the unctuous boss, and her Feride-self. She was a good mimic and soon her parents were laughing, but they were not fooled by her frivolity. They sensed something was wrong but knew that she would not say more. She was like a stranger now, disclosing nothing and always hiding her feelings behind a sincere-looking bland face. Her parents didn't like the situation.

"Why is she behaving like this?" Metin kept on asking. "What did we do to her? We never denied her anything. Are we being punished for whatever happened with Bill? Was there a promise or a proposal that we blocked?"

Helpless, Nermin would shake her head: "I'm only the mother. She doesn't confide in me anymore."

"But something is wrong, isn't it? She's not herself. What's changed?"

"Well, she's heartbroken, that's for sure. But I don't know why she's blaming us...it's not as if they were planning to elope and we stopped them! I don't understand it myself, Metin. Maybe, it's something else. Maybe we've put her on too high a pedestal and she feels disappointed in herself for not living up to our expectations."

"What expectations?" Metin said. "We've never had any reason to make her feel disappointed in herself. So what are you talking about?"

"Metin, her first love ended in failure. Her university dreams came to nothing when she failed the entrance exam. Her first attempt at getting a job was a fiasco. All her friends are getting married."

"She would too if she could only make up her mind and choose someone from her long list of suitors," Metin said, getting irritated. Unreasonably, thought Nermin.

"I'm just trying to explain...not that I understand the situation myself," Nermin sighed. They had no answers and they both hated being locked out of their daughter's life.

Meanwhile Neri wanted to talk to her parents but she did not know what to say. She was not yet ready to talk about Bill. She was afraid that if her parents said anything negative about him, she would never forgive them. And she didn't want to discuss Ismet because she didn't think he was worth talking about. He was just a casual someone, not even a boyfriend, who kept her occupied and her mind free of Bill. And she wasn't sure how she could tell them that for the second time in her life, her self-confidence had taken a jolt.

The first was Bill's rejection of her and the second was the hatred she had seen in the woman's eyes in that ugly room. She simply did not know how to process dislike except by blaming herself. This was an unfortunate side effect of the self-confidence her parents had meticulously instilled in her. They made her believe that she could always control what happened to her. So when things went wrong, she felt it had to be her fault and like her mother, Neri had a knack of doing everything in extremes. So far she had projected to the outside world the anger she felt for her broken heart. But now she was beginning to internalize it. Now she was thinking that maybe she was not worth loving and was just a superficial, coddled, spoiled girl...all looks and nothing else. What she did not know and could not imagine was that all these senseless introspections were simply making her more vulnerable and, thus, easier prey for Ismet.

15

The summer after her graduation, most of her friends got married at an alarming rate putting pressure on Neri to find someone too. Next in line was Leyla who had introduced her boyfriend to her parents, and they liked him. Bulent was an engineer, had completed his military service and had a good job—qualities most Turkish parents looked for in a prospective son-in-law. He was also a nice decent man with a good family background and their daughter, who had always been level-headed, wanted him.

So both families approved the union and agreed to let Leyla plan the wedding with her friends without any interference from them. Leyla invited Neri as well as Ceylan and Selma, two other good friends from school, to the Moda Yacht Club to go over the final details. The club was on the Asian side of İstanbul on the Sea of Marmara. It had a fantastic view of the Kalamış Bay and the Princes' Islands.

It was one of İstanbul's beautiful late August days, sunny but cool with gentle sea breezes. The sky was a clear azure and the sea a blinding shimmering expanse dotted with white sails. It would have been impossible for any person to be gloomy on such a glorious day, and even Neri was in a good mood. Besides she felt genuinely happy for Leyla. Her friend was marrying a good man.

They discussed the wedding in detail and everyone was given a task. Neri was in charge of assigning guests to tables. She had to work with Leyla closely to make sure that she was not going to offend anyone by seating them at the wrong table. Bulent had given them carte blanche regarding the seating arrangements which was very considerate of him since his family was paying for the wedding, as was the custom. Leyla's father had bought the couple's bedroom set, again per custom.

Ceylan had married a week after graduation and moved to Oxford where her husband was studying. She had returned to İstanbul for a short visit when she learned that she was pregnant. Her mother-in-law was vehement that Ceylan should stay and have the baby in İstanbul, arguing that made sense logistically and financially. But what irritated Ceylan most was her mother-in-law's assertion that Ceylan and the new baby would be a distraction to her son, slowing down his academic progress in Oxford— something she never failed to mention. After her own family had agreed with her mother-in-law, Ceylan, in sheer defiance, had declared that she was not going to sit idly and watch her belly grow. So she promptly went and enrolled in the School of Fine Arts since she had always been attracted to painting. As Ceylan was going to have her hands full with the school and the pregnancy, they had decided to give her the relatively easy task of overseeing the flower arrangements. Nauseous or not, she promised, she would make them perfect.

That left Selma who opted for a host of activities. This was a learning opportunity for her. Her own wedding was scheduled for mid-winter. Neri was beginning to feel like an old spinster and knew that eventually the conversation would turn to her determinedly single status.

"When are we going to attend your wedding" asked Selma, right on cue. "Can't you find anyone?"

"The problem," Leyla smiled, "is not finding someone. She just has too many suitors."

"Who she keeps on refusing," said Ceylan. "Why can't you decide?"

"She finds something wrong with everyone," Leyla said. "She is waiting for Mr. Darcy." They all giggled, including Neri. But Leyla was determined to get an answer.

"Ask her what was wrong with Emin. Every girl was drooling after him—tall, dark, handsome, and rich. Really, Neri, wasn't he perfect?"

"He was *too* handsome and *too* rich," answered Neri seriously. "And he had two bitchy sisters." They laughed as they knew the sisters from school.

"And Murat, what was wrong with him?" Leyla insisted.

"He was too nice and compliant, also not tall enough." Neri laughed. "I want someone who inspires me, who I can't dominate easily." She had thought half-seriously about Murat mostly because she admired people who played the piano well.

"What about Salih?" asked Ceylan.

"I always suspected he didn't have much between his ears."

"What do you mean?" said Ceylan, truly shocked. Salih was a friend of her husband. "He's a student at Oxford, for God's sake!"

"I rest my case," said Leyla.

On the way out, Leyla pulled Neri aside and warned her: "Neri, I hate telling you this over and over but beware of Ismet. He's no Mr. Darcy. If anything, he's Mr. Wickham!"

16

Ismet was the older of two sons. His father, Huseyin, was a self-made man who'd formed a construction company during the building boom years of Ankara. He never became as successful or as rich as he thought he should have but earned a good living. Huseyin owned a nice house in Bahçelievler, one of Ankara's prestigious residential areas, and he'd done his best to give his sons a good education. His oldest son Ismet had nearly got himself kicked out of Robert College but managed to graduate with an engineering degree. His younger son Mehmet barely finished high school before getting into trouble with women and gambling. Huseyin's wife Nuriye, who had brought him a good size dowry that started his construction business, had become fat and ornery. Huseyin was not a happy man and he made certain that everyone around him knew it.

Ismet had never been on good terms with his father. He knew he was a disappointment to Huseyin but he had never let the knowledge trouble him. He was too much of a hedonist to care. He knew how to manipulate people and had the luck of a good gambler. Just as he was looking for a job, the Americans had started coming to Ankara in droves. After World War II, President Truman realized the importance of Turkey as a buffer state to the Russians' expansionist goals and the two nations signed a number of military and economic aid agreements, opening the gates for a deluge of Americans to Turkey. The locals took to them. They were more colorful and friendly than members of other embassies. They had loud voices, huge cars, garish clothes, pockets full of dollars and an attitude of superiority that only people new to the game of imperialism could display, but they were likeable. They had tall, shapely blond wives and multiple screaming children.

Their arrival turned out to be a blessing for Ismet. His fluent English, familiarity with American ways after all those years in Robert College, and his engineering degree made it easy for him to find a lucrative job at an American company in charge of all their construction projects across Turkey. They were building large-scale communities for the military personnel and their dependents near Incirlik Airbase in Adana and another one near İstanbul in Yalova across the Bay of Izmit. There were silos to be built for the nuclear missiles along the Black Sea coast and facilities for numerous listening posts in Eastern Turkey. Although relatively independent, Americans still had to deal with the Turkish bureaucracy that was known to be excruciatingly slow and somewhat corrupt, a hangover from the old Ottoman system of patronage and favoritism.

After hiring Ismet, the Americans stopped experiencing those inconvenient delays that seemed to constantly handicap projects. Ismet had good connections in Ankara and knew how to work the system. He was a good middle-man, an efficient go-getter, and an effective palm-greaser. He was worth his weight in gold to the Americans who turned a blind eye to his shady dealings. They knew, for example, that he was in the habit of getting commissions from the Turkish construction companies for helping to secure contracts with the Americans. The fact that they were encouraging high-stake corruption in the Turkish system did not seem to bother the Americans. It was part of doing business.

Ismet was also very popular with the American wives. Every time a new family came into town, he helped them find a place to live and taught them where to shop and eat, even where to go dancing. In turn they smuggled him into the military Post Exchange (PX) and consequently the American goods he bought there increased his popularity with the Turkish girls. There were rumors that he had a way with women, including many of the lonely American wives.

Ismet's success was a source of distraction for his father. His son was fast becoming a well-known man-about-town which Huseyin resented and could not fathom. Ismet successfully dodged his father's curiosity and never answered Huseyin's questions about what he was doing at work and how much money he was making. Like mother like son, Huseyin thought. He could never get a straight answer from his wife either. Huseyin finally gave up all his inquiries, satisfied he did not have to worry about his older son. He had enough of a mess on his hands with his younger one.

Ismet was in İstanbul in May on business and had taken along one of the American women he had been dating on and off when they decided to go to the dance given by the French lycee. Once there he'd noticed Neri immediately. He could not take his eyes off her. There were other striking-looking girls around and some, he knew from experience, would even be more willing than this tallish, shapely girl with long legs. But it was her eyes that caught him. She looked happy and was smiling all the time but her eyes were full of anguish. For the first time in his life Ismet felt genuine curiosity, not how he could bed her but how he could ease the pain in her eyes.

When they were dancing, Neri was not responsive to his attempts at conversation. She did not seem impressed that he was working with Americans. She had almost scowled when he asked if there was anything he could get her from the American PX. He was stymied and was becoming nervous as a teenager. This is not like me, he told himself while trying to pull her close. Then, all of a sudden, the body yielding in his arms became as stiff as iron and her soft eyes flashed with anger and disdain. Ismet found himself blushing. He knew somehow he had lost the first round.

It took Ismet months of old-fashioned persistent wooing before Neri would let him kiss her. He had been careful to be patient and undemanding. He was also beginning to learn more about her. On their first official date, he had taken her to Kervansaray, İstanbul's hottest new nightclub. It had cost him a small fortune to secure a table. Everyone who was anyone in İstanbul society was there to hear the new American sensation Eartha Kitt who had become popular with her rendition of an old Turkish folk song called "Üsküdar". Neri seemed to enjoy the music but was not overly impressed with the lavish pretentious décor or with the overdressed crowd.

Ismet soon realized that Neri preferred eating at small fish restaurants that lined the Bosphorus. After a month of dating, he tried to give her a little gold pin which she politely refused. But when he brought her a record from the PX that was at the top of the Hit Parade that week, her face lit up. She was not like any girl he had met before, and he knew that one wrong word or act, she would dismiss him without a second thought.

Meanwhile this obsession with Neri was beginning to cost Ismet. His American boss was quite unhappy with his constant disappearing acts. Worse, some of the wives who depended on him for a variety of services were getting frustrated and complaining to their husbands. It was also costing him a lot of money. Once he had been forced to ask his father for a loan which Huseyin promptly refused. But Ismet's request also piqued the old man's curiosity. Why did his son need extra money suddenly? And what was he doing in İstanbul anyway? He could never get a straight answer.

Ismet could not remember exactly when he'd felt that something began to change in Neri's attitude toward him. She'd become more compliant, more open. After their first kiss, Ismet knew he had won the war. At the age of twenty she was still an innocent. That was as clear as day, but she was also curious and her body was craving for natural release and Ismet was here to please.

Thank you Mother Nature, Ismet said to himself, and thus began the seduction of Neri, or so Ismet thought.

17

Neri's acceptance of his proposal stunned Ismet. He hadn't thought of marriage and the proposal had come out of his mouth almost involuntarily. These past few months had been extremely frustrating for him. Every time he returned to Ankara, he'd made ferocious love to whoever had been available, leaving women spent and happy and himself edgy and more irritated. He wanted Neri with a different kind of fervor, one he'd not felt before. To conquer someone like her was a challenge he couldn't resist.

Neri was surprised at her answer too. She suspected she did not love him enough to marry him. Or did she? How do you know when you're in love? Had she really loved Bill or had it been just an infatuation, a sexual attraction? She was no longer sure. She was even less sure about Ismet. What she was feeling bore no resemblance to what she had seen in the movies or what she had felt for Bill. Ismet had not swept her off her feet as Bill had. Just the opposite, she thought, her feet had remained firmly planted on the ground. She'd never lost control and the seduction Ismet had initiated had amounted to no more than a few intense kisses which admittedly she'd enjoyed. He was a good kisser—not that she was an authority on the subject. She wondered if she enjoyed learning about kissing more than kissing itself, but she'd found his persistence appealing and satisfying. She needed to feel wanted and loved.

All the other young men she dated had treated her with kid gloves which she stubbornly interpreted as a lack of feeling for her despite the fact she could not blame them. They were doing what they were supposed to do: treat her like a well-behaved girl which she still was. Nonetheless, Neri resented being kept in the dark. If she was to remain inexperienced all the time, how was she to know if she was in love or if the right man had come along?

This was her friends' favorite subject back in school. They used to discuss what constituted a 'good girl' ad infinitum but the definition remained a mystery. Some argued that the concept was relative since there was a large gap between should and could. They were not supposed to kiss but they knew some 'good girls' who did. They were not supposed to neck but they suspected some had engaged in it. They all agreed that going all the way was a total 'No-No' but the rumors persisted about the sexual activities of a few girls who still claimed the stamp of propriety.

Nonetheless the fear of losing one's good name remained a suffocating and paralyzing fear they all shared as women, like an invisible choker they had all been born with which got tighter around their necks as they grew up, sucking all the joy of living out of them. The sexual taboos, even the minor ones, that permeated the Muslim culture weighed seriously on them. For Neri, one thing Turks were good at was inflicting shame. The taboos were in the air they breathed. They were in the unspoken expectations of even the most tolerant parents. They were in the eyes of family members, of neighbors, of strangers in the streets and the boys they knew. The boys had grown up in the same culture. They had been taught that there were two kinds of girls. You treated the good girls—'family girls' they were called—with respect. You did not mess with them and you eventually married them. The others you had your fun with, and then you discarded them like yesterday's newspapers.

Neri used to argue that this sort of thinking was irrational and unfair. She would ask what about men? Do they have to be virgins too to be marriageable? Who came up with these rules anyway? The imams who preached that the world had been created in a week? Did anyone know how many kisses it took before 'bad girl' was figuratively stamped on a girl's forehead? And what about the Europeans, the Americans? Were they all going to hell?

Once Neri had shocked her friends by asking if a woman was supposed to have sexual feelings and why the subject of a woman's sexuality was never discussed? Surely God created both sexes with the same feelings and needs.

Daring to ask such questions was nothing compared to the courage one needed to defy the sexual taboos deeply imbedded in Turkish culture. It required more than just wearing shorts or riding a bike. Yet with Ismet, she wondered, had she put a red letter on her chest and declared herself available?

Neri knew she had caved in when confronted with his singular intensity, an intensity which had finally made her feel wanted. In her inexperience, she had misjudged his lust for love. She'd thought that with such strong feelings Ismet would be the perfect man to mend her broken heart. On an unconscious level perhaps she also hoped that being a married woman would finally free her from the heavy yoke of moralistic expectations.

So she had said "yes". Yes to him and yes to the next step in life—marriage—that she was supposed to take and was curious about. But there were other reasons for her rushing into marriage with Ismet. He was safe. She was convinced that her lukewarm feelings for him would save her from the emotional cost of another unfulfilled and painful relationship—like the one she had experienced with Bill.

Plus marrying Ismet was the final act of rebellion against her parents. They had put her on a pedestal. She was angry and no longer wanted to live up to their expectations. She suspected that her parents had considered Bill an inappropriate husband. Well, she was going to give them a Turkish son-in-law. See how you like them apples! The fact that she might be destroying her life did not slow her down. On the contrary it seemed to spur her on. Neri needed purging and Ismet was her key to a living Purgatory. She never quite stopped to think why she settled for the wrong man.

Not too surprising, her parents did not greet the news well. What they'd discovered about Ismet and his family had not been reassuring, to say the least. Apparently, the father was a good businessman but was disliked by most of his employees. He was harsh and arbitrary—which upset Metin who was just the opposite with his workers. Worse, Ismet, they were told, was a shady character, a womanizer who was in too deep with the Americans.

Neri had shrugged everything off: "Ismet is a thirty-year old bachelor. What did you expect him to do, behave like a monk?"

"But Neri," her parents had argued, "youthful indiscretion is something, indiscriminate womanizing is something else. We heard ugly rumors about him that suggest a lack of character. Don't you have any worries?"

"None whatsoever," she insisted. "He loves me and he'll be a good husband."

Metin and Neri remained concerned but kept their worries to themselves, hoping for the best.

Huseyin and his wife met Neri for the first time when they came to formally ask her parents' permission for marriage. Neri had to admit that she couldn't possibly find two more different sets of parents if she'd tried, but her parents were successful in covering their true feelings through a mask of cordiality. Ismet's parents seemed happy and genuinely impressed. Interested in the decorations, Nuriye asked Nermin where she'd bought the beautiful curtains hanging in the living room, and Metin patiently explained to Huseyin his wine-making business.

Neri sensed the way she looked had surprised Ismet's parents, making her wonder what kind of girl they thought their son had caught. She'd wished Ismet was there to explain what his parents had expected but as was the custom, he had not accompanied his parents on this formal occasion.

Huseyin was indeed stunned and taking advantage of the fact that Neri and her parents were momentarily out of the room, he whispered to his wife: "How did Ismet get such a beautiful girl? They seem to be wealthy too. Do you think he got the girl into trouble?" For a split second, Huseyin even felt an unexpected respect for his son, but the moment passed quickly.

"Shush! They'll hear you. They fell in love, that's all there is to it. You always underestimate your son, Huseyin. Besides, I don't think they have more money than we do. Look how old the curtains are."

In the kitchen, Nermin and Metin were trying to hide their disappointment from Neri. While Neri carefully carried into the living room the traditional tray with tiny porcelain cups filled to the brim with Turkish coffee—a test all prospective brides perform when they first meet their future in-laws—Nermin pulled Metin aside. "I don't like this," she said. "This is not going to end well. Ismet's father looks mean and miserable, and I don't know what's bothering his wife, but she looks uncomfortable."

"I know but there's nothing we can do. Besides, they're not going to live with his parents. Tell Neri to make sure they find a flat in Ankara far away from his parents. I'm much more worried about Ismet. I hope he'll make Neri happy, but I don't know."

Neri's six-month engagement was marred with increasing doubts about Ismet. She suspected lying came easy to him. She also suspected he was seeing other women even after their engagement. But she convinced herself that these things would naturally change once they were married

Neri and Ismet had their wedding party at the Kervansaray and then they drove in a blinding snowstorm to a new hotel on the outskirts of the city that Ismet had chosen for their honeymoon. The next day, there was a 6.4 Richter magnitude earthquake in İstanbul and the huge crystal chandelier in the room where they held their wedding party the night before crashed down and killed two people and injured several others. It was an omen, everyone thought.

Ismet seemed amused by the incident.

18

Ankara surprised Neri. It was nothing like chaotic cosmopolitan İstanbul. It had been more or less a mud hole in the middle of the Anatolian plain before Atatürk chose it as the capital of the new republic. All the embassies from İstanbul were transferred to Ankara and a great building boom started. Wide avenues crisscrossed neat straight lines of streets. Official buildings, hotels, universities and parks mushroomed overnight. An opera house was constructed for the crop of singers being trained and new museums and galleries were opening daily. After some thirty years, the puny trees that were planted had grown tall and strong and gave the city a feeling of much-needed permanence and class.

It was an easy and spacious city in which to live. Its small population was highly educated, consisting mainly of government workers, military personnel, academics, foreign embassy staff and other professionals. The architecture of government buildings had a stark unfriendly Teutonic look, but the surrounding fields gave way to pleasant two-storied gardened residencies. Ismet's parents lived in one of these neighborhoods and Ismet and Neri, despite her parent's advice, ended up renting a small flat nearby, but the process had left Neri bitter and disappointed both in Ankara and in her husband.

The influx of Americans had changed the real-estate scene in Ankara. The owners preferred to rent to Americans. They were all afraid of the rumors about the possible devaluation of the Turkish lira and they were eager to get their hands on dollars. Neri and Ismet were rejected by one owner after another as soon as the owners realized that they weren't Americans. It made Neri angry to be treated this way in her own country and she couldn't understand why Ismet took the whole thing calmly and shrugged it off. Neri suspected that if Ismet had a place of his own for rent, he would do exactly the same thing, preferring American renters and their dollars instead of Turks. It was not a pleasant idea.

Her marriage was nothing like she had envisioned and Ismet the husband was very different from Ismet the boyfriend. She had entered the marriage with good intentions. Bill was not forgotten but neatly tucked away somewhere in the recesses of her mind. She wanted to be a good wife, a good homemaker, and a good daughter-in-law, all in that order. Although she knew nothing about how to run a house, cook, plan a dinner or entertain, she'd rolled up her sleeves and attacked each chore with determination. Soon she found out what she was good at. She had a flare for interior decoration. In less than two weeks, she had all her furniture bought by her parents in place and her curtains up. She had a pleasant living room with neutral-colored sofas and chairs, enlivened by pillows and a very expensive silk Hereke rug from her aunt and uncle as a wedding gift. She had oil paintings on the walls, fresh flowers in crystal vases and lots of books just like back home. There wasn't much in the flat reflecting Ismet or his taste.

She didn't enjoy cooking and didn't know how to do it. She finally bought two cookbooks, one Turkish, one American, and with constant hints and help from her mother-in-law, she became a confident if not a good cook.

Her problem was not the daily chores of marital life but her relationship with her husband and his family, mainly his father. First of all, sex with Ismet left a lot to be desired. It was all very business-like, leaving her cold and befuddled. It was hard to believe his reputation as a womanizer! As usual she thought the fault lay with her, and she even asked Ismet if there was something she was supposed to do? He did not answer but told her that such questions were inappropriate. Clearly even married women were not supposed to talk about their sexual needs. His lovemaking remained frustrating and she resented the fact that he was not concerned at all about her reactions or feelings. This bothered her greatly since she knew that not everyone was like him. After coming from her honeymoon and blushing with embarrassment, Selma had confessed that her husband's lovemaking made her toes curl and Ceylan had nodded smugly. Neri was the only one who had no idea what they were talking about, but she wanted her toes curled too.

Another thing she was beginning to resent was Ismet's lack of interest in what she thought, what she felt, what she wanted. He was not into talking or sharing. There was less intimacy now than when they were dating. He was secretive. She knew nothing about his job or how much money he made. He would make plans without ever discussing them with her. She was expected to obey and do whatever he wanted. He would come home and declare that they were going out that night. All she needed was to dress up and look good.

She didn't like going out almost every night. She felt like a cardboard figure, a possession that he just wanted to show off, and she hated the self-satisfied expression he'd get on his face whenever men stared at her with hungry eyes. She felt uncomfortable and cheap.

After becoming more acquainted with his family, Neri began to understand Ismet's behavior a little better. His father was a tyrant with a room-size ego, impervious to the feelings of others, and constantly in need of ego-stroking and reaffirmation. He ruled over his wife and two sons. No one dared to interrupt or contradict him. Instead, they all acted within the confines of the roles assigned to them. Nuriye was an obedient wife, a passive mother and a good cook. Although both grownup, Ismet and Mehmet acted like two quiet respectful children, never uttering a single word that could be interpreted as a challenge to their father. Beneath their submissive behavior, however, Neri could detect deviousness and resentment. There was venom underneath the smooth family façade.

A little incident during her first dinner with her in-laws stayed with Neri a long time. Ismet's younger brother Mehmet was the only one at home with Nuriye arriving much later. She kissed Ismet and Neri and rushed to the kitchen hardly saying a word. When Huseyin finally came home, he was peeved that the dinner was not ready and scolded his wife in front of everyone. Nuriye explained that she had forgotten the time while talking to the newlyweds. The blatant lie bothered Neri. Walking back home, she asked her husband about it.

"Well, my mother plays cards with her friends two or three times a week. My father disapproves because sometimes she loses a lot of money. So instead of creating a fuss, I guess she thought not telling him would be the best thing to do."

"But lying is not a good thing, right?"

"Your parents never lie to each other?" Ismet asked laughing.

"I don't know," she said, slightly offended. "I don't think I've ever caught them in a lie." That in itself was not true because just then Neri remembered how when she was only eleven her parents had lied about the accidental death of her German Shepherd dog. Instead, they told her they had given the dog to someone else who could take better care of him. After finding out the truth, Neri had been very upset at the deception. Now irritated at the memory, she stubbornly insisted that lying did not pay.

"Sometimes little white lies are necessary," replied Ismet.

"But your mother did not tell a little white lie. She also put us in a compromising situation. What were we supposed to do if your father asked us the truth?"

"Well, I assume you'd not put my mother in a difficult situation. Come on Neri," he smiled, putting his arm around her, "don't be so serious. It's not such a big deal, is it?"

Neri was getting more irritated by the moment. She knew she had told white lies herself now and then, so why was she so upset? She realized that what troubled her more than Ismet's cavalier attitude about lying was his sly, false deference to his father. She perceived it as proof of lack of integrity in his character. How could she ever believe him? How could she ever trust him? It bothered her that she had no answer. It also dawned on her that maybe the same deferential behavior was what was expected of her too. Maybe her survival as a wife depended on her becoming quietly manipulative and complacent like her mother-in-law. The thought made her shudder. She did not like the image. It was not her!

Neri wished she could talk to someone and ask for advice but everyone she cared about had been dead set against the marriage and had warned her about Ismet. This was her problem and she had to solve it herself, but how? So her first year of marriage did not live up to her expectations. It was like a bad movie which had been promoted with a very promising trailer but had turned out to be not worth the price of the ticket. Wasn't there more to life? Surely she could do better?

19

Neri's first cocktail party was said to be a great success but it left her somewhat unsettled. It was Ismet's idea to introduce her to everyone he knew by giving a cocktail party, a new form of entertainment ushered in by the Americans and quickly adopted by the so-called modern Turks. The traditional sit-down dinner was now considered passé. Cocktail parties, where guests stood shoulder to shoulder for hours as though packed in a tram gulping down black-market American booze, were in.

When she heard about their plans, Nuriye suggested a proper dinner party and she would help with the food, but Ismet insisted on the cocktail party format. Nuriye then warned not to invite too many people and not to mix their Turkish friends with the Americans.

"There'll be trouble," she predicted. "There's too much anti-Americanism nowadays."

"How do you know?" her husband snickered, never wasting an opportunity to put his wife down.

"You're not the only one who reads the papers Huseyin," she snapped back.

Good for you, Neri thought. But Ismet ignored his mother's sound advice and invited all his American coworkers and Turkish acquaintances to show off his prize possession, his wife.

Neri could hardly remember the first hour of the party which passed like a speeding train, all blurry faces and too much noise. She had a lot to do, welcoming people she had never seen before, passing the canapés her mother-in-law had helped her make, and seeing that everyone had a drink and was having a good time. She was constantly aware that her guests were scrutinizing her with interest, some unabashedly, some slyly. It was unnerving. What had they been expecting? But she liked her guests. They were all friendly and eager to talk to her, particularly the young officers who were begging her to teach them the cha-cha-cha, the new dance craze. Soon the party came alive with everyone having a good time dancing.

She was about to relax and enjoy herself when a new couple walked in. Ismet introduced them as Stanford and Sarah Wiley. The man quietly shook Neri's hand and moved to the far end of the living room away from the dancers. The woman was tall and blond and would have been strikingly beautiful except for small green eyes much too close together. She totally ignored Neri, kissing Ismet on both cheeks and hanging onto him with an inexplicit air of propriety. Neri instinctively knew she was not going to like the woman. She also felt slighted and could not figure out the reason for hostility the woman hadn't even tried to hide.

"Don't pay attention to Sarah, she's a difficult woman," said Maude, wife of Ismet's boss John Miller, who had suddenly appeared at her side.

"Who are they?" Neri asked, puzzled.

"Stan is the civilian contractor in John's office, in charge of construction projects. He's a very nice man. Just steer clear of Sarah. Anyway, congratulations Neri, this is a very nice party," Maude said. "You must be exhausted. May I call you Neri? That's your nickname, isn't it? How do you like Ankara?"

"It's interesting."

"People usually say something is interesting when they have nothing nice to say."

Neri tried to defend herself. "I've never been to a well-planned city before. Compared to İstanbul, everything is very orderly and easy to find."

"Dull you mean," teased Maude.

"Why are you giving our gracious hostess such a hard time Maude," asked John, putting an affectionate arm around his wife's waist.

"I'm not giving her a hard time. I just want to find out how somebody from such a beautiful city as İstanbul can get accustomed to living in Ankara, that's all."

"I know what you are doing Maude, you can't fool me. You're pursuing your devious plot to convince me to move my office to İstanbul, right? And you're hoping our hostess will badmouth Ankara, so become a conspirator in your plan?"

Neri looked at the Millers with interest. Maude was a nice-looking woman in her early fifties with salt-and-pepper hair and a soft Southern accent. Her husband was a tall, thin Midwesterner with a Henry Fonda face. He had a booming voice which Maude said he'd cultivated because of the immense distances it had to cover back home. Maude was from Savannah, Georgia, and they made quite a pair, John with his long strides and bold gestures, and Maude with her tiny ladylike steps and gentle demeanor. Their camaraderie reminded Neri of her parents, and she had a feeling that they were all going to be friends. God knows I need friends, she thought.

"Look, I love İstanbul, who wouldn't? I was born and grew up there, but it's a huge chaotic city. I went to a boarding school but whenever I decided to go home, it took me a long time: half an hour to forty minutes on the tram from Arnavutköy to Karaköy to take the twenty-five-minute ferry to Haydarpaşa on the Asian side, then thirty five minutes on the train to our home in Erenköy. But here everything is within easy reach."

"You went to college in Arnavutköy?" said Ayla Korkmaz, a dark slim vivacious beauty in her mid-thirties. "So did I." She was a professor of political science at the university, and her husband Mete was in charge of the government monopoly which produced and distributed cigarettes and alcohol. Ayla looked at Neri appreciatively but also with puzzlement, wondering how Ismet got such a well-brought-up girl to marry him. She was no friend of Ismet, having disliked him from the first moment she'd met him when he tried to seduce her as if he was God's gift to women. The stupid smug-ass, she thought. She'd always regretted not having had the courage to slap him.

Normally Ayla and her husband Mete would not have accepted Ismet's invitation but she had heard the good rumors about Neri and was curious to meet her. Now she was glad that they had come. Ismet's wife was a delightful young woman and worth cultivating as a friend. Besides, school loyalty demanded that they took care of each other.

"Don't you miss the sea and the Bosphorus?" Ayla asked.

"I do, every day," Neri sighed. "I close my eyes and see the emerald green waters and ruby sunsets of İstanbul. I miss it very much."

"Emerald green waters, ruby sunsets...You sound like a poet Neriman," chimed in Ayla's husband.

Neri blushed and looked up at him. "Don't pay any attention to me. I've had too many drinks."

"I think we all have," said Maude. "But I'm curious to know what jewel you think Ankara resembles?"

"A plain functional opal?" Neri suggested, making everyone laugh.

"It may be dull but you have to admit that it has a long and interesting history," interrupted a very tall man. Neri couldn't remember who he was.

"You're absolutely right," she said. "I've been reading about it, and I was amazed to discover that the first settlement goes all the way back to the second millennium B.C."

"Then it became part of the Ottoman Empire around the 14th century."

"Yes, but not before it was conquered and lost by the Greeks, Romans, Byzantines, Arabs, Seljuk Turks and the Mongols. Even Alexander the Great had it for a short while."

"I see you've done your homework, Mrs. Eloglu," said the tall man. Neri looked uncomfortable. The remark was a little condescending. She looked around for Ismet but he was nowhere in sight. Nor was Sarah Wiley.

"Don't mind him," John Miller interrupted. "He sometimes forgets that he's no longer in class in Princeton, putting his students down." Neri remembered what Ismet had said about the tall man: his name was Jack Horowitz but everyone called him 'the Professor', and he was in Ankara doing some research on Atatürk.

"I mean it as a compliment," said the Professor. "So many young Turks nowadays know nothing about their history. All they care for is the future."

"Reflecting on history is a luxury we cannot afford, Professor," said Mete. "Remember, we're busy building a new Turkey."

"You don't believe in learning from your past mistakes then?" asked the Professor.

"I do, but the government doesn't!" Mete replied, in his element now. "In the past, every time we tried to modernize, the Muslim clerics put a stop to it. Now the government is catering to the religious zealots again, hoping to broaden their base in the next elections. They're opening Pandora's Box and we'll all pay the price."

"But what about the freedom of religion? Some say that Atatürk was a little harsh in curbing the influence of religion."

"Yes, they like to paint him as anti-Islamic but you tell me, Professor, which serves the freedom of religion better. Atatürk saw to it that the Koran was translated into Turkish so that people could read and understand. Our Prime Minister declared that the only way to read our Holy Book was in its original Arabic which practically nobody speaks. If you can't read the Koran, it becomes impossible to challenge some of the strict behavioral and social codes imbedded in the Sharia. These commands would rule our daily life if we had – praise be to Allah—not become a secular country," he said to the amusement of the group. "Can you tell me if some of the restrictions applying to women are actually in the Koran? I don't speak Arabic but I've read the Koran in English and couldn't find a single sentence that said women should be covered from head to toe! Our current leaders seem to believe that ignorance is bliss."

"My father used to say that ignorant people are easier to control than others," said Neri.

"Like sheep," Mete agreed.

"You're bad mouthing sheep Mete," said Ayla. "It's unfair. They're not here to defend themselves!"

Professor Horowitz envied the Turks' knack of turning any heated conversation into light-hearted banter. Friendship always seemed to take precedent over principle. He took the hint, grabbed himself another large glass of bourbon and moved to the end of the room where Stan was sitting, reading a book.

"Very haunting music and lyrics," Mete meanwhile said addressing Neri about the new Nat King Cole record she'd just started playing. "What's it called?"

"*Lush Life*. The composer is Billy Strayhorn. Do you know him? He wrote music for Duke Ellington," explained Neri. At the mention of Strayhorn's name, Stan Wiley's head jerked up. For the first time he looked at her.

"Interesting and beautiful too, isn't she?" laughed Professor Horowitz. "Glad to see someone finally woke you up."

"I beg your pardon," Stan asked, puzzled and still staring at Neri.

"Nothing Stan. Go back to your reading. These are all Neri's books, did you know that? Ismet's brother told me. The record collection is hers too. She's really a very curious person." Stan listened, looking like a man who had stepped into the bright sunlight after spending years in a dark moldy place. He closed his book and moved near Neri and Mete.

"I heard you like Billy Strayhorn. How come you know about him?" For a second Neri could not remember who he was.

"I was interested in his music and found out about him. Did you know that there were some problems with Duke Ellington about proper attribution of his music. "

"I didn't know that. Who is your favorite American popular composer?"

Neri's brow crinkled up. "That's a hard question. I guess Cole Porter. But I also like George Gershwin."

"The pervasive influence of American music is incredible, isn't it?" Said Professor Horowitz.

"Sometimes underappreciated too. It has such universal appeal," responded Neri. "I believe jazz, as well as your pop music, is America's great gift to the rest of the world. It's enjoyed everywhere like your movies."

"Americanization of other cultures..." Stan said. "Is this a good thing?"

"Why not? Commonalities bring us together, and that can't be a bad thing, can it?" Neri commented.

"Don't forget American booze," said the Professor.

"And Mickey Mouse," said Neri.

"And cowboys."

"And blue jeans."

"And hot dogs."

"And hamburgers."

"Enough," said Stan, laughing, enjoying himself for the first time in a long while. Then he saw his wife glaring at him. He sighed and returned to his book.

While they were tidying up the flat after everyone had left, Neri got a whiff of Sarah's heavy perfume on Ismet. Suddenly, she felt an irresistible need to suppress a smile, visualizing herself as the wronged wife in a Barbara Stanwyck or Joan Crawford movie. This was no laughing matter. She should be feeling anger, betrayal, humiliation and even jealousy. But all she felt was confirmation of her unspoken fears. They'd told her he was a womanizer. What did she expect? That she'd be enough for him to change? No, she was not going to take responsibility for Ismet's inexcusable behavior. But shouldn't she at least feel hurt? The truth, the flimsiness of her feelings for her husband, stunned her. What had she done? She had no answer.

20

Two weeks before their first wedding anniversary, Neri's parents came for a short visit. They liked what she'd done with the house and even complimented her on her cooking! They had dinner with Ismet's parents, and Neri was proud of her mother who covered up her irritation at the way Huseyin had insisted that the men talk among themselves, keeping the women out of their "important" conversation.

Then they went to the museums, had dinner at Sureyya, the best restaurant in Ankara owned and operated by a White Russian emigrant, and saw an amazingly good version of Puccini's *Turandot* at the Opera House. Neri could see how proud her father was at the considerable accomplishments of the Turkish singers who were all recent graduates of the expanding conservatory. The Millers gave a party in their honor, and Nermin and Metin were happy to meet Neri's new friends.

The week passed quickly and Nermin was eager to return home. Throughout their fast-paced stay, she observed that Ismet appeared to be a doting, tender and attentive husband, but it all rang false. Nermin could tell that Neri was not happy but also that she was determined not to talk about it. It was hard for her to see her daughter so unhappy, and when Neri asked them to stay for her wedding anniversary party she refused, saying this was something she should celebrate with her husband alone. Neri wondered bitterly what was there to celebrate, not knowing that Nermin was asking the same question.

Saying goodbye to her parents at the train station was very hard for Neri. She was dying to run into their arms, beg them to forgive her and tell them she wanted to return home. But she could not. Instead she smiled, bought her mother magazines and her father the late edition of Ulus, the local newspaper which he enjoyed reading since it was brutally critical of the government. After waving to their daughter, in the split second that it took Nermin to move away so Metin could close the window, Nermin noticed the change in her daughter. The radiant smile on Neri's face was gone, replaced by a look of desperation only a mother could decipher. Nermin rushed to the window and cried out to her daughter, but they had disappeared from view as the train picked up speed.

Metin and Nermin sat in their compartment quietly for a long time, both disturbed and deep in thought. Finally, Metin broke the silence: "She is not happy."

"I know. It's Ismet and his family."

"Yes and from everything we've heard about him, I can't see him settling down with her, can you?"

"No, I can't. I wish I could have talked to Neri but as usual she avoided me."

"Me too," said Metin with a sigh.

"Is there anything we can do now? We made a mistake by not putting our foot down and preventing her from marrying him. I think that's what she needed and we failed her. I hope she's not destroying her life."

"Sure you're not being too dramatic? Things aren't as bad as that."

"Oh, Metin, you know you don't believe what you're saying. It's not just Ismet; it's his family. I felt like hitting you and his father during dinner at their home, the way you two excluded us from your conversation. You were rude and provincial."

"Well, what did you expect me to do? I couldn't tell the host that I needed permission from my wife to open my mouth, could I?" Seeing his wife's glaring look, Metin added, "Sorry, I know what you mean, but there wasn't anything I could do."

"Metin, we made a mistake in the way we raised our daughter. We taught her to rely on her own judgment, believe in herself and speak her mind. Now I'm beginning to wonder why the possibility never occurred to us that these qualities we valued and instilled in her could be considered totally dysfunctional by others."

Metin just stared blankly at her.

"I should have known that our culture does not value competent women who do not fit the quiet, compliant mold. Don't you think I know what some people say behind my back that I'm bossy and outspoken? I never cared what others thought because I've always felt safe and secure in our love but I should have prepared Neri for the real world out there. I blame myself for what's happening to her and for her anguish."

"Nermin, you're doing an injustice to yourself," Metin said, slipping an arm around his wife. "Just because you're not like other women doesn't mean there's something wrong with you. I love *you* and I hope Neri will soon discover in herself the same courage and determination you have. You're also being unfair to men. Surely you don't think I'm the only Turkish man who appreciates a woman who is independent and speaks her mind, do you? The trouble is not who Neri is but who Ismet is. I don't think she'd have had the same problems with other boys who wanted to marry her."

"You may be right. Ismet is from another world. His family is so authoritarian, so patriarchal. When Huseyin is around, his wife seems to vanish. She becomes part of the furniture and let me tell you, it's all an act because Nuriye's no dummy. This is her way of coping with her husband and her marriage but whether Nuriye realizes it or not, they're doing the same thing to Neri. She's fading into thin air. What are we going to do?"

"I don't know, Nermin," Metin said with a sadness he'd not felt in a long while.

21

Two things happened during her second year of marriage which pulled Neri out of the doldrums. First, despite the age difference, Maude Miller became a good friend. Then both Ceylan and Selma came to Ankara with their husbands who had been called up for military service, the three months of their officer training program. Neri helped them find a flat near her house and since their husbands were home only for weekends, the girls—they called themselves the girls, this despite the fact that everyone was married and Ceylan had a two-year old daughter—felt like they were back in school again.

Ismet was not happy. He knew the girls were dissecting him constantly. He could feel their veiled hostility every time they saw him. He also did not like the fact that they demanded so much of Neri's time, but he did not know how to stop them. So when John Miller decided to send Ismet to Diyarbakir to deal with a problem that was brewing there, he was relieved to be away from the girls' disapproving eyes.

Americans had a major military listening post in Diyarbakir. Although it was promoted as a joint base and a collaborative effort between the two governments, it was totally under American jurisdiction. Even the highest ranking Turkish officers were barred from entering the top secret base. However, the Turkish media had somewhat sniffed it out and they were trying to infiltrate the work crews, hoping to get some pictures of the powerful spying equipment directed at Russia. With the Cold War heating up, this plan to covertly obtain photographs could have been construed as a serious offense, a threat to the national security, but John Miller had convinced his superiors to deal with the problem diplomatically and quietly by sending Ismet who was good at dealing with delicate political situations. He was ordered to create as little fuss as possible and not to get his name in the papers.

Neri liked being alone. It was fun having her friends all to herself. They spent their time sightseeing, going to movies, and talking. It was therapeutic to open up to her friends and discuss her failing marriage. While commiserating obligingly, neither Ceylan nor Selma had been able to come up with any solutions. Many times during her weekly visits to Maude, Neri had thought about confiding in her too. Maude was nonjudgmental and kind like her mother, and a strong bond had grown between them, but Neri found it hard to discuss her marriage with anyone else but her old school friends. It was such an intimate subject, and she was afraid that Maude would find fault with her, whereas she knew the girls were a hundred per cent behind her.

The Millers lived in a new apartment building in Kavaklıdere where most of the foreign embassies were located. Their living room was spacious and uncluttered, with a few comfortable chairs and colorful antique *kilims* on the floor. Two huge copper cauldrons with big leafy plants stood on either side of the balcony, with its fantastic view of the city. There were exquisite, framed Turkish embroideries on the walls. The bookshelves were full of books on Turkish history and culture. Both John and Maude were learning to speak Turkish and Neri appreciated their interest in her country. She had met enough Americans to realize that this couple were different and did not fit the pejorative image sometimes heard on the street of the 'Ugly American.'

Maude liked her young Turkish friend. She had often considered warning Neri about Ismet but each time she'd considered it, she ended up rejecting the notion. How can you tell a newly-married woman that her beloved husband was a cad? She sometimes doubted Neri's love for her husband but why take the chance? Who knows what goes on behind closed doors, John kept on cautioning her.

Maude was still curious about Neri's marriage though: it just did not make sense. True, Ismet was useful in the office and helpful in many other areas too, and yes, he was charming. But she'd heard the rumors and suspected that he was unscrupulous, in two words, a liar and a cheat. Everyone except Neri seemed to know that Sarah was having an affair with him.

From the beginning, Maude had come to appreciate Neri and wanted to protect her from Sarah's continuing hostility. It was uncomfortable for everyone to hear Sarah's disparaging remarks, sometimes within Neri's hearing distance. Sarah would criticize Neri's English: "too pretentious, too British..." Neri's clothes: "Poor Ismet, all the money he's wasting on his wife's clothes. Who does she think she is, dressing like a little princess?" Neri's house: "All her furniture, copied from American magazines...I bet her parents still eat on the floor..."

They all knew Sarah had a bad temper but her hostility was puzzling. She should be the target of Neri's anger, not the other way around. Maude told John she would not allow Sarah to get away with such rudeness—at least not when she was around.

In the short while she'd become acquainted with Neri, Maude had come to appreciate Neri for her keen mind, polite manners and self-effacing humor. She was a good person and, she suspected, a romantic at heart, the daydreaming kind—the curse of the only child. Maude knew this because she was one herself. She also sensed that beyond Neri's bravura there was a naïve girl, desperately seeking a little understanding and guidance. This vulnerability had appealed to Maude's lonely heart. She loved her husband but their only child had died of polio as a toddler and ever since Maude had become drawn to orphans and lost kittens "in that order" her husband would tease her. In some ways, Maude saw

Neri as someone who one day would need her help. At the same time, Neri had a knack of making Maude feel young.

Today, Neri was even more radiant than usual telling Maude about the unexpected arrival of Selma and Ceylan and some of their antics while they were in school. She promised that she would bring them to tea as soon as possible. Maude had never seen her so animated. She looked like a teen-ager who had just secured a date to the prom with the captain of the football team. Did Turkish schools have football teams? Maude didn't know. It didn't matter really. It was nice to see Neri so happy.

As she was getting ready to leave, Neri stopped and asked Maude about Stan, Sarah's husband. "Can I ask you something about Mr. Wiley? He seems like a nice quiet man but so sad and distant. He never talks to anyone and looks depressed. What's wrong with him? Do you know him well?"

The question surprised Maude. Why the sudden interest in Stan? Was Neri trying to steer the conversation back to Sarah? Could Maude be honest about what was going on between Ismet and Sarah? "He's sad because of something tragic that happened to him," she answered. "About five years ago in the States he inadvertently killed two of his brothers. A car crash not his fault. Someone ran a light in high speed and rammed into them. Stan was in no way responsible for the accident. In fact, he almost lost his own life. You see, I think he still blames himself."

"I'm so sorry, I had no idea. Maybe the next time I see him, I'll try harder to talk to him. I thought perhaps he was not a friendly sort of person."

"If you try to be too nice to him, then he'll think you're addressing him out of pity. It's better to let him be."

"But that's a vicious circle, isn't it? Isn't there something we can do?"

Maude shook her head. Neri hesitated a second, then asked: "What about his wife? Why does she seem so angry all the time?"

"Sarah's not a happy person, Neri. I'm not excusing her behavior, but she's had her share of troubles too." The moment lingered. How do you justify cheating, Maude asked herself, to the wife whose husband you're cheating with? What a mess! "It's not well known but when Stan had his accident and was in the hospital for months fighting for his life, Sarah had a miscarriage. Afterwards Stan suffered from depression for a long time and was no help to Sarah when she needed him most. I think their marriage died then. As you've noticed, even now he is still very withdrawn. It must be hard for her or any wife to live with a husband who is so unresponsive." Neri nodded, for the first time feeling sympathy for Sarah, but the feeling passed quickly when she remembered the hostility she encountered every time she met her.

"I'm sorry to hear that she lost her baby," Neri said. "That must be a horrible experience. But what does that have anything to do with me? Why is she so rude to me? I don't know how to deal with her. She's making me uncomfortable."

"She's making everybody uncomfortable, Neri. There's nothing anyone can do. Just try to ignore her. We're all aware of the situation…" Can I mention that she's jealous of you because of Ismet, Maude thought, but lost her courage. She sensed that Neri was still not ready to discuss her husband's infidelity. "We're all on your side," Maude said, lamely.

Just then the doorbell rang and Sarah strode into the room. Speak of the Devil Neri thought. In her usual way, Sarah scrutinized Neri from top to bottom with the sneer she never tried to hide. It was as if Sarah was royalty and Neri was her slave! This time though Neri returned her gaze, unmoved. Then a wicked thought occurred to Neri and she smiled in a moment of malice. Sarah's tiny green eyes—too close together—inspired a nickname for her, Snake Eyes, and Neri knew the girls would approve.

Meanwhile Sarah was complaining that Ismet had promised to take her to the new jewelry store in Kızılay. She needed to buy a gift for Stan whose birthday was in two days. But now John had sent Ismet to Diyarbakir for "God knows how long" and the whole thing was very inconvenient "since I wanted to finish my shopping today." Then Sarah turned to Neri: "Perhaps you can help me with my shopping? It won't take more than an hour. I can give you a ride home too," she added, as though that would make the experience worthwhile.

The question caught Neri by surprise. This was the first time Sarah had ever addressed her directly and asked for a favor. Neri's cultural upbringing made it difficult to say no. It was rude to refuse a request, however unpleasant. Despite her better judgment, she nodded, thanked Maude for her hospitality and followed Sarah out. The Wileys' flat was just across the hall on the same floor. Unlike Maude's flat, Sarah's living room was cluttered with haphazardly chosen furniture. Heavy curtains, half closed, hid the view of the other buildings on the hill. A young village girl in baggy pants was bent over the floor collecting toys.

"Look at her! She hasn't even finished yet," remarked Sarah in an angry voice and switched to Turkish: "*Tamam, yok?*"

Neri hid her smile. Sarah's Turkish was atrocious and she had just put two unconnected words together. The girl blushed and said "*Ben her şeyi temizlemiştim ama ablanızın çoçukları gelip oyuncakları hertarafa yaydılar.*"

"She says she'd already finished all her chores and put away the toys when your sister's children came in and scattered them again," Neri translated.

"Excuses! She is always full of excuses. I hate these dumb village girls. Tell her to be quick. I'll go and see where my sister is. They're flying back home tomorrow."

Left alone, Neri noticed that the girl was in tears. She found out that her name was Tenzile and she had been working for the Madam, as she called Sarah, for four months. Tenzile said she'd replaced her older sister who got married. Neri asked why she was not at school? The girl lifted her head and stared making Neri feel ashamed for asking such a question.

"My family did not even let me finish grade school,' she said. "I've been working ever since I was eleven."

Neri gave Tenzile her card and told her to call if she needed anything. Just then Sarah returned saying she could not go out now but would appreciate if Neri could do her shopping for her and handed Neri a list.

Stunned, Neri realized that jewelry shopping had been a ruse. Sarah wanted to humiliate her by asking her to do her grocery shopping as if Neri was her maid! The enormity of the insult hit her hard. The woman must really hate me, Neri thought and felt diminished because she could not come up with a single response. She was not raised to be rude. She could not conjure up a single movie scene that would give her a clue about how to react. She could not slap her. She had never slapped anyone in her life. She could not resort to a verbal insult. Nothing came to her mind. So she dropped the crumpled list on the floor and walked away. Tears were streaming down her face as she ran down the stairs. As she walked out, she came face to face with Maude who was returning from the corner grocery store.

"What's wrong, Neri? What did she do to you?" But Neri just shook her head and ran into the street, flagging down a taxi. Curious and irritated, Maude took the elevator up and rang Sarah's bell.

"What did you do to Neri?" she asked, the minute Sarah opened the door.

"I didn't do anything. What are you talking about? There was a simple misunderstanding, that's all."

"Misunderstanding about what?"

"About shopping."

"What about shopping? Weren't you supposed to go to that new jewelry store in Kızılay to get a birthday gift for Stan? That's what you told us. So what was there to misunderstand?"

"How would I know? She is just a spoiled girl. She thinks she is better than everyone else. Probably her father is just a mid-level government bureaucrat anyway, dime a dozen and easily bought and sold."

Maude looked at her in amazement. The woman was something else. Why do they send such people to other countries to represent America, I'll never understand, Maude told herself. She had to talk to John about this whole incident. As she turned to leave she noticed the crumpled paper on the floor. She bent down and picked it up. When the significance of it hit her mind like a red-hot iron, she became so furious that she could not bring herself to say anything to Sarah. She thought it would be better to leave before the urge to hit Sarah smack on the nose became too irresistible.

Maude talked to John that night about the whole incident. John was reluctant to get involved.

"What do you want me to do? I can't talk to Stan about his wife's rude behavior. Even her infidelity doesn't seem to bother him. Why do you think he'd even care what Sarah does to Neri?" It was a good question. How can any man live with a wife who was having an affair with someone else and making no attempt to be discrete about it?

"I don't understand this Stan," Maude said. "He's still a young man, and he is a good man too. How long is he going to continue like this, dead emotionally and intentionally blind to what's going around him? It's such a waste."

"I don't know," John sighed. "I'm his boss not his therapist."

22

The girls were furious when they heard what Sarah had done and Selma said Neri should have punched Sarah on the nose. The other two looked at Selma in utter shock. She was known for her quiet manners and gentleness. For her to suggest that Neri should have resorted to such violence was absolutely unbelievable.

"Sure," Neri said, laughing, "and I should have kicked her butt as well."

"Why not?" Selma said. "The woman is vicious. She deserves it."

"Come on," Ceylan said. "What can Neri do? She can't respond in kind, that's not her."

"Why not?" Selma turned and faced Neri. "The woman is fucking your husband, isn't she? Do something about it." She had switched to English and the crude language stunned the other two. They had never heard Selma use a profanity before.

"Such as?" asked Neri.

"Get even!" Selma blurted.

"Who *are* you?" exclaimed Neri, shocked, "and what have you done to my well behaved friend? If I didn't know better, I'd say that you're suggesting I should have an affair with Sarah's husband? Are you nuts?"

"No, of course not, but you could make her jealous, can't you? Give her a taste of her own medicine? Put the fear of God into her? What's good for the goose is..."

"Stop it, Selma. You're talking nonsense."

"Wait a second," cut in Ceylan who was wearing her I-am-thinking-don't-bother-me-now expression on her face. "It is not a bad idea. Think of it this way. You can flirt a little... wait now, don't interrupt. We have all seen what women can do to men in that department. I'm suggesting just a little flirtation and see what happens. Besides, you'd be teaching Ismet a lesson too. So you'd be killing two birds with one stone."

"Would you two stop talking like this? What's with all these stupid sayings? I'm married so I can't flirt with anyone, least of all that poor Stan."

"Why poor?" both women said. So Neri had to tell them about Stan's tragic accident. That sobered them for a minute or two.

Then Ceylan perked up. "Think of it this way, Neri. Maybe the poor man needs a little loving care. I am sure he does not get it from Snake Eyes. So you'll be doing him a favor."

Strange as it seemed, the whole idea was beginning to intrigue Neri. Why had she asked Maude about Stan? Was she unconsciously concocting a seduction plan? She wasn't sure but her friends were beginning to sense that she was warming to the idea. So they kept on devising different scenarios to snare poor Stan when their fun was interrupted by a stormy-looking Ismet walking into the room.

"I need to talk to you," he said without acknowledging the others.

"Fine, but later. Can't you see we have guests? I wasn't expecting you back so soon. I'm glad you're back though. I have a lot to tell you."

Ismet had an uncanny sense of smelling trouble. He could feel the hostility emanating from the girls so he turned his charm on full force without getting anywhere. They were all set against him, including his wife.

After Ceylan and Selma left, a somewhat deflated Ismet asked what had happened with Sarah? "Sarah showed up at the office and made a scene in front of everyone telling them how rude you had been. What did you do to her?"

"What did I do to her? You should be asking what she did to me!"

"OK. What did she do to you?"

"Well, she asked if I could go with her to the new jewelry store at Kızılay and pick a birthday gift for her husband, as if we were bosom friends! So I couldn't say no. Then she walked me to her flat and gave me a grocery shopping list instead." Recalling the humiliating experience was too much for Neri. Tears were beginning and she did not want to show any weakness in front of her husband. She tried to laugh it off. "I guess she didn't trust her maid to buy her groceries. Perhaps she knew how obliging all Turks are, so she asked me. I'm sure she didn't mean it as an insult." The irony in her voice was unmistakable.

Ismet knew what Sarah was capable of. He could easily see her reverting to ugly tactics just to humiliate his wife. He had been forced to deal with Sarah's jealousy more than once. He looked at Neri. She was so beautiful and so sad. He almost felt guilty for exposing her to the likes of Sarah. He loved his wife more than anything, except himself, of course. He knew he was selfish and determined to beat all the odds to succeed in life. He had to show his father, didn't he? Neri was his Achilles' heel, his only weakness, and this marriage was doing no good either to himself or to Neri.

Ismet did not like protracted self-reflection. He was a man of action. Still it bothered him that he had taken this carefully brought-up fragile girl—yes, fragile, despite all her notions of independence and competence—into an alien world. Perhaps he should have left her in her family's protective cocoon. Trying to be worthy of her was turning out to be beyond his capacity, character, and, he admitted sadly, beyond his will.

"I'm so sorry, Neri," Ismet said and put an arm around his wife's shoulder and kissed her cheek. "I know Sarah can be cruel.

131

What she did was inexcusable, but she is a troubled woman. That's why I try to spend so much time with her." Was he treading on dangerous ground? Maybe he shouldn't have left such an opening for Neri to start asking questions about Sarah? But Neri did not respond. She was looking at Ismet with amazement. It was so rare to see Ismet show some concern for her feelings that she almost forgot about his relationship with Sarah. Neri sighed and let her head rest on her husband's shoulder.

Deep down she knew she was taking the easy option.

23

I smet and Neri were late to Korkmaz's party. Neri was always prompt but tonight she was taking her time. When she finally emerged from the bedroom, Ismet was stunned by her looks. She had a different hair-do and more makeup than usual. She looked glamorous but also dangerous. Ismet's heart filled with pride. No one has such a striking wife, he thought. All his guilty feelings about taking her out of the bosom of her protective family disappeared. He looked forward to showing off his wife.

The party was in full swing when they arrived. Mete and Ayla came over to welcome them, chiding their lateness.

"It's Neri's fault," Ismet said. "She took a long time dressing."

"But it was worth it," Ayla exclaimed, looking at Neri with admiration. Ismet turned and glanced at Neri as she was taking off her coat. She was wearing a simple sleeveless black dress with a low-cut V-neck, the back with the same deep cut. The dress was short, exposing her long legs. Her only jewelry was a star-shaped diamond antique pin given her by her aunt. She looked like an elegant model. Ismet had never seen the dress before. Then he realized it was one that she always wore, but usually hidden by a matching jacket. Why take the jacket off tonight, he wondered feeling uncomfortable. Neri looked like a different person with a promise of fire and heat under the cool surface which unsettled him.

Ismet was not the only one noticing the change in Neri. Several men quietly crowded around her. Maude wondered what she was up to. Her innocent young friend had become a femme fatale. She turned and saw Sarah glaring at Neri like a human volcano, ready to spew out red hot lava. Oh, oh, thought Maude to herself, trouble's a-brewing. She decided not to interfere but just wait and watch. Suddenly she realized that she had short-changed Neri by treating her like a wounded child. Clearly she was a grown-up woman and on her own war path.

All the men wanted to dance with Neri, including the Professor. She was having a good time while keeping a discreet eye on Stan. Like everyone else he was watching her with more than usual interest. Neri knew if she didn't act, she would lose her courage to implement the seduction plan the girls had devised. What a hypocrite I'm becoming she thought, pretending I had nothing to do with it. It's my plan too.

Neri now noticed that Maude had joined Stan in a corner. She told herself it's now or never. Take baby steps, don't rush into it, there's a friend at hand to rescue you just in case....So Neri slowly sashayed through the crowd while Maude watched her with growing amusement. She kissed Maude on both cheeks and asked how she was doing. Then Neri turned her radiant face to Stan and purred: "Hello, Mr. Wiley, how are you doing tonight? I didn't get a chance to talk to you yet."

"Thank you, Mrs. Eloglu. I am fine, but please call me Stan."

"Only if you call me Neri," she smiled, looking up at him sweetly.

I am glad she refrained from batting her eyelashes, Maude thought; she knew exactly what Neri was up to and she didn't blame her one bit. She decided to leave them alone. She excused herself and went to warn her husband John. Maude expected fireworks soon.

Meanwhile Stan and Neri were quietly staring at each other. She had never noticed how handsome and young he was, particularly when he was animated, as he was now. He was very tall with a trim body, dark hair, soft friendly brown eyes, and a deep voice.

"You have a beautiful name, Neri. Maude was just telling me it's short for Neriman. And thank you for allowing me to call you by your first name. I know that's reserved only for family members and close friends in Turkey."

"I'm surprised that you know our customs, Stan... Oh, I'm so sorry. That did not come out right. I just meant to say that most Americans know very little about our traditions."

"Please, don't apologize. I am acutely aware of our shortcomings. But I have lived in Turkey before." This was total news to Neri.

"You have?" she asked incredulously. "When?"

"When I was a teenager. You see my father was in the State Department and worked at the American Embassy here for a number of years before he decided that it was time for us to join him. We all arrived and lived in Ankara for over three years. This was in the mid-thirties."

"Oh, my God," Neri said, "that's incredible. There's so much I want to ask you. Please, can we just sit somewhere and talk?" All her plans to flirt with Stan were forgotten. "Tell me about Ankara," she pleaded. He seemed only too happy to oblige.

"When we first arrived in 1934, Ankara was still a small town. None of the residential areas like Kavaklıdere and Bahçelievler had been built yet. The main intersection of Kızılay was just in the process of being developed. Most of the town crowded around the Ulus section and the train station. The trees were little stumps, and you could see the top of the hill where the Roman citadel is now without all these shanties blocking the view. There were very few restaurants or hotels. But it was still a great city."

"1934," said Neri, in a voice filled with awe, "that's when a lot of Atatürk's reforms were being implemented?"

"Yes. Actually when we first arrived, your Assembly had just passed the surname law and everyone was scrambling around trying to find a name that would represent them. My father used to tell stories about families breaking up simply because they couldn't agree on a name, or neighbors quarrelling because they wanted the same surname. It was really a peculiar time. I never forgot the day the Assembly enacted the law bestowing on your president the surname of Father of the Turks, Atatürk. That was a very emotional day for the whole nation."

"I envy your memories, Stan. You lived our history. Please tell me more." Neri said.

"Well, some of the reforms that were passed while we were here included the one about dress codes. My father said that after wearing the fez became illegal, hat shops sprouted in Ankara like mushrooms." They both laughed. "Then of course the most important of all reforms, as far as I am concerned, was the one giving women the right to vote and run for elected office. You realize, of course, Turkey did that thirteen years earlier than France, don't you? So much for Western democracy!" Neri was spellbound.

"I am amazed you remember your time here so vividly."

"The reason is simple. I met my first love here."

"Oh, Stan, how wonderful! Was she an American? How did you meet?"

"No, she was our Turkish neighbor's thirteen year old daughter, two years younger than I was. I remember following her like a sheep dog. Every time she saw me, she would cover her mouth with her hand and giggle. I thought her the most beautiful girl in the world." He looked at Neri sadly. "If you don't mind my saying, I imagine she grew up to look like you." Neri was touched.

"That is the nicest thing anybody ever said to me. Thank you." They looked at each other. Neri felt a pang of guilt remembering what she had intended to do to the poor man just an hour ago.

Their tête-à-tête had attracted a lot of attention. It was not like Neri to spend so much time with a single person, and no one had ever seen Stan looking so happy or talking so much. Maude had

136

been watching Ismet and Sarah closely. Despite all her efforts, Ismet was not paying much attention to Sarah. He looked distracted, worried. His eyes were constantly on his wife. He finally started walking towards the corner where Neri and Stan were sitting.

"They're serving dinner now Neri, aren't you hungry?" he asked.

"Oh, Ismet, please sit down. Did you know that Stan had been in Ankara before? He has been telling me such interesting things about Ankara in the thirties."

"You were here before?" Ismet asked. "I didn't know that. Still let's all go and eat. We can talk later." With that he took his wife's arm and began leading her to the buffet table.

There was a commotion at their back. They heard Sarah's voice. "What were you talking to her about all night long, Stan? Leaving me all alone. Is this your way of punishing me?"

"Quiet, Sarah. No need to make a scene."

"Why were you talking to that woman? You know I don't like her."

"I didn't know I needed your permission. Besides, I was just telling her how Ankara was in the thirties."

"A likely story. I'm really mad at you, Stan."

"Time to go home, Sarah."

Neri glanced discreetly and saw Stan firmly pushing a red-faced Sarah out of the room. She smiled. She had not done anything to be ashamed of, yet she had managed to infuriate the Snake Eyes. Good!

Maude had seen it too. Too bad, no fireworks, she thought. But maybe that was for the best. She did not want her friend to get into trouble. You never knew what Sarah was capable of. She caught Neri's eyes; they nodded and shrugged their shoulders. They knew exactly what the other was thinking. Mission accomplished. But would there be repercussions?

On the way home, Ismet seemed agitated. He had the look of a man who shouldn't open his mouth but couldn't help it.

"Your behavior was strange tonight, Neri."

"What do you mean strange?"

"Didn't you notice? Everyone was staring at you."

"Isn't that what you want every time you take me out?"

Ismet looked at her sharply. "Why would I want everyone to stare at you?"

"How would I know? But that's the impression you give."

This was not the conversation Ismet had in mind. "I don't know what you're talking about, Neri. People were staring at you because you spent such a long time talking to Stan. It looked inappropriate."

"How long is an inappropriate talk with Stan or any other man, Ismet?

Ismet sighed. She was being deliberately provocative, Ismet thought. What was happening to his wife? She usually avoided confrontations. He also had a sinking feeling that if he pursued badgering her any longer, one way or another his behavior if not his affair with Sarah was going to surface. He wised up and kept silent.

24

They had just finished dinner and were sipping Turkish coffee at the house of USAID director Tom Wilkes and his wife Christie. It was a small group and they all noticed that Stan had come without Sarah again.

As usual the conversation was getting heated with Mete arguing that the Menderes government was not only dismantling every good program implemented by the previous administrations but was also damaging the chances of future administrations by politicizing religion.

"They are reverting to the old ways of using religion as a means of keeping people ignorant and manageable," Mete was saying.

"By opening religious schools instead of universities," Ayla added, "and by closing down programs that helped reduce our deplorable illiteracy rate."

"Which programs are you talking about?" asked the Professor, knowing very well which programs they were.

"Such as the urban programs designed to increase literacy and civic awareness as well as the rural programs offering agricultural and other farming-related courses," said Ayla.

"Yes, but I read some seriously negative information about these programs," Tom said. "Wasn't there some documentation indicating that they had been infiltrated by the communists?"

"Depends who you're talking to," Ayla answered. "I can cite you statistics to prove that the adult classes enhanced literacy rates and general knowledge. We don't know what impact the widely popular civic classes could have had on the general population by making them more involved in public affairs. But obviously the government became increasingly suspicious of them. We seem to be afraid of educating the masses. The same thing happened with the rural village institutes. What was wrong with teaching rural kids some elementary knowledge such as how to farm more effectively or how to fix a broken tractor?"

"Nothing was wrong with the intent but I heard that the fact that girls and boys were being taught together offended some people's religious sensibilities," Tom said.

"The same religious sensibilities that have interfered with all our modernization efforts and kept us a backward country much too long, you mean?" Ayla said with a sharp tone to her voice.

Mete interrupted. "Come on Tom, give me one incident, when a Turkish government has listened to what people say or feel. The imams were afraid of losing their grip on the villagers and they incited the pious among them, saying that it was against Islam to teach girls and boys together. And of course the aghas who own the villages were not happy to see anyone getting educated. Can you imagine, peasant kids learning to think for themselves! No, Tom, I don't think they closed these programs because of fear of communism or religious sensibilities. They closed them because an enlightened and free-thinking electorate scares them more than anything else."

"You know Tom, according to some journalists it's the Americans who are encouraging our government to go soft on religion as a deterrent to communism," said Ayla.

This is precisely where Tom had not wanted the discussion to go. "That's nonsense," he objected. "But you must agree Ayla that there aren't many Islamic nations in the world that have embraced communism."

"It's because most of them have despotic regimes, many of which, by the way, you support. Can't you see the relationship between oppressive Islam, ignorant populace, and undemocratic regimes," insisted Mete.

"You have a point, Mete," said the Professor. "Without an educated electorate, you have no hope of real democracy."

"Unfortunately we're still struggling to develop a good educational system," said Neri thoughtfully. "In middle school all I did was to memorize things. It was only after I went to the American college I realized that learning required understanding. My father used to say that our schools encourage rote learning but not thinking."

"As a graduate of a Turkish school, I agree with your father one hundred percent. I'm still learning to think," Mete said.

"Oh, yes, don't I know it" said Ayla, making everyone laugh. Here we go again, the urge to lighten the conversation, thought the Professor but he kept on prodding.

"Going back to religion though, I sometimes wonder if you young modern Turks fail to appreciate fully the hold religion has on people. Look at our past: it took Christianity centuries of bloody struggle before some sense of rationality and tolerance was allowed to creep into it. I'm beginning to think Atatürk was wrong in muzzling religion."

"Jack," sighed Mete, "you know our history better than any of us. Why do you say Atatürk was harsh on religion? All he wanted was to keep it out of the public arena. Our history has taught us that religion and state affairs don't mix. I can argue that Islam was one of the factors leading to the collapse of the Ottoman Empire."

"Never mind the Ottoman Empire," said Ayla. "Look what's happening in the world now. Almost the entire Muslim world suffers from poverty, illiteracy, and tyranny. You don't think the way Islam is practiced has anything to do with why these countries lag behind the West in every socio-economic and democratic measure, do you?"

"Such as?" asked the Professor.

"Such as gross domestic product, industrial output, book sales, modern amenities like telephone lines, health care, scientific research, human rights...shall I go on?"

"No, I get the picture," said the Professor.

"Turkey is the only Muslim country which has shown improvements in all these areas because of our secular constitution," continued Ayla.

"There's nothing wrong with Islam but everything wrong with the way it's practiced, if you ask me," said Neri. "Our Prophet Mohammed insisted that our faith was a personal bond between us and Allah and that no one should tell us how to practice it," Neri added, noting that Ismet was scowling at her.

"Are you religious Neri?" asked the Professor.

"You've got me, Professor," Neri laughed. "I don't think you can call me a religious person. At least, I'm not a practicing Muslim."

"What do you mean you're not a practicing Muslim?"

"Just what I said: I don't pray, at least not using Arabic words; I don't go to mosque, and I have no intention of listening to a religious man tell me how to live my life! However, I do believe in the need for religion. It seems to be a human condition. Like everyone else, I'd like to think there's a benevolent being up there somewhere, looking after us, giving us hope and resiliency. I think faith is a necessity, nourishment for our souls, you might say..." She was silent for a second, the others staring at her intently. "Our Koran dictates we should treat each other with compassion, justice and equality. But in practice, women are excluded. It's hard for me to condone this. So I don't believe what's usually propagated in the name of religion. I also don't believe in life after death and I certainly don't believe in heaven and hell, nor" she added with a smile and a quick apologetic look at her husband, "that men are superior to women."

"Good for you, Neri," said Ayla. Neri noticed that Ismet was no longer looking at her but watching Stan. She glanced at Stan and what she saw on his face made her blush.

"Sometimes I don't understand her, John," Maude was saying to her husband on the way home from the party. "She is not afraid of offending God with all her talk of not believing in life after death, yet she seems to be petrified of what others would say if she packs up and goes home to her parents."

"How do you know it's a lack of courage? She must be in love with her husband. Why else would she have married him? Besides I think you're always much too harsh on Ismet. He's not as bad as you think."

"What do you mean he's not as bad as I think? Are you condoning infidelity all of a sudden? You'd better fire him. He's becoming a bad influence on you."

John looked at his wife and laughed. They'd been married nearly thirty years and he still loved her. "Sure I'll fire him if that's what you want."

"Seriously John, I wonder why or how they got married. There's a mystery here and soon enough I'm going to solve it."

"You really like Neri, don't you?" John asked his wife.

"Yes, like a daughter," Maude answered but refrained from voicing 'like the one we lost.' Sometimes she dreamt that her daughter had grown up and become a lovely woman just like Neri, but with a better husband. Definitely with a better husband.

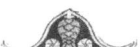

It was a good thing Ayla was driving because Mete was still fuming. "Why is it so hard to talk about religion with our American friends?"

"It's because unlike you, they're all deeply religious, Mete," Ayla said. "Plus they no longer have the problems with religion we face."

"I know. We need to go through the process of religious reformation that the Christians went through."

"And a long period of enlightenment."

"Don't hold your breath, Ayla. That's not going to happen in our lifetime and the only thing that's keeping us from sliding back to Sharia Law and a seventh century mentality is our secular laws that this government is intent on destroying."

"Many Americans I know seem to be uncomfortable with the notion of secularism. To them, it verges on sacrilege, as good as being anti-religious."

"I sometimes wonder if that does not serve their political purpose?"

"What do you mean?" asked Ayla.

"I'm beginning to give credence to the conspiracy theorists who claim that the Americans want Turkey to become more religious so that our faith could deter the spread of communism."

"I suspect our faith is perceived as a deterrent to nationalism too. I just gave a talk in my class about how nationalism is increasingly perceived as an impediment to the Western powers who still cling to their imperialistic aspirations."

"I bet that was not in your government-approved curriculum?" Mete said with an edge to his voice. Ayla nodded, her brow creased. The problems of her country upset her deeply, and they were goading her toward behavior both reckless and dangerous for a political science professor in a public university. Until now Ayla had been able to conceal her activities from her husband. But 'probably not much longer' she said to herself, worried. She was not eager to face the day when Mete would learn about her lectures that were sharply critical of the present government's policies. He was what the Turks called a 'modern' man with progressive ideas about women. He did not believe women should stay home quietly and do as they're told. He was proud of his elderly aunt who had shed her veil and joined the national forces fighting the Greek invaders in 1922. Mete still displayed the medal awarded to her by Atatürk for her bravery. Still, Ayla wasn't sure how tolerant he would be of his own wife's 'bravery'. She suspected he would call it foolhardiness! She sighed as she parked the car in front of their apartment building.

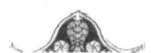

In the taxi going home, Ismet couldn't contain himself anymore. "Neri, what was all that talk about not being a good Muslim?"

"I didn't say I wasn't a good Muslim. I just said I was not a practicing Muslim."

"Isn't it the same thing?"

"Is it? I don't see you going to mosque or praying, yet you pretend to be a good Muslim whenever you discuss religion with your father."

"You're right, I don't do everything a good Muslim should do, but I believe in our Islamic tenets..."

"So do I but I suspect not in everything you believe, Ismet. Besides, isn't there something in the Koran about not judging people on their religious practices?"

"Is there?" Ismet laughed, deciding not to pursue the subject. "You're sure?"

"No, I'm not but there should be!" She decided not to argue. Religion was a murky, confusing subject for her. She believed in the existence of God but not in everything said in his name. Better not to discuss such things with anyone, she reminded herself but it was a subject that was becoming difficult to avoid with the increasing intrusion of religion into public life day by day.

25

The New Year's Eve party given by Mete and Ayla was a success with drinks flowing and people dancing. Mete worried that it was getting near what everyone was calling "the pinching hour" when Professor Horowitz threw away his serious and dignified demeanor and turned into Mr. Hyde, running after every female and pinching their bottoms. Even Neri had been subjected to his groping hands until she had learned to recognize the look and become adept at avoiding him which was not very difficult if you were good at sprinting because by pinching hour the Professor was drunk and totally unsteady on his feet.

Mete and John had a bet going about how many drinks it took the Professor to metamorphose into Mr. Hyde, but it was not easy to keep track of his drinks. The Professor used to be a bourbon drinker but lately he had been seen drinking Turkish *raki* too, making his behavior rather unpredictable.

"This is serious," Mete was arguing. "I've invited a lot of my colleagues tonight, some of whom are very uptight and old-fashioned. If he starts pinching their wives, we're going to have a serious problem on our hands."

"But what do you suggest?" asked John. "It's not even eleven. We can't ask him to go home yet. Besides we gave him a ride here, and I'm not going anywhere just yet."

"I'll try to keep an eye on him," offered Maude.

"This open bar of yours, John, makes it hard to know how much he's drinking," Mete warned. "Please Maude, make sure that he eats a lot of *meze*. We're not going to eat till after twelve."

Mete's open bar was stacked with black market bottles of American whisky, bourbon, gin and vodka in spite of the fact that part of Mete's job was to prevent the illegal sale of foreign liquors. But these drinks had become very popular, and like American cigarettes, they were sold openly at the corner grocery stores. A class of neuveau riche was rapidly growing on the sale of these black market goods.

Mete and John both suspected that Ismet was already involved in the black market business but they were keeping their concerns to themselves until they could find proof. If Ismet was implicated, however, it would present a serious problem because of their friendship with Neri. Their affection for Neri was complicating everything, including their treatment of Sarah. They had never been too fond of Sarah and now they were all trying to avoid her and her disparaging remarks about Neri.

They also worried about Stan. He was no longer morose but glowed whenever Neri was around. They watched the four of them with growing concern: Sarah, increasingly verbal and angry, flaunting her relationship with Ismet shamelessly to spur her husband to action; Stan oblivious to Sarah but coming alive whenever Neri was around; Ismet calm, collected, and devious as usual, but keeping an eye on Stan; and Neri, obviously starved for tenderness, responding to Stan slowly and cautiously like a traveler in the desert testing the water in an oasis before drinking it. The question on all their minds: would she drink it?

In any case, Neri had changed the dynamics of their group. It was buzzing with tension and the political problems, which the Turks were convinced were exacerbated by the Americans, were feeding on and fueling that tension.

Things were getting difficult for Neri too. She did her best to avoid Sarah as much as possible, but Neri was also becoming a little uncomfortable with Stan. She knew Stan was attracted to her; you had to be blind not to see her charmed effect on him. But Neri also knew that Ismet was keeping a closer eye on her and somehow this irritated her. She could not decide whether Ismet's attention was due to heartfelt jealousy, hurt pride or fear of losing a prized possession. At the same time, she couldn't face the feelings she knew she was developing for Stan. Their intensity confused her.

So far this evening she had been able to avoid Stan, dancing every dance with the young American officers and some of Ayla's academic friends, but she was getting tired and a little headachy with all the noise and the drinks. She needed a few moments to herself, so she went out into the corridor to find Ayla's study and to take a peek at her famous book collection.

The flat was huge, the rooms running into each other without rhyme or reason. Suddenly in the library she felt, without actually seeing, Professor Horowitz bearing down on her. Oh, oh, she said to herself, the pinching hour, and ran through the first door she saw. A couple stood in the middle of the dark room in a tight embrace. With a sinking heart Neri realized it was Sarah and Ismet.

For a second she couldn't breathe. This was not a movie scene. It was her own husband who was passionately embracing another woman. Her heart ached, out of jealousy or humiliation, she didn't know. All she wanted to do was to escape. She closed the door, barely escaping the Professor's hands before Stan appeared out of nowhere, grabbed her arm and pulled her through another door onto the crowded dance floor.

"Thank you Stan for saving me," she said looking up at him.

He bent down and smiled: "Any time."

They were being jostled by the other dancers while standing still in each other's arms. Suddenly, Neri had an uncanny feeling of déjà vu. Stan's height, lean body and arms reminded her of that brief moment years ago with Bill. She felt herself blushing at the memory and was afraid that Stan would misread her face.

The countdown to midnight began with everyone shouting the passing seconds and laughing. They stood there quietly, staring at each other. He was still holding her close. She could hear his heart beating. When the lights went out, she impulsively stood on her toes and kissed him. Stan pulled her tighter and kissed her back, hard and long. She regretted immediately what she'd done.

Neri knew she had enjoyed the kiss and did not feel any shame. Ismet and Sarah deserved a little of their own back. But she was not sure if it was the wish for revenge that had motivated her. Maybe Stan had reminded her of Bill and she had just wanted to go back to that April night, to imagine Bill's arms around her and taste his mouth again. Or maybe she had simply wanted Stan. What kind of a person was she becoming?

Before Neri could entangle herself from his arms, the lights came on and someone grabbed and kissed her on the cheek, wishing her Happy New Year! Other friends crowded round her, while the whole time Neri could feel Stan's eyes on her. But she could not read his expression.

Then suddenly Ismet was back, with the immediate smell of that perfume on him, and he was pulling her close. Neri felt dizzy with conflicting emotions and allowed herself to be swung around away from Stan.

Would her life go on like this? Was 1955 going to be another bad year?

26

Neri had an unexpected visitor. Nuriye had never come to her house unannounced before. She could feel apprehension creep over her. Was she going to be lectured about how to become a better wife? Or how Ismet could be a better husband? She realized she was gritting her teeth. She put on a big smile and invited her mother-in-law inside.

Surprisingly, Nuriye appeared more nervous than she was. After the usual polite queries about health and weather that opened up all Turkish conversations, Nuriye reached over and took Neri's hand.

"Neri," she said, "I want to talk to you about my son. I know he's not making you happy. I am not going to give any excuses, please do not misunderstand me. But you're an intelligent woman so maybe what I'm going to say will help." She looked at Neri pleadingly, as if asking for permission to continue.

Neri was stunned. She had not expected this. "Yes, please continue," she said in a small voice.

"You know I was only sixteen, Neri, when my parents forced me to marry Huseyin. I wanted to finish school but nothing I said would change their mind. Next year I gave birth to Ismet. Can you imagine it? I was a carefree girl playing with dolls one year and the next I had a baby of my own! I knew nothing about how to be a wife, let alone a mother. We were living in Ankara, far away from my parents, family, friends, everyone I had known all my life. I had no one to talk to. So I coped as best I could. Obviously not too well." Neri could hear the regret in her voice.

"Huseyin was no help. All he wanted was a house he could retreat to after a hard day's work, eat, and rest." She looked at Neri and seemed to be struggling to say something else but decided against it. Neri could guess though. Ah, yes, she said to herself, and a warm bed!

"Neither of us knew how to be a parent," Nuriye continued. "Two years later I had Mehmet. I thought I was in prison with two screaming kids and a husband who didn't say more than ten words to me each day. I don't remember when the verbal abuse started... No, Neri, not to me, to Ismet."

Neri felt a pang of understanding.

"It was probably when Ismet was thirteen or so, just about the time Huseyin's job started failing. He never raised his hand, but he was harsh. He denigrated everything Ismet did. There was nothing Ismet could do to please his father so after a while he stopped trying." Nuriye stopped as if unable to continue. She looked old and worn out. Neri did not know what to say so she asked if Nuriye would like to have a cup of tea, but she declined.

"No Neri, let me finish what I came here to do. You know I am not an educated person. I don't know if any of the things I'm telling you make sense. But they do to me. I blame Huseyin for the man Ismet has become. As much as he hates his father, he is an exact copy: selfish, insensitive, and only interested in making money. That's who they are. Their only goal in life is to make more money than everyone else. It is ironic that both have failed."

"Nuriye *anne*,"—the first time Neri had used the term 'mother' to Nuriye—"please, let me make you a cup of tea or bring you a glass of water."

"Water would be fine," she replied, wiping her tears.

"My son loves you, Neri. When I first saw you, I thought maybe you could save him from himself. I now realize that he

151

cannot be a better husband than his own father. We ruined him. He has inherited his father's worse traits. He feels entitled just because he is a man. Don't think of him as an immoral person. Our culture supports him. He is the head of the house. You cannot question him, least of all his behavior, particularly outside your home."

Neri shook her head. She did not know if she could excuse infidelity just because Nuriye said it was culturally acceptable. Besides, in whose culture was it condoned? She knew her parents would have never approved it. She kept silent.

"Neri, what are you going to do?"

"I don't know," she answered, honestly. "I've been thinking of going to İstanbul for a week or two. I miss my parents and they want me to come. Don't worry. I'm not going to discuss my marriage or this conversation with them. I just need to be with my parents for a little while...to think."

Nuriye got up to leave and kissed Neri on both cheeks. "Give my love to your parents. Talk to them, Neri, they can help you." She looked sad and lost. Neri could almost see Nuriye as the pretty sixteen year old girl she must have been, a girl like herself once, full of dreams for the future. She embraced and kissed Nuriye goodbye. It was after she closed the door that Neri realized she was crying.

That night, Neri told Ismet she wanted to go home to İstanbul for a short visit. His reaction was predictable. Angry, he told her he wouldn't even consider it. She glared at him and said that she was not asking for permission. She was going. He could not budge her.

After a sigh, Ismet said he'd get the train tickets in the morning.

27

Neri liked train travel. She particularly liked the night express that ran between Ankara and İstanbul. It was almost as elegant as the Orient Express which had introduced her to luxury travel. Despite the soot bellowing out from its stack, the night express was always clean. Her first-class compartment was spotless. The marqueterie walls with delicate flower designs were perfectly polished. The red velvet seat did not have a single stain.

Immediately the steward brought a vase for the flowers Ismet had bought her. Her husband was trying to be nice, or she thought cynically, he liked playing the part of the affluent caring husband. She thanked him and promised reluctantly that she would not be staying long in İstanbul. They said their goodbyes and she felt a growing sense of relief and freedom as the train gained speed.

An hour later she walked into the restaurant car, dazzling with heavily starched white table clothes, polished silverware, and crystal glasses. She was seated at a table for two and before she could even unfold her heavy napkin, she heard a familiar voice addressing her.

"Neri, what are you doing here? I didn't know you were going to İstanbul?" Surprised, she looked up and saw Stan standing by her table.

"Nor you," she stammered. This was going to be an unwanted complication.

"May I join you?"

"Of course." What else could she have said?

Stan sat across her and they both picked up their menus. The tension between them was palpable. She declined his offer to share a bottle of wine. They decided what they were going to eat and Neri let him order. The silence was becoming unbearable. They said each other's name at the same time and laughed.

"After you, Neri."

"OK, I want to apologize about what happened at the New Year's party," she began clumsily.

"You don't see me complaining," he said with a deadly serious face, but his eyes were twinkling mischievously.

Neri couldn't help but smile.

"I know but it was awkward, wasn't it? Can we just forget it?"

"I don't think I can, particularly when I want to know why."

"You know, you just reminded me of someone," Neri confessed.

"Your first love, I hope?"

Neri's head snapped back before she realized he was teasing her. But her reaction did not escape his attention.

"In a way," she said, "if you must know."

"Who was he? Tell me, it's only fair. I told you about my first love."

"I'm sorry Stan, I can't talk about it." She felt uncomfortable. How could she explain things to him when they failed to make sense to her? Sensing her discomfort, Stan felt an urge to take her hand into his but he resisted. He changed the subject and soon they were talking like two old friends. The tension was gone. Everyday it was becoming less of a mystery to Neri why it was so easy to talk to Stan. He was a good, compassionate and kind man. She wished she had met him before instead of Ismet. Her life would have been so different.

They stayed talking until the dining car was almost empty. Then Stan walked Neri to her compartment. In the narrow confined space, looking at her slender body swaying in front of him to the rhythm of the train was a pleasurable torture—one he knew he would gladly endure forever. She had ignited so many forgotten feelings in him. For the first time in years Stan was feeling alive. But a new fresh sadness had now begun to gnaw at him. He knew the situation was hopeless.

"May I see you at breakfast tomorrow?"

"I'm afraid not," Neri answered. "I have to get up early. I'm getting off at Pendik." She was glad her father had suggested this alternative to meeting her at Haydarpaşa Terminal where there was no car park. Stan looked disappointed.

A little formally, they shook hands and parted.

28

It's going to snow, Neri thought. The Sea of Marmara was steel gray, blending into the sky and obscuring the horizon. The Princes' Islands appeared way off in the distance like gray-shrouded ghosts, yet on clear sunny days they usually moved inland so close one could count the windows on each house.

The train was nearing Pendik. The steward tapped on Neri's door and asked if she was ready. He took her bags and escorted her to the door. She was surprised to see her mother on the platform next to her father. She knew they were both worried about her. She put on her best smile and walked into their arms. She did not even look to see if Stan was watching, although she knew he was.

The ride to Erenköy was uneventful, just conversation about how comfortable and clean the trains were. Neri came close to crying when she entered her old bedroom. Everything looked familiar. Nothing had changed, except her.

After lunch Neri told her parents she wanted to walk to Göztepe to see Leyla who'd had a baby boy recently. Nermin and Metin looked at each other and agreed. They knew their daughter would eventually stop avoiding them. They could wait. For the time being they were just happy she was safely back with them, if only for a few days.

Neri was greeted warmly at the door by Leyla's mother who, in the short distance to her daughter's bedroom, told Neri that it had been an easy childbirth and that Leyla was recovering fine. "I have every intention of keeping her in bed for forty days though. Such is the custom after the birth of a baby." She pushed Neri into the bedroom and closed the door.

Neri took one look at Leyla and started laughing uncontrollably. Leyla was in her "*lohusa*" attire, the post-partum period when all Turkish mothers are shamelessly pampered. She was in bed, dressed in a silk white nightgown and a blue hand-knitted bed jacket with a huge satin bow. A red ribbon held her long blond hair, and an evil-eye bead was pinned to her chest. The sheets were blinding white and intricately embroidered with tiny flowers. She was leaning against at least five puffed-up pillows. The whole thing looked ludicrous.

They were both choking with laughter, Leyla holding her belly and pleading, "Please, stop, Neri, stop. It's beginning to hurt."

Between giggles Neri asked: "How long are you going to stay in bed like this looking like a poor sheep dressed up for slaughter?"

"I am going to give my mother a few more days, then I'm going to get up and send her back to Ankara."

"Good," Neri said. "You look ridiculous. But I think you should keep your mother here a bit longer. You still look tired. Where's the baby, can I see him?"

Leyla never liked dilly-dallying. "My mother just put him to sleep. She'll now go out shopping. We have at least an hour to ourselves. Tell me how bad it is, Neri."

"OK," Neri sighed and started talking. At first, she only described her life in Ankara in lighter tones, cautiously omitting the humiliations and the unbearable loneliness. Eventually she broke down and told Leyla everything, including Ismet's continuing infidelity, the episode with Sarah, and even Stan. She was harsh about her own behavior too. She admitted that she had failed to learn to love Ismet, who was "so popular with so many women," she added bitterly. "Leyla, it's the first time in my life I feel like a total failure; I don't fit anywhere. I know I have inherited a little too much of my mother's defiant independence. This is something my father valued and admired in my mother. But the same quality is precisely what Ismet and his family don't like in me."

"Go on."

"They expect me to be quiet and submissive. I'm not supposed to have any thoughts in my head. How can I be happy with someone who expects so little of me? Maybe there's something wrong with me," she sighed, exhausted.

"You could have been happy with many men who wanted to marry you," Leyla said. "But you chose the wrong man. Let me tell you: there is nothing wrong with you. It's not easy to love someone you cannot respect. There's a lot that's wrong with Ismet." She refrained from saying "I told you so!" They looked at each other in silence. "Why don't you divorce him? Just pack up and come home? What are you waiting for?"

"I honestly don't know. I think about it, but just the idea of divorce paralyzes me. It's admitting failure and that doesn't come easily to me! I can't believe how pig-headed I was when I ignored everyone's warnings about Ismet, including yours. And I'm supposed to be an intelligent woman. What nonsense!" She looked lost in thought for a minute or two.

"So what can you do?"

"There's nobody in my family who's been divorced, Leyla. It feels like a shameful thing to do. I don't know how my parents would react to it. I don't want to be a disappointment to them."

"Neri, you're talking nonsense. Your parents love you and want the best for you. Do you think if they knew what you're going through, they'd ask you to stay with Ismet?"

"What am I going to do if I get a divorce? Do you know anybody who's divorced? Do I come and stay with my parents again as if I were a child? You know what happened the last time I tried to get a job?"

"You are over-dramatizing again, Neri, like you used to back in school. Do you remember the time when you flunked that university entrance exam? You thought that was the end of the world."

"Are you comparing my failing marriage to a failed exam?" Neri asked incredulously. She couldn't believe her ears.

"Why not?" answered Leyla. "In some ways they're both life-changing experiences. Think of it this way: if you hadn't failed that exam and gone to the university, your life would be totally different. You might have met someone nice or worse. Or you might have become a rich lawyer or a famous scientist. Who knows?"

"Who knows indeed?" Repeated Neri, deep in thought. "I wish I'd listened to you and all the others who warned me against Ismet before I married him. What a fool I've been!"

"So you have made a bad marriage. Learn from it. It's not the end of your life if you leave Ismet. Yes, go home. You'll think of something to do. How about enrolling at the School of Fine Arts? One time you were certain that you wanted to become a painter like Ceylan. Look how well she's doing. Her first İstanbul exhibit last year got rave reviews."

"I wish I'd seen her exhibit. You don't know how nice it is to have Ceylan and Selma in Ankara, even for a short time. They'll both be back here soon though."

"I know, but tell me about this Stan," insisted Leyla. "I presume he's tall, blond and blue-eyed?"

"You presume wrong," answered Neri laughing: "He's tall and dark."

"Well, then! He must have other qualities that make him so endearing."

"He is kind, considerate, warm…"

"And in love with you," interrupted Leyla.

"I don't know," Neri said thoughtfully. "I hope not. There is a strong pull, very strong indeed. Maybe it's our need to be close to someone. We both have lousy marriages." She blushed. "He is also very sexy. I feel attracted to him. Oh, don't look so disapproving, Leyla. You asked and I'm answering honestly. At least I think so!"

"I'm not disapproving at all. I'm trying to understand. You're keeping something from me. Out with it. This is no time to be coy, Neri. You know I'm not going to judge you."

"OK. I kissed him at the New Year's party and it felt wonderful. At first I thought I did it because in a strange way he reminded me of Bill. Now I'm not so sure."

Leyla was silent, thinking. "Are you falling in love with him?"

"No, unless a person can love two people at the same time."

"Is that possible?"

"I don't know Leyla, but why not? Do we have such puny hearts that we can only be in love with one person at a time? Can't we love different people at the same time for different reasons? Right now he seems to be meeting a need in me, the need to be appreciated and understood. He's considerate, caring and interested in me, not in my looks. He listens to me. When I'm with him, I feel like my old self, and I don't have to pretend to be someone I'm not. And he made it very plain that he cares for me. I'm going to shock you, I know, but it's an incredible feeling to see a man you like hum with desire every time you're near him. It's sort of empowering. I hate to admit it but I seem to crave that feeling."

"You're in love with him, face it," insisted Leyla.

"Maybe but not as much as I still love Bill. My feelings for him remain unchanged, still strong, still overwhelming. But the truth is simply that Stan is here, he's real and he wants me while Bill is a long ago dream. Stan and I are always thrown together, and the strong sexual feelings he stirs up in me are very confusing. The sad thing is that under other circumstances it would have been easy for us to make a life together but that's impossible now. He's no cheat, Leyla," Neri added emphatically, "and neither am I."

"I'm glad to hear that."

But Leyla looked as if she needed convincing. How long a person like Neri brought up in such a protective and close-knit family can survive without love and understanding, Leyla was wondering. Neri was like an exotic bird whose wings have been clipped. Did she realize how vulnerable she was? Was she going to make another mistake by getting more involved with this Stan? What would Ismet do?

"I've made too many mistakes," Neri was saying, "and missed my chance at happiness. I have to face the fact that love's not for me."

You're such a romantic fool, Leyla thought. It was ridiculous for a person like Neri to expect so little from life. Yet here she was in a mess of her own making. Leyla didn't know how to help her friend.

"Listen," Leyla sighed. "You can't change what's written on your forehead. But I know you'll find the happiness you deserve one day. Just wait and see."

Neri stared at her friend, wanting to believe her more than anything else. I'll wait and see, she promised herself.

29

Neri woke up with her mother's voice calling her, but she was still groggy. She had slept well without tossing and turning for the first time in weeks. She felt rested and at peace. She groaned and lay the pillow over her head.

"Neri, wake up. Ismet is on the phone."

She peeked at the clock. It was not even eight yet. "Why?" she asked. Nermin laughed. It was so nice having her daughter back home.

"How should I know? Ask him," she said. Despite her laughter, she sounded worried.

Now Neri was fully awake. She pulled on her robe and ran downstairs. Because of the hovering chestnut and pine trees, the first floor living room was always a little dark. But this morning the whole room was bathed in an eerie light from the wide windows. Neri gasped with delight. It was snowing. Outside was a fairy land, covered with at least a foot of snow. She always liked snow. Her childhood memories came pouring in: chestnuts on the fire, sitting on her father's lap listening to stories, her mother over-dressing her with sweaters, woolen hats, scarves, and mittens...All she had wanted to do was to wake up feeling safe once again in her parent's home. Now Ismet's call had ruined her day.

"Yes, Ismet, what is it?" she asked with a deliberate yawn.

He came right to the point. "Did you know Stan is in İstanbul?"

"Yes, I saw him on the train last night."

"Did you know he was taking the same train?" The anger was beginning to surface in his voice.

"How could I know?" she snapped. She was beginning to get irritated.

"No one in the office seems to know why he decided to go to İstanbul yesterday. The trip was scheduled for next week. Did *you* tell him you were going?"

"What are you suggesting, Ismet?"

"I'm not suggesting anything, but people are curious and are talking about it."

"You mean Sarah is talking, right?"

"Don't bring Sarah into this Neri. What's the matter with you? What does she have to do with this?" Now he sounded furious but also a touch defensive.

Neri had had enough. "I'm bringing her into this conversation because she's a cheat, and she thinks everyone else is too. Well, I have news for you both. I'm not."

With that Neri banged the phone down. Later she wondered at having the gumption to do what she did. Was she angry at his intrusion into her only safe haven? Or was it because deep down, although she had not done anything yet, she was beginning to feel guilty about Stan? Surely she would never act on some of the fantasies creeping into her mind since the New Year's Eve party. She knew her daydreams were a reaction to the loneliness she felt. The emotional vacuum in which she was living with Ismet had become unbearable. She had reverted back to her age-old habit of daydreaming to shun reality. She knew it was not healthy. And it would cause her trouble, as it had in the past. But daydreams were all she had, or so it seemed to her suffocating mind and heart.

While they were having breakfast, the lights went out. Then the phone shut down. That pleased Neri: no more irritating calls from Ismet. It was still snowing and it looked very cold outside.

Yusuf, their old cook, came in and lit the wood stove in the living room. When they'd moved to İstanbul, Metin had spent a fortune putting central heating in the house, but the generator was erratic and was not working again. Neri loved the old stoves and she was glad her father had agreed not to throw them away. For Neri they were works of art. The living room one was covered with majolica rectangulars of pale green with a pink-and-white tulip design. The woods flamed up quickly and unlike the dry, noisy heat of central heating a nice soft warmth spread throughout the room.

Neri knew going out was not an option. She could not avoid talking to her parents indefinitely anyway. Sooner or later they were going to ask her what the problem was. Maybe the best time was now, sitting in the familiar room in the glow of the wood stove with snowflakes swirling outside the windows.

Nermin smiled at her. The loving concern on her mother's face broke Neri's heart. She got up and kissed her, lightly touching her lips to her forehead, the tip of her nose, and finally her cheeks. She could not remember when she had started kissing her mother like this but it was a special tradition they shared, affirming their strong bond.

Encouraged, Nermin asked: "Neri, are you going to tell us what's going on?

"You know we've been worried about you," Metin added.

Neri had been dreading this moment for months now. She did not want to tell them about Ismet's infidelities. She was afraid what her father might do. The emptiness, the loneliness she was feeling, when put into words, sounded melodramatic like the whining of a spoiled child. She tried to explain as objectively as she could the lack of connection she felt with her husband, the lack of intimacy, and the frequent outings when she felt like a trophy on display.

"Most of the time I feel like I am being used. He doesn't care who I am. He only cares how I look. When we go out and the men

164

are looking at me, he gets a funny self-satisfied smug expression on his face that makes me sick. I feel like...I am invisible." She had nearly said, "like a whore."

Nermin and Metin looked at each other horrified. Could the strong bond between parents and children make it possible for them to hear their children's unspoken words? Neri had a feeling it could, and it did.

"I would not complain if we had a different, strong, loving relationship. I would have been happy to help my husband in any way I could, but we live like strangers. We never have any real conversation. Sometimes I think he knows nothing about me. Worse yet, I don't think that he feels the need to know me. It's sufficient that I am there for his use. He might as well have bought himself a slave!" Neri tried to laugh.

"Neri, doesn't your husband's infidelity bother you?" asked her mother. Neri was shocked. How did they know?

"I don't know what you've heard, annecığim. He did have a bad reputation before, but he has given up his old ways ever since we got married." What a liar she had become!

Metin had been silent all through out the conversation. He now looked at his wife. They knew exactly what was happening in Ankara. In fact, they knew more than Neri realized. But there had to be a reason for Neri's reluctance to talk about her husband's deplorable behavior. Metin had never liked Ismet. He would like nothing better than kicking him out of Neri's life, and a few well-placed punches on Ismet's chin would not be too bad either, but it was his daughter's life and her decision how to handle it. Besides he did not want to humiliate Neri any more than what he suspected she already was feeling. So he changed the subject after reassuring her they would support any decision she might make. Neri was wise enough to read the unspoken message in that promise.

Meanwhile, they had no idea how long before the electricity and telephone service would be restored. Everything was unpredictable in Turkey, so people coped by helping each other, including strangers. This was something embedded in their culture and religion. Life for most of the population was tough. The country was still struggling to provide for its citizens after centuries of neglect. Mutual reliance was the only way to ease the pain of coping and family and friendship ties were life-long. Except sometimes for marriage!

The least Neri had expected was this empathic bond to develop between her and Ismet. In its absence, the loneliness was killing her. She did not know how much longer she could turn a blind eye to Ismet's infidelities. She could not accept, as Nuriye did, that it was a man's prerogative to cheat. It was not. The whole thing was sordid and humiliating. It was eroding her self-respect. She had to admit, however, that her apparent inability to act decisively did not reflect well on her self-respect either. Maybe it was time to stop thinking about saving her marriage and to start considering a divorce.

Or maybe if she could act more compliant and overlook her husband's infidelities, her marriage could be saved? Why was it so difficult to become more obedient and less demanding as expected by his family? And what about Ismet? Maybe he was unhappy too and deserved better.

Neri realized that all these maybes were giving her a headache without offering any solution. What she needed in this weather was to dress up, go out and make a snowman. At least that would bring relief, some child-like optimism. So on her way out, she grabbed the largest carrot she could find in the kitchen; she intended to stick it on the face of Ismet the Snowman!

30

Because of the snow, Neri stayed nearly two weeks in İstanbul. Ismet's daily phone calls started the minute the lines were repaired but he seemed subdued, deferential and uncommonly considerate. He even encouraged Neri to take as much time as she wanted which, of course, made her suspicious. Determined not to dwell on her troubled life in Ankara, Neri managed to have a good time, talking to her parents, reading her favorite books, and listening to music which brought back warm memories of her childhood.

After the roads were cleared, they took the car ferry to the European side of İstanbul to visit her uncle and aunt in Maçka. Her aunt, who could only show love by feeding people excessively, had prepared a five-course luncheon with Neri's favorites.

In the ferry on the way home, Neri watched the incredible silhouettes of St. Sophia and the Blue Mosque against the setting sun. Blanketed with snow, they loomed larger than life. The golden crescents on top of their large domes shone against the ruby-red sky. The dark towers of Topkapi Palace looked less sinister. Neri envisioned the plight of the harem women and felt slightly better about her own problems. Everything was relative, wasn't it? The snow had a softening, cleaning effect on the whole world, even on Neri's troubled thoughts.

Before leaving İstanbul, she promised Leyla that she would confront Ismet but without admitting she was unsure how to do it. What was the proper way to talk to a cheating husband? None of the movie scenes she remembered helped. They were usually too dramatic. She couldn't see herself sobbing, screaming, or pleading. Her heart was not broken, just her dignity. She realized how little she cared for her husband. She had given herself and her broken heart willingly, hoping Ismet would heal, protect, and teach her to love again. It had not happened, and no amount of talking was going to convince him to change his ways and give her what she needed. She decided to act like a stiff upper-lipped lady in a British film and wait just a bit longer.

When she arrived in Ankara, Ismet met her at the train station with a big smile and a long hug. He looked genuinely happy to see her. Neri wondered whether Ismet had thought that she wouldn't return at all. He also appeared a little nervous, talking continuously, even mentioning how much Tenzile had missed her. This was odd because Tenzile was still a sore subject between them. Ismet did not want Neri to hire the girl after she had shown up on their doorstep, crying and complaining that she could no longer work for Madam Sarah.

Neri had not budged, hiring her one day a week and then with the help of the janitor who knew everybody's needs in the apartment complex, she had found her a four-day cleaning job with a new couple who had moved into the top-floor flat. The husband was a reporter with the Ulus newspaper and had a very young and very pregnant wife who was delighted to have Tenzile work for her. She showered her with clothes now too small for her, and overnight Tenzile was transformed from a village girl with baggy pants into a smartly-dressed city girl. Neri noticed Tenzile still covered her hair with the silk scarf she'd given her.

When they arrived home, Tenzile gave Neri a big hug. She loved Neri as her protector and "*abla*"—older sister. Tenzile said that she had bought tangerines which she knew Neri loved, cooked

Neri's favorite dish for lunch, cleaned the house and changed the sheets on the bed, the last with a furtive glance at Ismet who was in the other room.

Late that night, after she had endured Ismet's love-making and just before falling into sleep, Neri remembered Tenzile's words. What did she mean? Why did Tenzile feel the need to tell her that she changed the sheets? She knew it was going to be another one of those sleepless nights, listening to Ismet snore.

31

Ankara was buzzing with the recent delivery of dry milk and cheddar cheese to lactose intolerant Turks as part of the American aid program. Turks did not drink milk but usually got their vitamin D from yogurt. With Turkey's wide variety of delicious and high-quality dairy products, most people could not understand why the Americans would send them some flat-tasting orange-dyed cheese.

Soon it became a big joke. Newspapers were full of cartoons depicting fat-bellied Turkish men in diapers drinking dry milk. No one wanted to look a gift horse in the mouth, but even so the subject lent itself to easy ridicule.

Years ago when US military aid had first arrived, the journalists kept relatively quiet when they discovered that the much anticipated and needed aid turned out to be World War II broken-down surplus trucks and used military equipment shipped from storages somewhere in Germany. Eventually a black market for spare parts and a legitimate repair-and-restore industry developed making the Turkish generals sigh with relief and any criticism of US aid unnecessary. But the millions of dollars worth of dry milk and cheese was the last straw.

Whenever the group met, poor Tom tried to defend USAID policies and explain the ins and outs of how his government worked, how aid decisions were made, and the influence of the American farm lobby on the US Congress. Not used to the idea of a responsive government, Tom's sell fell on deaf ears.

The newspapers were having fun feeding the gossip mill with all sorts of wild stories: villagers stuck with tons of dry milk were using it as animal feed and animals were mysteriously dying. The orange dye in the cheese was making pregnant women lose their babies. Then the bombshell, namely that Americans had put something in the milk to make Turkish men impotent. That did it. No one in the countryside would touch the cans of dry milk and cheese even if you paid them. Strangely though, just about that time, American cheddar cheese started appearing on the grocery shelves of the big city stores and the rumors immediately started that someone was making a lot of money by flooding the market with American cheese and selling dry milk to restaurants. This is when Ismet introduced Abdullah Okun to the group.

It was an unusually warm Sunday and they'd all met at the tennis club for a rematch pitting Neri and Stan against Ayla and Mete. Halfway through their game, Ismet showed up with a short man, impeccably dressed in a suit. Since everyone else was either in shorts or casual dress, he stood out like a sore thumb. His ferret eyes lit up when Ismet introduced Neri as his wife. He sat near her and tried to dominate her conversation. Neri wished she was more conservatively dressed. The man made her feel naked.

While they were leaving the club, Maude asked Ismet who Mr. Okun was.

"He's the one who got the dairy contract from the USAID office. Ask Tom about him. He is responsible for distributing all the dry milk and cheese you've sent us." Ismet missed the look Tom and John gave each other and continued. "He's from Kayseri and he's a really shrewd businessman. He knows his stuff." Neri could hear the admiration in Ismet's voice which bothered her. What did her husband have to do with this man? But she knew that he would not answer if asked. It was men's business!

Lately Ismet was getting on her nerves more than usual. Nothing had changed between them. Little by little the tenderness he had shown upon her return from İstanbul had disappeared. Also whenever Stan was around, he seemed determined not to leave her alone which in turn made Sarah more belligerent than usual. Neri was beginning to see the whole thing as mildly amusing. It seemed to her that they were all second-rate actors caught up in a bad play. She felt sorry for Stan. He was the only one who appeared puzzled, looking for a better script, but Neri knew there was no such thing, and the play had to end in a fiasco, the sooner, the better, she thought.

32

It must be safe to assume that some traditions that have seemingly lasted forever have a reason for their longevity. The insistence of Turkish parents that no daughter of theirs will marry a man unless he's finished school, done his military duty and is reasonably well-employed was one of those tried-and-true traditions. Unfortunately more and more young girls were opting out of carefully-arranged alliances in favor of "love marriages" regardless of their grooms' qualifications. Both Ceylan and Selma had made such marriages but both had sufficient financial resources to accompany their husbands to Ankara for their military training but this is when their luck ran out.

After finishing military training, assignments of new officers in Turkey are carried out by lottery. Ceylan's husband drew a small isolated post on the Russian border as his next assignment and Selma's husband drew a small town in Southeastern Turkey. There was no way for them to take their wives along. After they left, the girls packed and got ready to return to İstanbul, feeling both listless and depressed. They hated the idea of spending the remaining eighteen months of their husbands' military service all alone by themselves under the thumb of their parents.

Neri tried to cheer them up but their mood remained sour. Finally Neri and Maude came up with the idea of a last night on the town: first, dinner at the Millers, then to the jazz club *Intim* to hear the new quartet that was getting good reviews. Luckily for Neri, Ismet was away in Diyarbakir on business.

The Millers decided to keep the party small. They did not want this farewell dinner to turn into one of their bottom-pinching wild parties and had no intention of inviting the Wileys. Sarah did not get along with the girls. The first time she and the girls had met, the negative vibrations emanating from Ceylan and Selma were obvious to all, not that anyone could blame them. The girls had almost snarled at Sarah like two cougars protecting their cubs.

Maude wanted a nice, quiet, friendly party. Definitely no drama or excitement. But then John told Stan about their plans and when Stan appeared on the night of the party at their door looking sad like a lost puppy, Maude just couldn't say no and asked him to drive the girls.

When Stan came to pick Neri up, she was surprised and upset at the same time. He was stirring all sorts of emotions in her and the more she wanted to appear normal, the more she seemed to make Stan aware of his effect on her.

Neri wished she wasn't wearing her sleeveless black dress again. She was afraid it would remind Stan of the night they had kissed. While helping her with her coat, she could hear his rapid breathing. She knew she had to be very careful and not act like a lovesick teenager.

"Ceylan and Selma are waiting in the car. I went and got them first," Stan said, trying to put her at ease.

"Thank you, I hope that was not an imposition."

"You're right. Escorting three beautiful women is indeed an imposition!"

She laughed. "Well, enjoy yourself. They're all leaving tomorrow."

"But you're not," Stan said straight to her face. Neri blushed, a small tremor going through her entire body. She put her head down, hiding her red face. Fortunately, the street was dark and they had come to the car. Getting into the passenger side to sit next to Stan, she ignored Selma and Ceylan who were making faces at her. Soon, however, they all got into some friendly banter and the tension she felt eased up. She had no idea what Stan was feeling but he was in top form, entertaining and charming. He had come a long way from his morose days.

Maude's dinner was a great success. Without their husbands, all three young women were feeling liberated, regressing back to their old schoolgirl selves. The stories about their student days on top of the hill on the Bosphorus had John and Maude doubling up with laughter. Stan was laughing too, but Maude noticed that now and then he had the oddest expression on his face, like a little boy looking at the train set in a store window, knowing he could never have it.

After dinner Stan offered to continue with his chauffeuring duties. "This is such a rare pleasure for me," he pleaded, "escorting three beauties."

"Be careful what you wish for Stan," teased Selma. "If you give the apple to the wrong beauty, you might start another Trojan War."

The club *Intim* was already jam-packed when they arrived. All eyes turned to the three young women as they entered the semi-dark room. Neri, tall and beautiful, her eyes sparkling with joy, was half-turned laughing at something John had said. She radiated a quiet sensuality made unexpected by her elegant appearance. Ceylan was dressed in a velvet dress, long sleeved and buttoned-up so it looked like a school uniform, but one that emphasized her hour-glass figure. Her long blond hair shone against the deep green of her dress and her light eyes appeared yellow, like those of a prowling cat. Selma was wearing a tightly draped red dress which showed her tall slim body to perfection. She too was a beautiful woman with an Oriental-looking face, high cheek bones and large slanting eyes. Her dark hair was cut short, framing her pale oval face.

They were escorted to the only remaining empty table at the back of the room, next to a bunch of noisy American pilots from Incirlik airbase who stared at the girls openly. The dance floor was full of couples slowly swaying to the spine-tingling wail of the lead saxophone player. The drinks they ordered had been hardly served before one of the American officers from the next table approached John.

It turned out that they had met before. It was clear that the young man was asking a favor. All the others at his table were quiet, intensely watching the interaction. John turned to Neri and said that the young officer was asking permission to dance with her. Stan made a move which John restrained by gently placing his hand on his shoulder. The move did not escape Neri's attention. She felt apprehensive about dancing with Stan. Better an unknown danger than a known one she said to herself and got up.

"My name is Neri," she said, shaking the young officer's hand.

"I'm Bill," he said, startling Neri. Wasn't there any other name in the world? She didn't want to be reminded of Bill. She wanted to forget him *and* Ismet and have fun for just a little while. That was all she wanted.

Before they could join the other dancers, Neri saw with amusement that two more officers were heading toward their table and Ceylan and Selma soon joined them on the dance floor. From that moment, the night became a blur. Between dances they hardly had time for drinks, but they must have, because they were all getting merry except Stan who looked glum.

On the dance floor, John leaned closer to his wife's ear. "What's wrong with Stan?" he asked.

"I don't know," Maude replied.

"What's going on between him and Neri?"

"What do you think is going between them?"

"How should I know? You're the expert. Why isn't he dancing with her or with the others?"

"Why don't you ask him?"

"Yeah, sure," John said, breaking into laughter. This night is a great success, he was thinking and everyone is having a good time, except poor Stan. What was wrong with him?

When they all returned to the table, John decided to give everyone a break and told the pilots "Time out, gentlemen. You know where the bar is." There were groans of protest but they followed the friendly advice since they were all outranked.

"Thank you," Ceylan said to the Millers, "for making us feel like youngsters."

John laughed hard. "Anytime you old ladies need some fun, you can call Uncle John."

"Please," said Selma, "the next time you are in İstanbul, look us up. We'd love to show you our city. Come in April. İstanbul is its best in the spring."

"I hate April," muttered Neri, quite tipsy. They all stared at her.

"*April is the cruelest month, breeding lilacs out of the dead land*," quoted Ceylan in a nasally British accent, teasing Neri. The Americans were baffled.

"What's going on?" Maude asked.

"It's Neri's favorite line of poetry. She loves T.S.Eliot," explained Ceylan.

Stan felt as if someone punched him in the stomach as he remembered the next line: "Mixing memory with desire." Whose memory? Whose desire? Then it dawned on him that the obstacle to attaining Neri, which he wanted more than anything else in his life, was not her insipid husband but the memory of her first love. How do you fight a memory? The answer was simple: with desire!

"What's wrong Neri," asked Maude. "You look sad."

"I'm going to miss them," Neri sighed, looking at her friends. "They were my life line."

"We are your friends too. John and I love you like a daughter."

"Come on everybody," complained John, "this is a party not a funeral...Wait, better be prepared girls. Here come the boys, again."

Before the American pilots could reach their table, Stan grabbed Neri's hand and literally pushed her to the dance floor. She did not resist when he pulled her into his arms, nestling close to his chest. Neri's yielding so willingly had the strange effect of frustrating him. He pulled her closer. Stop thinking about him, Stan felt like shouting in her ear. *It's my arms that you feel now. It's my body heat that's making you tremble. Look at me. See me. Not him, whoever he is.* But just having her so close was enough. He closed his eyes and bent his head to hers.

A peculiar thing now occurred. Neri's inhibitions disappeared and she let her body melt into his. His strong arms felt wonderful, sexy and safe. She was tired and a little bit drunk. She put her head on his chest. She could hear his heart beating as loud, she smiled, as the Ramadan drums that during the month of fasting wake the pious before dawn. She found the sound soothing. Stan's lips were gently touching her hair, then her temple. She was afraid to move. He bent lower and brushed his lips softly on her neck just under her ear. She flushed with shame at her feelings.

All the admonishments about how a proper girl should behave were threatening to engulf her. Neri pushed them aside rebelliously and rose up on her toes, burying her face in his neck. Her warm breath sent shivers down his spine. He whispered her name. For a second her arms crept up to his neck; she was trembling. Just as he was pulling her closer, she stopped, forced his arms to slacken, and stepped back.

"I can't...*we* can't, Stan," she murmured, hardly audible.

"Why not?" he complained. He wanted her and he knew she wanted him too.

She stared at him with eyes full of desire, compassion, and regret. He braced himself.

"I'm too vulnerable," she whispered.

33

The next night, the Millers drove Neri and the girls to the train station. Ceylan was upset because the baby had an ear infection and was crying nonstop. She had her nose in Dr. Spock's Bible for new mothers and was trying to figure out what to do, ignoring Maude who was doing her best to assure her that there was nothing to worry about.

Selma still had a bad hangover. She kept on saying that she deserved it. A married woman acting like a teenager! She looked at Neri as if she blamed her. Neri was quiet, looking downhearted.

John was amused. He had never seen them so despondent before, and he could not for the life of him understand what all the fuss was about. They'd a wonderful time last night, except for perhaps Stan. John had been unsuccessful in making Maude talk about Stan and Neri, but tonight he was determined to get the story.

After the tearful farewells, they drove Neri home. She was preoccupied, not interested in talking. Her brow was creased. She looked as if she was losing whatever battle she was waging inside. John walked her to her door and bent and kissed her on both cheeks in the Turkish style. Immediately she was reminded of Stan. The night before he had kissed her goodbye in the same polite way and said she could "count on him always," while looking sad and lost. It had broken her heart.

"Cheer up, Neri!" John was saying. "You'll see them soon enough."

"I know John. And thank you for the ride. Please tell Maude I'll give her a call tomorrow."

John walked to the car and sat down staring at his wife. "OK, spill it out. What's going on between Stan and Neri? Ever since last night, they're both acting miserable. Don't say you don't know, and don't say it's nothing either, because I saw you watching them while they were dancing, or whatever it was that they were doing."

Maude sighed. She looked worried. "I don't...OK, I won't say I don't know. But really John, I know as much as you do. We all noticed their mutual attraction, and who can blame them with the spouses they have!" She sighed again. "One thing is certain though: she's brought Stan back to life."

"I know," agreed John. "Everyone in the office has noticed the change in him. He looks happy, but he's also troubled."

"They both are. It is an impossible situation. They're both married. I don't know how difficult it is to get a divorce in Turkey but you can be sure Sarah will give him hell if he asks for one."

"It's gone that far, you think?"

"Well, here we go again. I don't really know! Why are you asking me these impossible questions?"

"But you saw how they were dancing."

"Yes and I also saw that Neri pushed him away, however reluctantly. I have a feeling their connection has become too much, too overpowering. I think Neri is trying to cool it."

"Well, good luck to them both, they'll need it. It's really too bad though. They're perfect for each other. They could have made a wonderful couple."

"I know," said Maude, feeling sad for both of them.

It was another sleepless night for Neri. She was tossing and turning, trying to get the image of Stan's face out of her mind. Last night on the way home, he'd asked Neri what she'd meant by being too vulnerable. She couldn't answer. How could she admit to him that she didn't know if she was attracted to him because of who he was, a compassionate lovely man or because she was starving for affection and understanding? She was ashamed to be so needy, so weak. Did it imply anyone would do? She hoped not. No, she knew it wasn't so. Still her so-called vulnerability was humiliating.

She cursed the situation they were in. She knew exactly how hurt Stan was. She knew that feeling only too well. She suspected her need had blinded her to the possibility of damage she would inflict on both of them. She had tried to justify her behavior by rationalizing that he was a considerate, caring, understanding man, all the things her heart yearned for and all the things her husband had not been able to give her. But she knew that wasn't the only reason.

Lying in bed, Neri laughed bitterly. Still pretending to be a prude, aren't you? she reprimanded herself. How come you're not admitting how sexy you find him and how you can't stop wondering how it would feel in bed with a man you find attractive? She remembered Leyla's advice. She had to make a decision about Ismet, or she knew the next time she may not be able to say no to Stan.

Not for the first or the last time, it was morning before Neri was able to fall asleep.

34

Nuriye had once remarked that one positive consequence of the arrival of the Americans was the ever increasing number of antique shops in Ankara. It was true: every time Neri and Maude went shopping, there was a new antique shop looking just as grimy and dusty as the old ones.

Neri enjoyed these outings with Maude. It was like treasure hunting; you never knew what you would find. Today Maude had uncovered a bronze mortar and pestle set which might be over eight hundred years old and according to the label 'genuinely belonged to a Seljuk Turk.' Maude bought it, saying that even if it wasn't authentic, it was still beautiful.

Neri had stopped buying months ago. She no longer wanted to spend her husband's money; plus the money her parents had given her stayed untouched for a rainy day which she feared was coming soon. She no longer had any hope of saving her marriage.

Finished with their shopping, they started walking toward Ulus. There was an unusual noise in the air—like a lion roaring in the distance—that they hadn't heard inside the quiet shop. People were hurrying around in all directions. They turned into the main street and before they could realize what was happening, they were caught in a sudden melee. They were jostled from all sides by frightened people who were trying to extricate themselves from a wave of human bodies with a mind of its own, carrying them forward against their will.

Then they saw students battling the police. The noise was deafening. Someone grabbed Maude, pulled her and Neri into a shop, and then quickly closed the iron security gate and the internal door.

"Mrs. Miller, what are you doing in the middle of this?" the shop owner cried. "Haven't you read the papers that the students were planning a demonstration today?" Only then did Maude recognize the Armenian rug merchant from whom they'd bought most of their rugs and kilims.

"Thank you for saving us, Mr.Hazazyan." She said." I had no idea, I'm afraid. What are they protesting?"

"Mostly the Menderes government but I'm sorry to say, also the American presence, Mrs. Miller. I don't really blame them for being angry at the government though."

"Why don't you blame them?" Maude was curious.

"Because the government is playing with fire by encouraging Islamic fundamentalism. History has taught us that it's a mistake to stir up religious feelings. It's making us very uncomfortable." He seemed reluctant to continue. Just then Maude heard Neri gasp. She turned and grabbed Maude's hand, pulling her close to the window.

"Look," she said, pointing to a group of students trying to protect a well dressed woman from the police. It was Ayla.

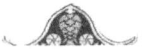

That night, when they all gathered at the Miller's house, Mete and Ayla were still continuing an argument from hours earlier.

"Please somebody," Mete was imploring, "tell Ayla she can't put herself in danger like this, protesting in the streets."

"But aren't you the one who said we should get involved and not just sit back and talk?"

"Yes Ayla, but in class not in the streets. You're a teacher; teach your students to become active participants in our civic affairs. Make our elections honest. Isn't that enough for you?"

"Again, aren't you the one who always argue democracy doesn't depend on elections alone and we need to constantly monitor government to ensure transparency and honesty?"

"Yes, yes, I said all that but I wish you would have ignored what I said like you usually do with everything else I say." Mete sighed and put his hands up in the air in a sign of defeat. "I just don't want to see you get hurt Ayla, that's all."

"Or go to jail," murmured Neri, holding Ayla's hand. "I admire your courage but Mete is right. You may be more useful in your classroom than in the streets."

"How did you get so many students to protest?" asked Tom.

"We weren't that many when we started. Then we noticed others joining us. I didn't recognize them. I'm certain they weren't students and they were the ones throwing stones at the police. They were also the ones with anti-American slogans, not us. The question is who organized these provocateurs and why?"

"All the more reason for you not to get involved, Ayla," pleaded Mete. "Things are getting ugly."

"Mete is right," said Neri. "Please Ayla, try to be more careful for your own sake and for the sake of your students too. You don't want to get them into trouble, do you?"

"Did you all see the latest poll in the newspaper? Anti-Americanism is on the rise," said John.

"Well, that's no surprise, is it?" said Ayla with a sharp edge to her voice. "That seems to go hand in hand with your aid program."

That was almost rude, Tom thought, surprised.

"What does American aid program have anything to do with our problems?" asked Ismet belligerently, entering the conversation for the first time.

"I can give you a long list, Ismet," said Mete. "But just for starters, how about aiding and abetting corruption and eroding our sovereignty?" He gave Ismet a hard stare.

"It doesn't do any good blaming others for our own shortcomings," insisted Ismet.

"Well, I hope the time of reckoning for those who are exacerbating our shortcomings will come soon," Mete replied, irritated.

John realized Mete's anger was not only directed at Ismet whom he blamed for participating in the black market and other corrupt activities but also at himself for not knowing how to stop his wife from endangering herself. He discreetly signaled Maude to start the dinner. Recently, most of their discussions were getting too heated for his taste and he hoped to distract his friends from serious topics by plying them with the expensive French wine he had just bought at the PX.

Tom had been listening to the conversation closely. Turks loved arguing and he was learning a lot from these arguments. They also valued friendship so that even the most heated arguments ended with a joke and a hug. But not tonight: there was too much tension and anxiety. He could not blame Mete for worrying about his wife. Ayla was playing with fire. From everything he had been reading, social unrest was on the rise in Turkey. People were frustrated with the government's inability to provide jobs and services.

In the old days, when poverty and lack of amenities were shared by so many, people suffered silently and accepted their common fate. But now the growing difference between the Haves and Have-Nots and the blatant corruption making some rich at the expense of others were together fueling anti-government feelings.

Similarly, the secular-minded military, liberals and academics were upset with the government's coddling of religious sects, those same sects with a long history of impeding any improvement in everyday Turkish life. Members of these sects were busy testing the limits of their newfound rights and privileges by protesting co-ed schools, introducing religious subjects into text books and vandalizing Atatürk's statues and pictures. In between these two groups, labor unions infiltrated by the communists were staging protests and strikes, crippling the nascent Turkish industry. So both the Cold War and—Tom had to admit—the American presence were increasing pressure on a tense situation already fraught with danger.

Maybe it was time for Tom to return home. He knew he had become too fond of his Turkish friends and Turkey. His usefulness as an observer required interaction with the locals but he was no longer sure of his objectivity. Still, he had good insights and an interesting opportunity had presented itself lately. Although his reports had been very thorough about the well-educated Turks, particularly the so-called 'secularist elites,' he had not been able to make any sense of the more traditional religious Turks. They just did not make friends with foreigners. Those working in the office maintained a strictly official relationship, hiding behind a bland, respectful, bureaucratic façade. It was frustrating.

Now this man called Abdullah Okun had been introduced to their group: he was from a small town, a product of a religious school and he appeared to be eager to be one of the boys. So Tom was eager to know what made Okun tick. Unfortunately, however, he was also suspected of siphoning US aid products into his company and selling them illegally. In fact, he had made a fortune in a very short time. Tom's office was cooperating with the Ankara police, keeping a close eye on him. He did not yet know how Ismet was involved but it did not look good.

John and Mete were also helping the police. The black market business had become too big to ignore. Besides, it was the responsibility of Mete's office to stop the illegal sale of American liquors and cigarettes. John had asked Mete to question Ismet and find out about his involvement with Abdullah Okun. After dinner, Mete told John and Tom that his earlier conversation with Ismet had not gone well.

"He's a slippery son of a bitch. I told him point blank that the police knew Abdullah Okun was involved in black market activities and that he should stay away from him. But Ismet *insisted* that Abdullah was an honest businessman and not involved with anything illegal."

"Do you believe him?" asked Tom.

"Of course not. I even suggested that if he was involved with Abdullah, this would not look good for me because of our friendship and that was why I was concerned. He just pooh-poohed it!"

"Well, that's it. You warned him. That's all we can do," said John. "But I hate to think what would happen to Neri if he ever gets indicted and goes to jail."

"I don't know," Mete answered. "Let's keep this to ourselves. Our wives will kill us if they learn we're involved in getting Ismet implicated."

"Maybe it's the best thing for Neri anyway," Tom replied. "She may finally decide to get rid of him."

"Amen," said John.

35

Neri and Ismet had had one of their worst fights when Ismet told her he wanted to invite Abdullah Okun to dinner. Neri could not believe her ears.

"You want to invite him to our house for dinner? No way. I don't want that man in our house."

"Listen, he is a business associate of mine. I need to soften him up. Besides he's been asking to see you *and* our house."

"I bet he has," Neri answered, really irritated now. "Haven't you noticed how he looks at me? He gives me the creeps."

"Neri you're exaggerating. Abdullah is a very kind man."

"Right, one that would like to eat me alive. That's what Ceylan said."

"You pay too much attention to Ceylan. You're not at school anymore. You're my wife. And I want you to be nice to him."

Neri looked at her husband, shocked. How could he say something like this? "Ismet, believe me. You don't want that man anywhere near me."

"What do you mean by that? What did he do to you?"

"I don't want to talk about it. Please take my word for it: Abdullah is not a nice man. He has no respect for me or for you."

"Neri you have to tell me what he did to you." Now Ismet sounded agitated.

Neri did not know how to explain why Abdullah's insistent stare made her feel undressed.

"Ismet, he makes me feel uncomfortable. Every time we meet, he insinuates how much money and power he has. Why? It's none of my business."

"So what? Is it against the law to brag about how much money one is making?"

"But it's more than that, don't you see?" How could she explain to him why Abdullah made her feel so cheap? Ismet should have seen what was happening and he should have come to her protection, Neri thought bitterly. Instead he was insisting there was nothing wrong with Abdullah. So, blushing furiously with anger and embarrassment, Neri was forced to describe the incident at a recent party when Abdullah had cornered her and boasted how he could be "useful" to Ismet.

"I must admit I was surprised that he refrained from saying 'if you are nice to me,' but the implication was crystal clear," she said.

"You must have misunderstood him," Ismet responded flatly. "You have this tendency to dramatize everything. Let's forget all this foolishness. Just tell me which night we can have him over?"

That was when Neri made her decision. She went to the bedroom and closed the door.

Early next morning before Neri could act upon her decision to leave her husband, Leyla called from İstanbul, all excited. Bulent was going to Oxford to attend a three-day conference and Leyla was going too and she wanted Neri to come along.

"Mother is going to take care of the baby. Plus I already talked to your parents and they agreed that this would be a good break for you. You need a little vacation. We'll be there just for four days. Think of it, we'll be in England in April! We can even take the bus to Stratford-upon-Avon and see where Shakespeare lived. Come on Neri, what do you say? Your parents will pay for the trip."

"I'm coming," Neri said without any hesitation.

Later that night they heard about the riots in İstanbul. All the shops in Beyoglu belonging to the non-Muslim minorities had been ransacked. No one had been hurt but the absence of any police during hours of rioting was a question the government could not or would not answer.

36

Neri leaned against the headrest of the airplane seat and tried to forget last week. After the fury of the ugly fight about Abdullah Okun subsided, Neri realized that she needed time to talk to her parents and find a lawyer before she could leave Ismet. But first, Leyla had called with the news of the trip to England. So Neri put everything on hold, admitting to herself that she was once again being a coward and avoiding trouble.

She had never thought of herself as timid. Her self-image used to be that of a strong and decisive person, but the years under Ismet's roof had been enough to erode her self-confidence to the point where she was constantly questioning herself. Getting away, even just for a few days, was exactly what she needed. She looked at Leyla. For how long had Leyla been speaking?

"So what do you think Neri? Isn't that a good sightseeing plan?"

"I'm sorry Leyla, what were you saying?"

"You weren't listening, were you? You have such an irritating habit of vanishing in the middle of a sentence. Oh, don't look so hurt like that, I love you warts and all. I was just talking

191

about our tentative plans. I think we should take the whole day tomorrow for sightseeing Oxford. The next day we can arrange for a trip to Stratford-on-Avon. What do you say?"

Neri lowered her voice so that Bulent would not hear. "I can't," she whispered. "I can't leave Oxford."

"Why not?"

"I did something stupid, Leyla."

"What did you do? Come on Neri. What did you do?"

"I sent a letter to Bill telling him where and when I was going to be in England." Neri looked worried. She knew Leyla was going to explode.

"You did what?"

"What's going on?" asked Leyla's husband from the other side of the aisle. "You two OK?"

"We're more than OK Bulent. Just read your paper." She turned and stared at Neri, weighing the consequences of her behavior. Finally Leyla relaxed and held Neri's hand. "What's the chance that he'd get your letter? It's been five years. He might have moved. He might be married with children. For all we know, he might be dead at sea!"

Neri winced. "Oh, Leyla, don't be so morbid, please."

"No but really, what's the chance he'd get the letter?"

"Very little, I guess. Even if he gets it, what's the chance that he'd respond or be interested after all these years? I know I did a stupid thing, but I've thought of nothing else once I knew I was going to England. Just the idea that I might see him again was too tantalizing, too overwhelming, too tempting. I don't think I could have lived with myself if I *hadn't* sent the letter. Oh, don't look at me like that. I know what you're thinking and I'm sick and tired of everybody telling me how over-dramatic I am!"

"Neri, you don't look good. What's the matter? Bulent, does Neri look OK to you?" Bulent leaned over his wife and stared at Neri. She looked green.

"I think she's getting nauseous," Bulent said alarmed. "I think she's air-sick."

37

He saw her first. After waiting in the lobby of the Reynolds for hours, he saw her enter through the hotel's double doors. She was just as beautiful as ever. No, even more. She was no longer a girl but a grown up woman with a new magnetism, demanding attention. Bill could not take his eyes off her and realized with a stab to his chest that whatever had occurred during those insufferably long five years had not made her happy.

Neri was clearly sad. The twinkle in her hazel eyes that once so mesmerized him was gone. Her face was no longer animated but cool and distant. Bill felt the emotion physically in his throat. He stood, scraping his chair, and the noise attracted her attention. Neri glanced at him and froze. Suddenly her face broke like the sun. Her smile, her eyes, her whole body radiated with delight and happiness. It was so intense that he could not look directly at her. He was shocked, but her reaction told him what he needed to know. In three long strides he was at her side and kissing her.

Neither remembered how they got to her room. She was not even sure they spoke a word. All those years of yearning were too powerful. Kissing and exploring each other's body consumed them until the last thing she remembered before losing her senses was her curling toes.

Later she was not sure if she was asleep, dreaming or half-awake. She was six or seven, clinging to her mother's hand, and they had just come out of a movie in İstanbul. It was snowing and big flaky shapes were swirling gently down. There was a gypsy woman opposite the theater selling flowers, wearing a thin sweater. Neri was worried, thinking that the poor woman must be cold. Then her mother bent and picked up the last bunch of white roses the gypsy had, handed the woman more money than she'd asked for, and pulled Neri away.

They turned the corner to Beyoglu when Neri smelled the chestnuts. She looked at her mother pleadingly. Nermin smiled and nodded, and they stopped before the chestnut vendor. He took off the black conical lid of his stove, exposing plump chestnuts roasting on tin, glowing from the charcoal fire beneath. He placed about a dozen chestnuts in a small brown paper bag, twisted the top and handed it to Neri. Neri clasped her cold hands around the warm bag. Just as her mother was handing the money to the chestnut vendor, a white petal escaped from the bunch of roses in her hand and fell onto the hot tin. It lay there, as white as snow and as pure. It curled and started sizzling silently. Then in the blink of an eye, it flared up and was no more.

That's exactly how she had felt all night long, sizzling and burning. She'd also had a strange sense of emancipation as though doing something she shouldn't: something that was against all the rules and regulations about how to be a good girl had ironically freed her. She felt as light as a bird and smiled. Her dreams and reality had finally merged, making her whole at last.

Caressing lips touched her nose gently. "Don't pretend you're still sleeping," she heard a voice saying. "You just smiled. I know you're awake." He kissed her tenderly and then with passion. Neri opened her eyes. It did not feel a bit strange that she was lying naked in his arms. It was the most natural thing in the world. In fact it was much more natural than everything that had happened to her in the last five years.

"Why did you stop writing?" she asked. Bill put his head back and laughed. "Good morning to you too," he replied and kissed her again. "And how long have you been married?" Her lips quivered. Was she married? She had forgotten. "I guess we need to talk," Bill continued, playing with a strand of her chestnut-colored hair, "but I'm ravenous, aren't you? Let's have breakfast."

They went down and while waiting for their breakfast in the dining room, Leyla appeared.

"You must be Leyla," Bill said, getting up and pulling a chair for her.

"And you must be Bill. Glad to meet you after all these years," Leyla answered, scrutinizing him unabashedly.

Neri could see that Leyla liked him. She knew Leyla would approve of anyone who made her happy. But it was hard not to like Bill. He looked good, dressed in gray slacks, white shirt and a navy-blue crewneck sweater that deepened his eyes. Leyla avoided Neri's face to save their mutual embarrassment.

"Where's Bulent?" Neri asked to break the awkward silence.

"He wanted to see the famous Oxford library, the Bodleian. You know how he's obsessed with books. I guess you'd want to cancel our plans for the day, right? You two spending the day together?"

"Yes, I hope so," said Neri, "but what about dinner tonight?" While Bill was watching quietly, the two made plans for dinner after which Leyla got up and left, but not before telling Bill that she was really happy that he was there, so Bill knew he had an ally in Leyla and he had a feeling he would need her support. The ring on Neri's finger was burning a hole in his heart, and he knew he still had many obstacles to overcome.

They decided to go for a walk by the river. It was a sunny day, unusual in the middle of England's April showers, as if the Gods were on their side. The air was crisp, smelling of fresh flowers. They sat on a bench and watched the swans glide by. Bill had his arm around her shoulder and was nuzzling her neck.

Without warning she said: "Bill, I need to know why you stopped writing."

"I know but it's very difficult to explain. Most of the first year after we parted, I wavered completely between bliss and despair. Sometimes those five days we spent together felt totally unreal. I used to go over and over every minute we spent together and still could not believe it. The intensity of my feelings for you continued to shock me, but there was no one to encourage me, no one to support the plans I was making to change my life."

"I did."

"I know, sweetheart, but Captain Reilly kept telling me that you were beyond my reach and that your parents would never let you marry a poor Englishman. He talked at length about the difference in our culture, social standing, and religion. I started questioning those things myself. Nothing seemed to work out the way I thought it would. As I wrote to you, I was hopeful in the beginning that I could leave the merchant marines, find a part-time job and start the process of going back to school. But being away at sea all the time, it was impossible to line up any part-time job. It was also difficult to study for my qualifying exams. I started feeling desperate as if I was losing control of my life, that there were too many obstacles I was unable to overcome. Then an incident happened."

"What incident?" Neri asked, waiting for the worse.

"Remember the time I went to London on business?"

"I remember well. You wrote me three letters in one single week you spent there," she answered, smiling.

"Well, something funny happened. I met a young officer from another ship line at the hotel's bar one night, and I asked where he usually traded and he said 'the Black Sea.' Well, I happened to say I wanted to get onboard a ship going to İstanbul. He asked me why, so I laughed and said I had met a girl whom I wanted very much to see again. He asked me where I had met her, and I promptly said a place called Tekirdağ. Well, darling, you could have knocked me down with a feather when he said 'It's not Neriman Ersoy, is it?' When I said yes, he laughed and said he knew you, and asked whether you'd remember the fireworks display?"

Neri had been listening with increasing dismay. Now anger took over. "His name was Archie, wasn't it?" If Archie had been there, she could have easily killed him with her bare hands!

"Yes," Bill said.

"Nothing happened, let me explain..."

"You don't need to explain anything, sweetheart. I know nothing happened, but I'm ashamed to tell you what Archie told me upset me more than it should have and I made the mistake of telling Captain Reilly. Of course he jumped to the wrong conclusion and from that moment on, he never failed to remind me that you were just a young girl having fun, and that you didn't love me."

"That's not true. I do love you."

"I wish you told me that, but in your letters you were always a little distant. I could never be sure of your feelings."

Neri was silent. She knew he was right: she'd never been able to tell Bill how much she loved him. She cursed her upbringing and her culture which had taught her not to reveal her feelings. She was not a shy person, so why had she never told him openly? Was it fear of tempting fate or just a ploy she'd learned from the way the Turks played the game of love? Whatever, it had backfired.

"I'm sorry," she whispered, her head down. "I was too young and stupid. But I loved you and I still do, Bill, with all my heart."

"I hope so," he laughed, "or it would be very hard to explain what we've been doing since yesterday."

Seeing her blush made Bill laugh even more. She always made him incredibly happy, and in a strange way powerful, like the Greek gods he'd been reading about. Look what he had achieved in the last few years of struggle—and he now saw it was all for love. He bent down and kissed her hard, his heart overflowing with contentment.

"Not knowing exactly how you felt," he continued, "I made the worst mistake of my life. I gave up on you, and I gave up on myself. I became despondent and no longer believed I could escape my rut. Even my mother said you were too young and what you felt was probably a crush. I'm not blaming you but I couldn't sense in your letters the kind of intensity of feeling I was looking for. They were more like pen-pal letters than love letters. Maybe you were just being modest, I don't know, but I eventually convinced myself that it was impossible, that breaking off would be the best thing and that I should let you move ahead with your life. Since then I've regretted that decision every single day, and I'm sorry for the pain I've caused us."

"It's my fault too. I wish I'd been able to write to you what I was feeling. In a strange way, I thought you knew. You see, I used to imagine us together meeting somewhere somehow, talking, revealing how much we loved each other and making love...yes, don't look so surprised. Nice girls have dirty dreams too, you know?" The mischievous sparkle was finally back in her eyes. "Those daydreams were so real, I was sure you knew exactly how I felt. Childish, isn't it?"

"If daydreaming can be called childish, I was childish too. But reality turned out to be better than my wildest dreams, Neri." He stared at her eyes full of love and passion for him. At that moment, he had no doubt that eventually they were going to be together and that all his plans, mocked and derided as impossible by others, were going to come true.

"So when did you start going to school?" Neri asked.

"Three years ago my sister fell in love and decided to get married, giving up her plans to get a university degree. We thought she was too young but couldn't change her mind. She insisted I should use the money I'd put aside for her education for myself. My father said I should too. He'd read somewhere that these new electronic machines were the thing of the future and soon all ships were going to be equipped and run by them, making navigators like me obsolete. He wanted me to go back to school and learn a new profession."

"Wise of him, don't you think?"

He smiled. "Yes, very wise. So I left the merchant marines, studied and passed the qualifying exams, and enrolled in an engineering program in York—that's why I was late in arriving here. I didn't get your letter until yesterday. Anyway, I'll be receiving my master's degree next spring and my doctorate in less than two years. By the way, I'm taking courses in literature too—

my secret passion." He didn't mention how this plan was something he'd promised himself in Tekirdağ, staring at her family's bookshelves. Neri stared at him with awe. He sounded full of confidence and ambition.

Although Bill expected Neri to have moved on with her life, he confessed that there was "still a part of me that would simply not give up on you. So I always held on to the idea that I would return to Turkey one day and find out how your life turned out." To date, he'd not been able to afford the trip, but he'd never given up hope. "I knew I had to return to Turkey. It was like an obsession. Even if we could not be together, I had to come and see you one more time. But here we are, together here in England..." He took her face in his hands and shook his head in wonder. "I never thought this could be possible. This is better than my wildest dreams."

"What happened to your girlfriend?" she blurted, startling him. He remembered the last time Neri had asked him about his girlfriend. It was ages ago but felt like yesterday. The memory made him smile, a response that was not what Neri had expected. She looked at him, worried.

"She's married with children," Bill said. "She thought I was trying to live a pipe dream. Besides, loving you the way I did, I couldn't settle for anyone else." She liked that answer and showed him how much with a kiss.

"Neri, are you going to tell me about your marriage?" He asked gently, pointing at her wedding ring.

Neri decided to be honest and told him how devastated she had become after his letters stopped and how she had started misbehaving. She told him about her rebellious moods, her indiscriminate dating and how she'd met her husband, Ismet. She couldn't tell him exactly why she'd married him but she tried to explain her need to punish her parents and, perhaps more importantly, herself. Neri spared no ugly details of her marriage, including Ismet's infidelities and her failure to be the wife he wanted her to be. Talking to Bill was cathartic: she bared her soul without pretense and felt as if a heavy weight had been lifted. But she had omitted telling him about Stan. She didn't know how to explain *him*.

Bill couldn't bear to hear Neri blame herself. He was devastated to realize the damage caused by his actions. All he now wanted was to make her happy. He suggested they return to the hotel.

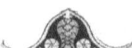

Despite Neri's apprehension, the dinner that night went smoothly. If Bulent disapproved of Neri's behavior, he didn't show it. Bulent and Leyla treated the awkward situation as if it was the most normal thing in the world, and Bulent was warm and friendly, asking Bill about his studies and future plans.

Leyla could sense Neri's discomfort but she was also beginning to detect something else on her face. At first, she thought Neri was upset because the next morning they would leave Oxford, but it was more than that. Although her face still glowed, her eyes were shadowy, hiding some desperation.

"*Nen var*, Neri?"

"Nothing," Neri shrugged.

"Something's bothering you, what is it?"

"It's really nothing. You're imagining things."

Bill was looking at them intently, as if he understood Turkish. He took Neri's hand, turned it over and kissed her palm. His eyes were clouded.

When they were getting ready to part for the evening, Leyla surprised everyone by pulling Bill's face down and kissing him goodbye on both cheeks. She also whispered something in his ear. He smiled.

When Bill and Neri returned to their room, they were both subdued, their lovemaking more tender. Their worlds that had collided twice were again on separate paths. Neither had the courage to talk about it yet.

In the middle of the night Bill woke up and found Neri staring at him. "What...what's wrong?" he asked sleepily.

"Nothing, I just want to tell you about Archie. I know I don't have to, but I want to."

He kissed her, wide awake now. "If you insist."

"It was the October after you showed up in Tekirdağ. I was home again on holiday and excited that my parents were going to take me to the Governor's Ball celebrating our National Day. It was my first ball and I had a lovely new gown."

"Wish I could have seen you."

"Wish you were there instead of Archie," she replied, tartly. "Anyway, we were sitting with the governor and his wife when the governor pointed at the British officers he had invited to the ball. They were sitting at a table across the dance floor, drinking and looking bored. The governor said something about no one talking to them and asked my father whether he can borrow me for a little while?

"My father did not object, and the governor took me over and introduced me. I remember him joking that he was leaving me in their care for a little while, stressing the 'little while' bit. Their captain was a nice man, much younger than Captain Reilly, and he asked me to dance, which I did. Then his first officer whose name was Archibald something asked me to dance too. The fireworks started in the middle of our dance, and he suggested we go out to the balcony to watch them. I knew it wouldn't look proper, but I didn't want him to think that we Turks were backward country hicks so I said OK. By the way, the balcony was nothing like the ones you see in romantic movies, dark and secluded. It was narrow, about two feet in width, and the double doors were opened behind us so that we were in full view. Not more than a minute or two passed before my father appeared and apologized to Archie saying that I had promised to dance the first tango with him. After the dance, my father took me back to our table and that was that. I'd never given a second thought to Archie until now!"

Bill kissed her. "Poor Archie," he said. "Maybe he was frustrated because he didn't spend more time with you. Or he felt like boasting to put me in my place. Who knows? Let's forget about him. Did your parents ever say anything about me? Did they know we were corresponding?"

"Sometime after we started writing, my father said he heard from my school's American administrator saying that I was receiving frequent letters from a sailor on a British merchant ship and asking if they should destroy the letters? My father told them to mind their own business."

"Good for him," Bill laughed. "What about your mother?"

"She never said anything but she watched me closely. When I got your letters, I'd disappear for hours, reading them in my room. Afterwards I'd appear, looking absolutely in high heaven. If your letters were delayed for whatever reason, I'd get short-tempered. I hated it when you went to Australia and I didn't receive any letters for a long time. I know my mother worried about me but she did not interfere. During that first year, I became a little withdrawn, I think."

"Oh, come on," Bill objected. "You kept on telling me all about the parties you were going to which I assume was with lots of boys."

"I think I was trying to make you jealous," Neri laughed. "But seriously, you don't know how many hours I spent all by myself walking by the shore watching the sunset. My mother tolerated all my moods but when she saw how heartbroken and destructive I became after you stopped writing, she tried to help but I was beyond help then."

"Neri, I'm so sorry. I never meant to hurt you."

"I know, and I never meant to disrupt your life the way I did, but what can you do? That's life, isn't it?" They looked at each other a moment before he took her into his arms. He had the uneasy feeling she had just said goodbye but the feeling just slipped away.

When Neri woke the next morning, she found Bill staring at her, frowning as if afraid to say what was on his mind.

"Neri, I'm still not making enough but next year I'll have my degree and a better job. Don't go, stay with me. We can live on the money I earn now if we're careful. Please Neri, we'll find a way for you to divorce your husband and then we can get married. When I get my doctorate, it will be easier for me to get a job in İstanbul and we can go back and live there. I'll do anything you want but just say you'll stay. I don't think I could bear to lose you again."

"I can't stay, and you must," she said, shaking her head sadly.

"Why? *I know you love me and I love you.* Aren't all these years of torture enough? If for a moment I thought you were happy with your husband, I swear I would have never mentioned this. But you are not. You are a grown woman now. Talk to your parents. Maybe they won't object to me if you can explain how unhappy you are. I'm sure they want you to be happy. But whatever you do, don't ever leave me."

He talked and talked, trying to convince her. His eyes were getting desperate while the lines by his mouth looked carved in marble. She could not say yes. She said she couldn't divorce her husband and he should forget her, find a nice English girl and be happy. Bill couldn't believe his ears. It sounded crazy to him but she was resolute, sobbing and shaking her head no. He could not understand her stubbornness. He had changed his life without any hope. Now everything he'd ever dreamed of was in his arms, and yet Neri would not acquiesce. She would not even give him a glimmer of hope.

"Why Neri, why won't you marry me?" Bill pleaded.

She stared at him with so much love that he thought his heart would explode.

"Because I'm pregnant," she whispered.

38

Nuriye was certain that Neri's problems with Ismet were simply going to evaporate with the arrival of the baby. She had been taught motherhood was the only possible source of happiness for women—not that her sons had given her much joy—so she was convinced it would be enough for Neri too. Neri did not argue with her mother-in-law. She could not believe that having a child with Ismet was going to make any difference. If anything, she feared, it would be another source of friction. Neri had a feeling that his idea of parenting and hers were mindsets apart.

Maude had pretended to be delighted at the news when Neri told her. But it was evident that she did not see the baby as a solution either. Neri suspected that most of her friends were thinking along the same lines. Nevertheless they had all put on happy faces and congratulated her and Ismet warmly.

Stan was a different story. He looked at her long and hard, sensing the glow on her face was due to something more than the baby. He had asked her about the Oxford trip more than once. She had lied, feeling ashamed and uncomfortable. Meanwhile Ismet had not even noticed the change in her. He looked relieved, convinced that he no longer had to worry about Neri leaving him.

During the first few weeks of her returning to Ankara, Neri began to fear that she was losing her mind. She felt she had split into many conflicting personalities. Neri, *mother-to-be*, was content. With each raging hormone preparing her body for impending childbirth, she was beginning to feel that being an '*anne*' would be enough for her.

But Neri, *the wife*, was far from content. She was full of venom with ugly vengeful thoughts and ready to turn Ismet to stone with one hateful stare. Similarly, Neri, *the daughter* was full of shame and remorse. She was sorry she was a disappointment to her parents and she was sorry that she had failed to live up to their standards. The single day she had spent with them before returning to Ankara had been very hard. She had tried to hide from them the fire of ecstasy that was still burning in her from her short time with Bill. She didn't know how successful she had been but Neri did not want to see her parents until she could pretend that the brief encounter in Oxford was only a daydream and this *Neri*, who belonged to and still yearned for Bill, did not exist. But this *Neri* was larger, more real and more immediate, looming over all the others. She tried to push that *Neri* down, but she would not be diminished or take a secondary role. It was amazing how easily all her friends in Ankara had failed to detect this particular *Neri*, except Stan of course. Those brown eyes of his could read every emotion she was feeling. It was uncanny and she tried to avoid him without appearing rude and uncaring. She simply couldn't face him without blushing.

On the plane back, Neri told Leyla everything that Bill had accomplished in recent years, his hopes for the future, slipping in his proposal for their life together and her refusal. Leyla listened quietly without interrupting. She was not surprised when Neri told her about her pregnancy. She had already guessed it. Leyla stared at her friend and then kissed her cheek.

"Don't make any hasty decisions right now, Neri. You can't fight fate. But I know in my heart of hearts that it's going to turn out all right for you."

Neri was already desperate enough to believe her.

39

The Menderes government was playing a dangerous game, pitting the moderns against the reactionaries and the secularists against the fundamentalists. The continuing erosion of secular principles was beginning to show its effect. There were increasing reports of harassment of women for dressing improperly. Incidents of vandalism of Atatürk's pictures and statues were becoming widespread. The unrest in the country was growing. The İstanbul riots had shocked most people. The newspapers kept on asking the same questions: where were the police, and why hadn't they intervened in time? Did the riots happen with the blessing of the government? The official investigation was going on, but few people had faith in the procedure or in the conclusions it would create.

The Menderes government was also handling its critics harshly. The Prime Minister seemed to have forgotten all his earlier promises of respecting the rule of law and the freedom of press and speech. Journalists and ordinary citizens were being jailed on the flimsiest of accusations of "insulting the government". Corruption had become rampart. Some said it was because of American aid and the dollars pouring into the country. University students were becoming bolder, demonstrating frequently. Several had been jailed along with two professors from the political science department of Ankara University. Everyone in Neri's group of friends was afraid that Ayla might any day join her colleagues.

Abdullah Okun was finally in trouble. The Ulus newspaper had a huge headline one day: "Dairy King Going to Jail." When Stan saw it, he immediately walked over to the Miller's flat. It was early in the morning and the Millers were having breakfast. Stan translated the article written by a reporter whose name sounded vaguely familiar. But more importantly something about the way the reporter told his story bothered him.

"You're right, this is a puzzle," John muttered. "It sounds as if the reporter knows more than he's telling."

"Yes, he does," Stan said. "He's protecting someone and someone we know." They all stared at each other. "But I don't know *why*, do you?"

"What's the writer's name again?" said Maude. "Isn't he the young reporter we met at Neri's some time ago, the one with the pretty wife and the new baby who live in the same apartment building? Your old cleaning woman works for them, remember?"

"Yes, of course," replied Stan, still confused. "But why would he cover up Ismet's involvement?"

"Do you need to ask?" John chuckled. "Neri!"

"Right. Neri more or less adopted the reporter's wife when they moved in. She found them a maid, she drove the young woman to the hospital when her husband happened to be out of town, and she's been helping them ever since the baby arrived. How could her husband reveal Ismet's involvement with Abdullah Okun and end up hurting Neri who has done so much for them?" Maude smiled. "I guess in Turkey loyalty counts more than ambition. What a country!"

"Indeed," said John.

For a while the newspapers were full of stories about how Abdullah Okun had "milked" the US aid process. When he was finally jailed, Neri was relieved that she would never have to see him again, at least for a while. No one stayed in jail too long: there was always some political excuse for amnesty. She suspected that just before the next elections he would be freed with countless small and big time criminals as well as political prisoners.

What Neri did not know was how close Ismet had come to getting implicated alongside Abdullah Okun. Nor did she know how Huseyin had come to his son's aid, probably for the first time in his life, and pressured the prosecutor who was from his home town to look the other way. John and Tom were astounded to see how easily Ismet had avoided jail. The shady functioning of the Turkish judicial system was still a mystery to them.

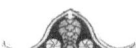

During their weekly tea-time, Neri and Maude talked about Abdullah Okun's demise. Neri even told Maude why she had disliked the man so much. This was the first time she had revealed something personal in a long time. Ever since she had come from England, Maude had sensed an invisible barrier between them, keeping Neri at a safe distance. Neri seemed less spontaneous, less transparent, and more deliberate in her speech, lapsing into long silences. Maude worried about her friend's mental health but did not know how to approach her.

"Neri, are you feeling all right?   You don't have any problems with your pregnancy, do you?"

"No problems at all, why do you ask?"

"You are not like your old self. You seem to be subdued and preoccupied all the time. I worry about you. Is there anything I can do?"

"Dear Maude, my only problem now is my ever-enlarging body," laughed Neri. "The minute I buy a maternity dress, I seem to outgrow it instantly!" She glanced outside and noticed that it was getting dark. There were few snow flurries and it was not even the end of September. The radio was broadcasting about a freak storm from the Siberian steppes which had arrived earlier than expected. Neri said she'd better go home before the weather got worse, then kissed Maude goodbye.

There were no taxis on the street. The air was icy cold, hurting Neri's lungs, so she decided to walk quickly down to Kızılay. She would take the bus to Bahçelievler if she could not find a taxi there. She pulled her coat's collar around her neck. The coat was already too small to cover her belly.

Neri saw that patches of ice had already formed on the sidewalk. Long slender icicles were beginning to weigh down the branches. The radio had said that many trees, still covered with leaves, were going to be damaged.

She was the only person in the street and the sidewalk was slippery but she didn't worry. With her flat shoes, Neri knew she could keep her balance. She remembered how quickly she had learned to roller-skate in Paris when she was a child. She started going down the hill, half sliding, half walking, as graceful as a gazelle except with a protruding belly. She was smiling broadly, feeling lightheaded and happy for the first time since she had returned from England.

Soon she caught up with a group of soldiers who were trying to keep some resemblance of military discipline while marching on the slippery surface of the street. They were in total disarray. Some were clumsily hanging together, others were helping their sergeant who had fallen down. They looked at Neri with open admiration, whistling and cheering. They must have been new recruits and they couldn't have been more than eighteen years old.

Neri smiled and waved as she passed by. Then she heard a loud grinding noise. She stopped, turned and looked. A big military truck was coming down the hill sideways. It had two small American flags up front, and she could see the driver's terrified face. Then a bizarre change affected Neri. She became deaf. She could hear nothing except the pulsing blood in her ears, and her eyes began tricking her, slowing things down to an unnatural pace. She watched every detail with great precision. The truck was plowing over the young recruits, scattering some around, cutting others under its heavy tires. It had no intention of slowing and was coming downhill like a diabolical metal monster.

Neri was frozen in place. She could not move. But she could feel the snowflakes on her face. Then her hearing came back. She heard an eerie screeching sound get louder and she watched calmly as a motorcycle veered onto the sidewalk to avoid the truck that was sliding over the bodies of the young soldiers. For a split second she locked eyes with the young man on the motorcycle. His looked defeated, resigned, and then Neri entered a blissful darkness.

40

She was dreaming but she did not know it. She thought she was back in Paris roller skating in the Jardins des Tuilleries with her French friend. She could not remember his name. But every morning when her mother brought her to the park, he'd be there waiting for her and they'd go roller skating together. As usual he was holding her hand and talking to her, except his voice sounded like Stan's.

Was he saying "Wake up Neri?" No, it couldn't be. He must be saying "hold my hand." She turned and looked. It was Stan. And she was no longer eight years old. They were skating together. She did not know Stan could skate.

She again heard him say "Neri, wake up. Please, wake up." What a funny thing to say, she thought.

Suddenly she realized she was at the edge of a steep cliff. She shook her head. There was no cliff at the park. But before she could stop herself she was off the precipice, skating on air. That was a lovely sensation. She closed her eyes and drifted into oblivion.

Neri woke up again, feeling irritated. She didn't know how much time had passed. She wanted to cling to the black nothingness that was comfortably familiar. She tried to hang on, but even the darkness was receding. She then realized she was underwater. It was cold and dark. She did not know which way was up. There was no light coming from the sky to guide her. She did not know how much longer she could hold her breath. She thought she heard a voice. Was it Stan again? She looked toward where the voice had come from. She saw a tiny pale light. She started kicking her legs as hard as she could. She swam and swam until her lungs were on fire, but the light stayed small and far away. She sighed and let her lungs relax. Returning to that darkness was preferable to this hopeless struggle to breathe. She felt a warm familiar breath tickling down her neck, smelled a familiar scent, felt strong hands clutching hers. She opened her eyes. Stan was leaning over her, looking relieved.

"Oh, Neri, you've come back," he whispered, before she heard other voices. Everyone seemed to be talking all at once. Then a young man in white coat entered and emptied the room. She noticed Ismet was not there. He came in much later. She did not like his smell. It reminded her of Sarah.

Neri stayed at the hospital for another week. She had concussion, broken ribs and a badly strained ankle. She had also lost the baby.

The day after she was allowed to go home, Neri packed her bags and returned to İstanbul.

41

Her parents were unaware of what Neri had gone through until she appeared at their doorstep one morning. They did not even know she was coming to İstanbul. They were happy to see her until they learned what happened to her and the extent of her injuries. Like everybody else they had been reading the newspapers about the terrible accident in Ankara. They had no idea that the single injured woman who had witnessed the accident was their daughter. No name was mentioned in the newspapers.

When Huseyin called them about Neri's hospitalization, he gave no details, saying only that they should not come to Ankara and she would talk to them soon. It was probably the first time Huseyin had ever carried out anybody's orders. Although groggy with pain killers most of the time, Neri had convinced him and her friends that any news about her and the baby should not be given on the phone.

Of course, Nermin and Metin were not satisfied with Huseyin's explanation and were worried to death. They had called Nuriye, then Ayla whom they'd met previously in Ankara. But everyone repeated the same thing as if well coached: nothing's wrong, just a little accident, and she'll call soon. No one in the group understood Neri's persistence in keeping her condition secret from her parents. They all thought her parents should have been informed and should have come to Ankara to be with their daughter, but they had all bowed to Neri's wishes. What they didn't know was Neri's decision to leave Ismet, especially now their baby was gone, a decision which she wanted to explain to her parents at home in İstanbul.

Her parents, now in shock, listened to Neri talking about everything: her accident, her injuries, the loss of her baby, and finally her decision to leave Ismet. She'd glossed over the brutal death of the young soldiers. She could not bring herself to talk about it yet.

Nermin held her daughter tightly in her arms with tears streaming down her cheeks. This time it was Neri who tried to console and soothe her mother. Metin was so upset that he was pacing the floor as if each corner was one of Ismet's limbs. He did not know why he was so furious with Ismet. The accident wasn't *his* fault. But Metin knew that if Ismet had not entered his daughter's life, Neri would still be a happy and healthy woman.

It did not take them long to realize that Neri was ready to collapse. Metin carried her to her bedroom and they tucked her lovingly into bed as they'd done hundreds of times. They kissed her, watched her doze, and closed the door. On the other side they stood, hugging each other and crying silently.

The next morning Ismet came. His belligerent manner became instantly deferential after he saw Metin's face. Nermin left them alone in the living room. Yusuf, their old cook, was sitting on the bottom of the stairway, brandishing a huge copper ladle. Despite the tense situation, Nermin started laughing.

"What are you going to do with that ladle?" she said, addressing Yusuf. "Beat Ismet to death?"

"I'm going to stop him from going upstairs, that's what I'm going to do," the old cook said in his most defiant voice.

"It's all right, Yusuf. Nothing's going to happen. He is not going to see Neri. Metin won't allow him. Go back to the kitchen."

"I'm going to stay here as long as I want." He said, pleading now.

"Suit yourself," laughed Nermin and went up to see her daughter. She was still sleeping. The doctor had advised them to let Neri sleep.

Ismet left in less than an hour. He looked defeated. But his mind was already back in Ankara, trying to figure out a way to appease his father. Huseyin had become furious when Ismet told him that Neri had left him. For a split second Ismet even feared that his father was going to hit him, but Huseyin just kept shouting that if he had known what a stupid incompetent son Ismet was, "I would have left you rot in jail." Huseyin would not calm down and repeated that if Ismet knew what was best for him, he'd immediately go to İstanbul and get his wife back.

His mother, who was crying silently, nodded her head in agreement. Nuriye did nothing to calm her husband down. On the contrary, she seemed to feel that Ismet deserved every insult his father was throwing at his son.

Ismet worried about his job too. He knew everybody's sympathies were with Neri. He could not figure out why but they all seemed to hold him responsible for Neri's accident. What did he have to do with that horrible accident? Nothing! Ismet knew, however, that he was at a crucial junction in his life; he had just escaped going to prison and he had to weigh his next move very carefully. He did not remember Neri until he entered his empty home.

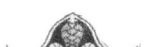

Meanwhile Metin told his wife that he had convinced Ismet, and nicely he emphasized with a smile, that a quick divorce was in the best interest of them both and that he'd make all the necessary arrangements.

"What about her things?" Nermin asked.

"I told Ismet I'll go to Ankara next week and take her personal effects home. I told him that he was welcome to furniture and anything else except what belonged to our family."

"Good. She'll be relieved to know that it's all over, or will be soon."

215

"How is she doing?'

"Still sleeping," Nermin sighed. It was very hard to see her lovely daughter so still and lifeless in bed.

42

The turmoil in Ankara that Neri left in her wake was considerable. With the exception of Stan, no one seemed fully aware of the extent of their affection for her. The horrible accident and her involvement had stunned them all.

On the day of the incident, it was Maude who first suspected that the injured woman might be Neri. A colleague of John had arrived upon the scene while Neri was still lying on the sidewalk. He did not know her. He had tried to help but when the ambulances had arrived, followed by the American Military Police, he was told to leave. He knew the accident was going to be a diplomatic nightmare. He decided to go to the Millers, knowing John would be home soon. He was telling Maude about what he'd witnessed. When he was describing the young woman whose face he had noticed in that horrific scene, Maude's face had turned ashen and she had started crying, but she soon collected herself, wrote a note to her husband, and left.

There was only one good hospital nearby, and Maude had to try there first. If not there, she knew she would try every hospital, every clinic, every back street in Ankara until she found Neri. And she did, at the very first try. In the hospital they first thought Maude was the accident victim's mother. They did not know the victim's name. There was no bag, nothing to identify Neri when she'd been brought in. The receptionist said the patient was in the emergency room and they were treating her, but she didn't know for what. Maude sighed with relief—at least, Neri was alive—and started making phone calls. Maude would recall later with surprise that the first person she called was Stan.

John and Stan arrived together, breathless and white-faced, followed by Mete and Ayla. Stan was frantic, stopping every nurse asking about Neri's condition. He looked so worried and heartbroken that nurses went out of their way to reassure him. His genuine anxiety appealed to them as well as his good looks and perfect Turkish. After what felt like a very long time, a nurse appeared with a big smile on her face.

"Mr. Stan, good news. No surgery for your wife. They moved her to a room. You can go and see her in about ten minutes." They all stared at each other. No one had remembered to call Ismet.

The next two days, during which Neri remained unconscious, were unbearable. There was nothing to do but wait. Dr.Yavuz, who was in charge of Neri, was pleasant and forthcoming. He kept them all informed, but he remained puzzled about the connection between the tall American and the young woman with the Turkish husband. The American was kind and considerate. He came early every day with the older woman. He took time to console the young village girl who arrived every morning, sobbing uncontrollably. Every day he stayed by the patient's side until her husband showed up.

At this point Dr.Yavuz began to realize it was only when the husband was away that the tall American would stand by the patient's bed, holding and caressing her hand and talking to her. The doctor could swear that she sometimes responded to his voice but never to her husband's. Dr. Yavuz was young himself and newly married. He told his wife that he had "never seen such devotion" in his life. He was "a hundred percent sure the American was madly in love with the woman and that was a good thing." The doctor had no medical proof but he would bet his license that if anyone could wake her up, it would be the American. And it was.

Stan would remember to his dying day the way Neri looked at him when she opened her eyes. She peered at him with an intimate smile that made him blush. If she hadn't just woken from a two-day coma, he would have felt they had just gotten out of bed together. Then the moment passed, and he knew it would never return.

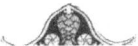

After Neri had left Ankara so unexpectedly, without saying anything to anybody, Maude told John about a 'Stan-problem'.

"Stan's too far gone," Maude said. "Frankly, I never realized how deeply he is in love with Neri. What are we going to do about it?"

"Why do we have to do anything? How is it any of our business?" said John, ever the practical man.

"Oh, John, how absurd you are sometimes. Of course, it's our business. I thought you liked Stan."

"I do, but it doesn't give me the right to interfere with his life, does it?"

"Yes it does! Why do you men insist on being so obtuse? Let me explain it to you. You should know by now that everybody in your office, including the doorman, heard rumors about what happened at the hospital. Anyone, any blind man, who had seen Stan with Neri, knows how much he loves her. And Neri's husband—remember him, your Ismet—works in the same office, your office. Hate to add to your problems but Sarah has probably also heard every detail by now, and you know what a bitch she can be."

"Sarah is no longer our problem," John replied with a smug smile on his face. Probably for the first time in his life he knew something that his wife did not.

"What do you mean?" Maude asked suspiciously.

"Stan sent her home a few days before the accident. They're getting a divorce."

Maude sat down hard, totally surprised. This was really unexpected. How had she not noticed that Sarah was no longer around? She started smiling and John knew why.

"You're not thinking of playing the matchmaker, are you?"

"No, it's too soon. Well, maybe... Why not?"

"I think we should let them be. Anyway, Neri will need a long time to recuperate. That poor girl has gone through a lot ever since she came to Ankara. I bet she'll never want to see our city ever again." They exchanged a glance and both knew what the other was thinking.

"When are we going to İstanbul to see her?"

Maude got up and kissed John. Every now and then it was good to be reminded why she'd married him.

43

Neri's family and friends closed ranks around her. They came and sat with her, gossiped and talked about insignificant things, never asking questions. She felt their love and concern, but she was still incapable of responding. What happened in Ankara remained unreal, behind a thick fog. She did not want to look at it. She could not bear to think of it. They told her she was getting better. She had color on her cheeks, they pointed out. Her appetite was back, her mother boasted. Neri listened. She was sure they were talking about someone she knew, but who was she?

Metin pulled all the strings he could and obtained an early court date. Leyla, Ceylan and Selma all went as witnesses. They told the judge that the marriage was not working. The husband was not contesting the divorce because he was the root cause of all the problems. He had been unfaithful to his wife from the beginning. The female judge was sympathetic. She asked Metin why his daughter had not appeared in court. He told the judge of the extent of Neri's physical and psychological injuries as a result of the accident in Ankara. She asked whether or not Neri was capable of making a rational decision to divorce.

Metin had come prepared. He gave the judge a report about Neri's mental stability that he had obtained from a well known psychiatrist in İstanbul. The judge declared Neri and Ismet divorced due to irreconcilable differences. She did not bother to hide her smile when she saw the three young women jump with joy, hugging each other. The judge had a good feeling about this decision, 'not a bad way to start a long day on the bench', she thought.

When Metin told his daughter that she was divorced, her response was a single tear, rolling down her cheek. She tried to smile but failed. She turned her back and went to sleep. Nermin and Metin stared at each other. One step at a time, they thought.

Next week Metin went to Ankara and gave the divorce papers to Ismet at his parents' house. They talked about the arrangements for Metin to pack Neri's things and take them back to İstanbul.

Tenzile was waiting for Metin at the door. She was newly married and was no longer working but wanted to help. Soon Maude and Ayla arrived, followed by Stan who brought in some packing cases. They all went to work. There was very little for Metin to do. They seemed to know what belonged to Neri as well as he did. It pleased Metin to see how much these people knew and loved his daughter.

Stan was one person Metin could not figure out. They'd met him at the Millers' while visiting Neri, but what was he doing here? Why wasn't he at work? Then he noticed that Stan was sitting on the floor next to the bookcases and was looking at a family album with a sad expression on his face. It was a picture of Neri as a young girl taken on top of the hill at school. She was smiling without any worries, full of life and promise. Metin immediately understood the depth of the man's feelings for his daughter. It was the second time he had seen that look. He felt pity for the poor man. He did not think anything good would come out of his devotion either. Maybe covering young girls from head to toe was not such a bad idea. God forbid, he muttered, shaking his head at the thought.

Before leaving Ankara, Metin went to the cemetery and said goodbye to his granddaughter.

44

Whatever they did, Neri remained out of reach, morose and unresponsive. She spoke only when spoken to. She was not interested in eating unless they encouraged her to the table. All efforts of Yusuf to please her with her favorite dishes failed to whet her appetite. She would give him a crooked smile of thanks but leave her plate half full.

Their family doctor kept on reassuring them. "Let her be. Let her rest. She'll snap out of it in her own time." But it was already a month since she'd appeared on their doorstep. As far as Nermin and Metin were concerned and despite all the optimism they displayed in front of others, they were worried. Their daughter was not back to normal. Then Metin had a bright idea.

Neri opened her eyes one morning and saw her parents standing by her bedside, giggling. She couldn't understand why they looked so cheerful. Then her father handed her something small and soft like a ball of yarn. She looked down. It was a gray tiger-striped kitten with green eyes. Neri and the kitten eyed each other for a second, then she said: "Tekir?"

The cat started purring loudly. Nermin could have sworn that the cat had even smiled! Then Neri clasped the kitten to her bosom. She was beaming. Thank goodness, no more dark, cloudy days, Nermin thought.

Neri didn't go to bed that day. She and the kitten were busy playing and bonding, Tekir following Neri wherever she went. Metin told Neri that he had found the kitten in the neighbor's yard. Tekir was a stray, and the neighbors had fed him once or twice. They were delighted that Metin was going to adopt the kitten and yes, he had looked everywhere. There were no other cats starving outside.

Nermin was extremely affectionate with her husband that day, kissing him on the cheek every time he went by, attracting Neri's curiosity.

"What's going on? Did I forget somebody's birthday?'

"No, just a normal day," laughed Nermin. "Everyday reminds me what a clever husband I have."

Neri looked at her father. He was strutting around like a self-satisfied peacock, chasing the kitten every now and then. Neri shook her head. She did have weird parents, no doubt about it.

Later that day when Leyla arrived and saw the little kitten in Neri's lap, she crinkled her nose in disgust. She was not a cat person but she quickly realized that in a single day the kitten had achieved a miraculous change in Neri, one the humans hadn't managed in a month.

So Leyla decided to be nice, bent down and tried to pat the kitten. Tekir stared her in the eye and spat with such unexpected force that Leyla leapt back as if confronted by a five-hundred pound Siberian tiger.

"You can't fool them," Neri admonished her. "Cats know instinctively when you don't like them."

"Oh, OK. You can have him. I hope I don't hurt your feelings or his," Leyla hissed, "if I never go near him again."

Metin and Nermin were watching Neri and her friend, smiling broadly. Things were finally back to normal, *Maşallah*, and they hoped it would stay that way, for a while, *İnşallah!*

45

The repercussions of the tragic accident wouldn't go away. It remained a diplomatic nightmare. Americans insisted that since the driver was a member of the US Armed Forces, it was within their jurisdiction to investigate and determine fault. Turks on the other hand argued that the accident happened on Turkish soil and was their responsibility. Five Turkish soldiers had been killed and seven others critically injured. The tire marks and the bodies of the soldiers clearly indicated how the incident had occurred. The American driver was at fault. The only thing left to determine was how fast the truck had been coming down the icy road and whether or not the driver was intoxicated. But the Americans had whisked the driver away from the scene before the Turkish police could question him. The Turks weren't even sure of the driver's name.

Of course, the Turkish press was adding fuel to the fire. Nationalistic fervor was being stoked and even the most rational Turks were feeling outraged. Whose country did they think this was? Was Turkey a colony of America?

Those critical of the Menderes Government were using the incident as direct proof of the government's apparent inability to influence Washington and protect Turkey's sovereignty. In the middle of all this was Neri as the only possibly reliable witness. The young motorcyclist was still in the hospital and his memory of the accident was limited. He could not remember anything except that one moment he was swerving to avoid the sliding truck, and the next he was sliding onto the woman on the sidewalk, and that was that, nothing more. All the injured soldiers could remember was the noise they had heard just after waving to the same young woman.

Both Turkish and American authorities had been in touch with Metin, trying to get an interview with Neri. Then a reporter discovered Neri's identity and now her name and face were all over the newspapers. Metin was getting telephone calls from reporters daily and the military police wanted to question her as soon as possible. With Neri feeling much improved, Metin decided it was time to put an end to all this unpleasantness. So he brought the subject up. Neri's reaction was surprisingly mild: she simply continued stroking Tekir the kitten and agreed to "get it over with."

The day of the interview, Metin and Nermin were more nervous than Neri. They feared that the stress of the day would be too much for her. Since they've never had an experience like this before, they did not know how to prepare her or themselves for an ordeal.

At the appointed time, two black cars stopped in their driveway and five men got out. The Americans were in uniform, Turks in civilian clothes. They introduced themselves. The Americans were members of the US Armed Forces legal staff with one speaking Turkish. The Turks didn't indicate which office they represented but Metin thought they looked like military intelligence. The Turks spoke English and after an initial word with Neri, they agreed to conduct the interview in English.

At the beginning Neri found the questioning process grueling. She couldn't bring herself to talk about the accident directly; it was easier to describe the chill in the air, the ominous sky, and the icicles on the trees than the horrible details of the accident. The Turkish investigator let her ramble on. American lawyers were impressed with his technique and kept quiet. Finally, little by little, the Turkish official got her to the point when she first heard the truck coming down the street.

"What did you do then?"

"I turned and looked. Actually I was half turned anyway. I was waving to the soldiers."

"What did you see?"

Her face crumbled up. Tears were beginning to well up in her eyes. Nermin made a move but the Turk signaled her to stop.

"I saw the face of the driver in the truck. He was very young and very frightened."

"What was he doing?"

"I think he was trying to control his truck but he knew it was impossible."

"Why?"

"It was coming down sideways."

"Do you know why?"

"It was slippery. The road I mean..."

"Before you turned and looked, could you tell from the noise if the truck was coming down the hill fast?" One of the American lawyers opened his mouth as if to say something but Neri had already answered:

"No, I couldn't. Besides how could the truck come down fast while going sideways?" She looked at them with her innocent eyes. There was moisture at the end of her long lashes.

"Then what happened?"

"What do you mean what happened? Surely you know what happened. The truck hit the soldiers. It went over them." Now she was sobbing silently. Nermin could not take it anymore. She went to her daughter and held her tightly. She was looking at the Turkish man ready to kill him.

"Would you like to have a glass of water, Neriman Hanım?" asked the man in Turkish. She shook her head.

"Then what happened?"

"Then I saw the young man on the motorcycle. He was coming fast on the sidewalk. He hit me, and that's all I remember."

The American lawyers asked more questions, walking her through the same scene over and over. But she could add nothing new.

"How old was the driver of the truck?" she asked while they were leaving. The question surprised them.

"Nineteen," said one of the Americans. "Why do you ask?"

"What a burden to bear the rest of your life." Then she stared at her parents: "All the Turkish soldiers were young too, maybe even younger," she said, her face collapsing again. "They just looked like boys."

46

The snow was long gone and the storks were back. The bare trees were beginning to show a faint taint of green. There was a fresh smell of grass that was itching to grow. The urgency in nature to renew itself was contagious, encouraging the birds to chatter loudly. The backs of old people seemed straighter, the smiles of young couples brighter and the sea breezes softer. Long, lazy beach days of summer were around the corner.

The world was waking up, except for Neri. She ate, slept, smiled, and talked, but to her parents and friends she still seemed hollow, as though she was still hibernating. Neri was animated only when playing with Tekir. She refused to go out. The sound of traffic made her cringe.

Nermin and Metin were at a loss. It was now six months since the accident. They knew there was nothing wrong with Neri physically but they could sense her silent anguish about the death of the young soldiers and her own baby. And now she'd developed a fear of going out. They didn't know how to make her feel that the world out there was not wholly dangerous but good too. They gave her love and comfort and they waited. She was young. Eventually she would recover. That was the law of nature.

The catalyst turned out to be her friends from Ankara. The Millers and Stan unexpectedly showed up one morning. The Millers had come to see her once just after Neri had returned home, but they'd left heartbroken after realizing her condition. Maude did not want to remember how Neri looked then in bed without any hint of life in her eyes. She was happy to see Neri's face lit up when she saw the large box of lilacs they brought her. She held them close to her face smiling and asking where they found lilacs so early in March.

Maude laughed and said Stan had "blackmailed someone in the PX" to search all over the US.

"I know they're Neri's favorites," Stan said quietly.

By now Metin had told Nermin about Stan, but she needed no telling. Stan's love for Neri was so apparent as to make everyone else in the room feel like a voyeur. Nermin looked at her daughter. She was basking in his love, shedding the protective layers she'd built around her. The awful storm that had lingered over their house for so long was finally moving away.

During lunch they chatted about everything but never about the accident. John was hilarious describing some of the rumors that had resurfaced after the Dairy Scandal had ended with Abdullah Okun going to jail. It was clear that, like Neri, her parents knew nothing about Ismet's involvement with the scam.

Metin served them his new award-winning wine which he was now exporting to Germany and promised John that he would take them to see his factory whenever it was convenient. He boasted that he had become a wine guru to a large number of young men who were in his training program, and some of his graduates were on the verge of becoming well-known vintners themselves. Nermin complained that although her husband was supposed to be semi-retired, he was busier than ever, with trips to Europe to expand his export business. She said she enjoyed these trips and would accompany him more often if it wasn't for the travel restrictions the government implemented to protect the Turkish lira.

After lunch, while they were drinking Turkish coffee, Maude pulled Neri aside to talk to her alone.

"All your friends in Ankara are still worried about you. We were relieved to hear that at least the ordeal of questioning by the police is over. Was it very difficult?"

"It was," Neri sighed, "but they were very nice and considerate. I don't think I was much help though; I couldn't add anything new. How could I? Everything happened so quickly." She looked despondent, and Maude quickly changed the subject.

"Do you know that Ismet is no longer working for John?"

"No, I didn't. Why?" Maude decided not to say anything about how close Ismet had come to going to jail with Abdullah Okun.

"He is working with his father now. They just landed a huge construction job with the municipality."

"Ismet working with his father? I can't believe it. Good for him!" Neri laughed. She did not seem to carry any ill feelings toward her ex-husband which irritated Maude.

Neri glanced at Stan who was deep in conversation with Metin. "How's Stan doing?"

"Much better now that he's no longer married," Maude confided. She was glad that they had finally come to the topic of Stan.

"What?"

"Didn't you know? Sarah returned home last fall, just before you were hospitalized. I guess they finally thought it was time to sit down and face their problems, and Sarah agreed divorce was the best option. They've been divorced for two months now. I am happy for him. He should have done it years ago if you ask me."

"Poor Stan," Neri said, glancing at him again. He caught her eye and smiled, somewhat perplexed. Maude decided to take matters into her own hands.

"Poor only if you don't have any feelings for him, Neri. You know he's still in love with you, don't you?"

Neri blushed and hid her face behind her hands. Stan was watching them and looking worried. Meanwhile Nermin who was approaching Maude and Neri with a bowl of chocolates now retreated. She did not want to break up their conversation. It looked important.

"I do," Neri answered, choking with emotion. "I know he loves me. I love him too but not enough. He deserves someone with more to give than me . . . . I can't."

"Why can't you, Neri? Do you love somebody else?"

"I've always loved somebody else. I should have never married Ismet. I can't do the same thing to Stan. He deserves better," she repeated. She looked ready to cry.

"Then I think you should tell him."

"But I think he already knows. I don't need to tell him. He seems to know me, what I'm feeling, what I'm thinking, without me saying anything." Neri knew this attentiveness was one of the things that she had found so attractive about him.

"So where is this other person?" Maude asked hesitantly. She had a feeling now she was treading on sensitive ground. She didn't know how to explain to Neri that she was not being nosy but she just wanted to be reassured that one day Neri would finally find the happiness she so richly deserved, something Maude wished with all her heart.

"It's a long story," Neri smiled and Maude knew she was not ready to talk about it yet. I can wait thought Maude. Just then Stan appeared by their side, hushing their conversation.

"May I borrow Neri for a little while?" he asked. Maude smiled and moved away towards the others.

"Neri," he continued, "the Millers' car is picking them up any minute. They're going to stay two more days in İstanbul. I think your friends Selma and Ceylan have made plans for them. I have to return to Ankara tonight. Can we take a walk or something?"

"Yes, of course we can," she nodded.

After the Millers left, her parents were surprised to find out that Neri was going out for a walk with Stan. She's over her fear, thank God, thought Nermin but after they watched their daughter put on her coat and leave with the young man, they looked at each other perplexed. Haven't they gone through this before? Was more emotional turmoil on the way?

Metin placed his arm around his wife's waist and sighed. "I hope she knows what she's doing."

47

They could feel the cool sea breezes all the way up in Erenköy. They headed downhill, walking in the middle of the asphalt road rather than the narrow sidewalks. There was hardly any traffic except an occasional bicyclist all bundled up.

Stan was looking around with interest. Large trees hid most of the houses behind high walls, giving the street more of a European than American flavor. From what Stan could see, they weren't small houses but resembled Victorian mansions with intricately carved lattices and turrets. As though in sequence, they were surrounded by pine, chestnut, and other tall trees he couldn't name. Stretching up the long lawns were elaborate flower beds of rose bushes, hydrangeas, and other plants waiting to blossom. Stan noticed some houses had orchards in their backyards: fig, walnut, mulberry and other fruit-bearing trees. Some even had small vineyards.

There was a natural harmony between the weathered-down old houses and their surroundings which appealed to him. It was disappointing to see newly-built apartment blocks with their bland gray facades disrupting that natural harmony. Neri did not like them either.

"Most of these beautiful old houses will probably be gone in a couple of years," she explained. "İstanbul is growing very fast, now we have a new real-estate deal destroying our neighborhoods. It's a very ingenious deal, actually."

Stan smiled. "Tell me."

"Well, businessmen from the Black Sea region are coming with their pockets full of money and making offers that most people find hard to refuse. They take your land, tear your old house down, and build an apartment building in its place. Say the building has five stories and each story has two units. They usually take six units for themselves and give you the rest. Suddenly, without spending any money, you become the owner of four flats. Sometimes they give you cash upfront and pay your rent while the construction is going on. After it's over, you have a flat to live in, however tiny in comparison to what you had before, and renting the rest brings you a steady income that you didn't have before."

"Let me guess what happens next. The builders get rich by selling the flats they own and move to the next house to demolish."

"Exactly. Everybody is happy except that every year more trees are cut down, more vineyards and orchards are ruined. My father says each spring he hears fewer nightingales. Also, the place is getting more crowded. There is more trash, more noise, and more commotion. It's a mess. I hate to see these beautiful places disappear and it's happening all over İstanbul."

Stan gazed at her in amazement. He had never seen her so angry, nor so talkative.

"Turkey is changing fast, Stan, and I'm worried about it. I think it's irresponsible to argue that every change or every new thing is a good thing if you don't consider its consequences and side effects. For instance, and please Stan don't misunderstand me, I'm not blaming your country but did you know that every tractor we receive from the US economic aid program tends to displace up to ten farm families? In recent years, hundreds of thousands of villagers have moved to İstanbul and other big cities. Every time you turn your back, there's a new shanty town mushrooming up with largely rural, uneducated people the cities can't absorb. There aren't enough jobs, and these places are breeding grounds for trouble."

"Surely that can't all be blamed on the US."

She didn't like his tone but continued. "Not directly, I agree, but it's an unplanned consequence of your economic aid program that has left us with serious problems. You see, jobless people living in crowded unsanitary conditions seem to be vulnerable to easy manipulation, some by communists, others by religious extremists. There are rumors that the minority shops in Beyoglu were ransacked by these people. That was a disgusting, deplorable incident, and it's really sad that many shop owners have decided to quit and not reopen their businesses. My father says that large numbers have already immigrated to other countries. Many of these people have been in Turkey as long as we have if not longer. It's such a shame!"

Her face was flushed; she was breathing hard. Stan was beginning to worry that the walk might be too much for her after months of bed rest.

"Neri, what Turkey is experiencing is not all that unique, is it? Many developing countries face similar problems. The transformation from an agrarian to industrial economy is a long process and tends to displace large populations of rural people."

"You're right of course, but we're a new republic with serious political and educational problems. We don't yet have an established culture amenable to sustain democracy. Concepts like equality, freedom of press and speech remain alien to most Turks. Atatürk was right when he once joked that he implemented all his reforms 'for the people, despite the people!'"

"I've never heard that but it sounds like an accurate description of his accomplishments."

"Stan, when you lived in Ankara in the thirties, you must have noticed that we had a unity of purpose. Most people believed in Atatürk's dream of modernization for our country and embraced his Western orientation. Now we are splintered into groups, each with a different and increasingly conflicting agenda. I think Turkey is going backwards and no one knows how to stop it. Oh, well, the lecture is over. We are already in Caddebostan."

Stan knew they were near the sea. He could smell the salt in the air and after dusty Ankara it was a wonderful fresh smell.

"I want to show you a place that was very important to me while I was growing up," Neri continued, making Stan's face light up like a little boy who had been handed a precious gift.

They were at the end of the road facing a tall wooden gate. He was not prepared for the scene on the other side. It was a large tree-covered promontory twenty some feet above the sea level and enclosed by a white picket fence. In the middle were light-blue painted wooden tables and chairs. The overhanging tree-canopy framed a small, outdoor dance floor.

The place had rustic charm and the view was incredible. On one side, there was a small bay full of colorful boats. On the other was a long crescent-shaped beach with fine silvery sand. Brightly colored cabins stretched away to another bluff jutting into the sea that supported a magnificent old mansion, its intricate woodwork darkened with age. In the distance the Princes' Islands shimmered like jewels in the Sea of Marmara.

"What a beautiful place," Stan said, slowly taking in the entire scene.

"In summer this place is very popular. In the morning mothers bring their children to play, and in the afternoon families come in for tea. Every night there is live music and dancing. When I was growing up, this is where I spent most of my summers, swimming," she said, pointing at the curving beach.

"Now I know where we are. I saw pictures of you on this beach."

Neri looked up in disbelief. "Where...how?" she asked.

"Back in your flat in Ankara when I was helping your father pack your things, I happened to come across your family album." He looked at her surprised face and added: "You don't mind, do you?"

"No, of course not, why should I mind? Let's sit a while, OK?"

He nodded happily. He would have jumped into the freezing sea if she had asked him. Didn't she know the power she had over him?

Neri ordered two teas from a young boy who had appeared out of nowhere. They sat at a table facing the sea. Stan noticed another couple on the far side, holding hands and huddled together. He envied their intimacy. He could imagine how romantic the place would be on a moonlit summer night. He wished he could be here with Neri in summer but as far as he was concerned, it was romantic enough even in the cold. He could feel contentment rising in his bones. He was grateful to Neri for sharing this magical little corner of her world.

They stared at each other a long time without speaking, afraid to break the mood. Their tea arrived in small tulip-shaped glasses, nestled in tiny metal trays. Each tray had three small cubes of sugar. The hot glass burned their fingers.

"This happens to me all the time," Neri was laughing. "That's why I like my tea in a porcelain cup, however untraditional that may be."

"I don't blame you. I've had more than my share of burnt fingers and lips." Suddenly, he reached out and grabbed Neri's hand.

"Neri, did Maude tell you I'm divorced now?"

Neri's face turned bright red. "Yes," she stammered.

"Does it mean anything to you?" He was still holding her hand and was leaning nearer so that his breath was warm on her face, making her tremble. She was surprised to realize that he still had that effect on her. How long was she going to remain so needy and so desperate for love? She couldn't bear to think about it. She also did not know how to answer him.

"Neri, you know I'm in love with you. What I'm trying to ask so clumsily is if there's any chance for us?" Hadn't she heard words to that effect before? How many times did she have to hurt, or get hurt?

"Neri, please say something." She heard the desperation in Stan's voice and responded without thinking.

"Stan, you know you're very dear to me," she started and stopped, seeing the change in his face. He looked like she'd just punched him. "No, what I mean is, I actually do love you. But I'm in love with someone else. Rather I never stopped loving someone else. I cannot be with you. I cannot do that to you. I love you much too much for that."

"Love me a little less and be mine," he said. They sat there for a full minute, Stan looking down, and then they burst into uncontrollable laughter.

"Oh, God," Stan said. "That came out so corny." He was still laughing, yet he managed to add: "But I meant every word of it. I'd be the happiest man alive if you agreed to marry me with half your heart Neri!"

"Oh, Stan, please, you deserve better than what I can give you." Her eyes were brimming with tears.

"Neri, I know I can make you happy. Won't you at least agree to give us a chance to see if I can change your mind?"

"Stan I know all of you thought Ismet was the wrong person for me. But did you ever stop to think that I might have been the wrong person for him too? I should never have married him when I knew I couldn't love him with all my heart. I can't do the same to you. I simply can't. I'm sorry because I know what a wonderful person you are."

"But not wonderful enough to marry, right?" he interrupted gently. "Who is this person you still love Neri and why aren't you with him?"

She knew he deserved an answer.

"His name is Bill and..."

"He's an American then?"

"No, he's English and we met years ago when I was only eighteen. He was...he is my first love, and I've never been able to get over him."

"Did you ever see him again, Neri?" But he already knew the answer. Neri blushed and before she could answer a childhood memory rushed in.

When she was about five, she and her cousin Alp had lied about breaking an antique vase while playing ball indoors. After her aunt took Alp upstairs to be punished, Neri's mother led Neri to a full-length mirror.

"Look how red your face is, Neri." She said. "You have an internal clock that makes you blush every time you lie. So don't ever try to lie to me or anyone, OK?" Neri knew there was no way she could lie to Stan and get away with it.

"Yes, I did see him again," she said.

"When you were in Oxford," Stan said, without it being a question.

Neri broke down and told him everything, at least almost everything. He listened quietly.

"He's a lucky man, Neri, and I know he'll find a way to come to you one day. I would too. Believe me, I'm happy for you, Neri."

She couldn't tell Stan she didn't believe Bill would ever come back. Without warning, she leaned over and kissed him on the cheek: "Thank you," she said softly. "We better get back."

"Am I ever going to see you again, Neri?" Stan asked.

"I'll let you know before coming to Ankara."

"You're coming to Ankara?" This was welcome news.

"Yes, I am."

Stan was about to ask why but the reason dawned on him. So he just kept quiet.

48

The next morning, Metin and Nermin were surprised to see Neri already at the breakfast table with a plate full of toast, jam, and cheese. Tekir was curled on the next chair, watching her and purring his little heart away.

Despite their gentle prodding, it soon became clear that Neri was not going to reveal anything about what passed between her and Stan the day before. It was still hard for Metin and Nermin to get used to this closed-mouthed version of their daughter who had, once upon a time, always been eager to share everything with them.

"If you haven't made any plans for this morning, I want to go and see Leyla," declared Neri. "She hasn't left her house since her mother returned to Ankara. And I miss her."

"Hasn't she got any help with the baby yet?" inquired Nermin.

"I don't know. Before leaving, her mother lined up a couple of prospects for her to interview, but I have a feeling she's being too cautious."

Nermin laughed. "She's still a new mother. Trust me, a week alone with the baby, even the most unsuitable helper will start looking good. Give her our love."

Neri kept a fast pace up the hill to Göztepe. The exercise made her feel good. She hadn't realized how much she missed the simple act of walking. For the first time in months she felt full of life if not hope. She was trying to teach herself to live without expecting too much.

Leyla's door was opened by a nervous-looking girl. She tried to lead Neri to the formal living room, but Neri told her that she was a close friend, and walked straight to the bedroom where she could hear Leyla cooing to the baby.

This time the sight of Leyla did not make her laugh at all. She was a mess. She was feeding the baby. Her long blond hair, unwashed and unkempt, was in loose braids. She had dark circles under her eyes and looked exhausted. She smiled when she saw Neri and put her finger to her lips. The baby was about to sleep.

After she put the baby in his room, Leyla turned and kissed Neri. She smelled of sour milk. Neri took her by hand and pushed her to the bathroom.

"Go take a shower, for goodness' sake. I'll watch the baby."

While Leyla was in the bathroom, Neri called the young girl and told her to clean the bedroom and change the sheets. The girl's demeanor changed. She smiled and went to work with a vengeance. When Leyla came back wrapped in a towel, she could not believe her eyes. The room looked tidy, clean and fresh smelling.

"How did you manage all this?"

"I didn't do anything. Fatma did it all by herself."

"She did? Maybe I underestimated her."

"No maybes." Neri said. "That girl is a miracle worker. I bet she is good with babies too. She told me that she has four brothers, one just a year old."

"Oh, OK. I'll see how well she does with the baby. I was about to get on my knees and beg my mother to come back but Fatma is a better solution."

They went and sat in the living room after Leyla had a long talk with Fatma. The girl was no longer nervous but eager to work.

Neri guessed that she thought Leyla did not like her and was going to fire her.

Leyla was curious about the Millers' visit. When she found out Stan had come too, she wanted to hear every word. "Too bad I wasn't there. I've been dying to see your irresistible Stan for a long time. Are you still stuck on him?"

"Yes, I'm still stuck on him but not in the way you mean. He's a lovely man and I wish I'd met him years ago."

"Even before Bill?"

Neri was silent for a while, thinking. "No," she sighed. "I'll never regret meeting Bill."

"Neri," started Leyla, very serious now: "I think you should let Bill know that you're divorced."

"Oh, God!" sighed Neri. "I can't."

"Why not? Don't you think he'd want to know?"

"No, I don't. Don't interrupt. Just let me finish, OK? Before leaving I made it very clear to him in Oxford that there was no future for us, that I was pregnant and was going back to my husband. I made him promise to go ahead with his life. And I vowed over and over again that I would too. He agreed."

"Under duress though, right? The guy has pined after you all these years. Do you think he is going to forget you in a single year, particularly after Oxford?" Neri blushed. "Anyway, did you? Forget him, I mean?"

"No, I don't think I'll ever forget him. Even someone as nice and decent, and—I might add—sexy as Stan is couldn't make me forget Bill."

"So why do you think Bill would forget you? You still think you're not worth loving. You know Neri, sometimes I feel like killing that stupid Ismet. He really made you doubt yourself. Trust me, Neri, you are lovable, and not just Stan, but your favorite Bill loves you too. You should write to him." She smiled.

Neri sank lower in the armchair. It was clear that she had an internal dialogue going on and not a calm one. She shook her head.

"Leyla, I've managed to hurt too many people. I know you don't like Ismet. But did he deserve what he got from me? I don't really know. Then there's Stan. It all started as fun and games but suddenly, we were involved. And what was my motivation? First, I convinced myself it was to get revenge, then I lied to myself pretending that he reminded me of Bill, while all the time I just needed his attention and love. Let's face it, I used him. What sort of a person does that make me? I know I'm not a bad person but I've made bad choices. Now I want to do the right thing, at least with Bill." She looked determined but sad.

Leyla looked unconvinced. "You can't just give up."

"But I want Bill to be happy. You met him in Oxford. He's such a lovely man, inside and out. He's changed his life for the better with a lot of struggle and he has a bright future. Leyla, Bill will meet someone there, a nice English girl, and marry. That's what I wish for him... a nice English wife to make him happy."

"You're kidding yourself with this act of nobility! Life is not a Noel Coward play! Denying yourself is not going to make you happy and you know it. What are you going to do, become an old maid? You're not even twenty-five. How old *are* you?"

"None of your business!" snapped Neri. Just then the baby started crying.

On the way back home, Neri kept on going over what Leyla had said about Bill. Was Leyla right? It was a tempting suggestion to contact him, but what if Bill had started a new life? Did she have the right to mess it up all over again? Besides, she was afraid. She had convinced herself that the loss of her baby was God's punishment for her behavior in Oxford. Giving up Bill was the only way she knew of repenting for her sins. Yet every time she remembered Bill's body and the sound of his voice, her resolve weakened and her hopes intensified.

49

It was a bone-chilling day in Ankara, not unexpected in early April but making every breath a chore. Wrapped in layers of warm clothing, Neri was still shivering. The sun was bright but failed to ease the cold at all. She wished it would disappear. Its reflections on the white tombstones and the snow were blurring her vision. She was also getting lost in the cemetery.

They had given her detailed directions at the gate but the snow-covered lanes were hard to identify. She did not know if she was walking on the path or stepping on unmarked graves. The thought really bothered her. She was about to turn and ask for help when the sun glinting on a solitary shelf of marble caught her eye. She walked slower. When she saw the name, Neri's legs gave way and she fell on her knees, sobbing uncontrollably.

"Hülya," they'd called her, a wisp of daydream, gone in the blink of an eye. Here was Hülya...Neri did not know how long she knelt there crying. A hand was touching her shoulder, shaking her.

"*Abla, Abla,*" the taxi driver was saying. "Please get up. You are drenched. You're going to catch your cold. Please, *Abla*, let's go now."

Neri looked at him, and for a moment she didn't know who he was. Then she remembered. She had taken a taxi from the train station to the cemetery. She had told him to wait at the gate and she would be back soon, but she had no idea how much time had passed. She now smiled gently. This young man, about her age, was calling her "older sister." When had she become an older sister?

They walked to the car. The taxi driver was still worrying about her wet clothes. He had an old run-down car. He turned the heater on full but it wasn't generating much heat.

"*Abla*," he said, "if it's all right with you, I'm going to stop at this roadside coffeehouse and get you a cup of tea. I know it doesn't look like much but it is a clean place. A cup of tea should help, don't you think?"

He was nearly pleading. She nodded. He disappeared into the shack and a minute later he returned with an old man in baggy pants.

"*Abla*, won't you come in? He has a wood stove inside and it's really warm. Maybe you can dry your coat while you're drinking you tea."

Neri nodded again and followed the two men. She felt good being told what to do. The place was smoky. There were others there, all village men sitting at tables. They tried not to stare at her, but she could see pity in their eyes. So near the cemetery, they must see a lot of grieving people, she said to herself. They took her coat and hung it on a chair near the stove. Someone pulled a chair out for her, next to the heat. Piping hot tea in a glass cup was placed in front of her. She sipped it gratefully, not feeling the scalding liquid.

She was getting sleepy. She could hardly keep her eyes open. She heard the taxi driver calling her.

"*Abla*, your coat is almost dry. Do you want to go now?" Neri got up, put on her coat like an obedient child, and realized that her legs were unsteady. The taxi driver and the old man rushed to hold her up. They helped her into the car. She heard the old man say *"Başınız sağ olsun"*—the traditional Turkish condolences. She looked at him. She hadn't noticed before, but the old man had pale blue eyes. They were compassionate. She forced herself to concentrate and get a hold of herself. She touched his hand.

"Thank you so much," she murmured. "I'll never forget your kindness."

He smiled sadly and squeezed her hand with such understanding that she found her eyes beginning to tear up. As the car got back on the highway, she turned and looked at the building, ramshackle and leaning dangerously to one side but so warm and comfortable inside.

Neri slept till late afternoon. Then she got up and called Nuriye. She was not sure how Nuriye would respond but she was friendly. Neri asked: "Who named my daughter?"

Nuriye admitted it was her and sounded worried but Neri assured her that it was a very good name, adding she could not have come up with a better name herself and thanked Nuriye. She knew it was more than likely the last time she would ever talk to her.

Neri went down to the hotel's coffee shop for some tea and a small sandwich. The starched table clothes, shiny silverware and flowers in little crystal vases all seemed oddly out of place. Her eyes searched for the taxi-driver, the old man, crooked wooden tables and the red-hot stove that had so warmed her heart just a few hours ago.

"Where has everyone gone?" she whispered.

Neri was not sure she could bear to meet the group as planned, but she had to do it. She needed to thank them. They'd all been so kind and caring during her stay at the hospital. They were now as dear to her as her school friends.

On the way out to meet Stan who was waiting in the lobby to drive her to the Millers' house, Neri happened to glance at her face in the mirror. She stopped and looked at it without recognizing it. It was the face of a stranger, someone she had seen in a dream...or someone from the past who had been a mother for too brief a time. What was real to her now? She straightened her shoulders and shook her head. She did not want to see that face any more.

Her short stay in Ankara felt too long. Mostly, she felt 'out of sorts' with her friends. She didn't know why. Maude sensed her discomfort and said to John afterwards that it had been a mistake for her to come to Ankara. She was not yet ready to face the remnants of her old life with all its painful memories. Neri knew she would never come back.

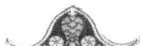

Listening to the soothing clickety-clack of the rail tracks, Neri remembered why she'd always liked trains. She abhorred standing still. Yet ever since she'd married Ismet, it seemed to her, she'd done nothing but stood still. She laughed bitterly. Did she want to stagnate or go on with her life? Do we have a choice, she wondered?

She made a resolution. She would not dwell on the past ever again—at least not consciously or continually. She knew her internal turmoil would go on. How much longer, who knew but she did not want to guess or think about it.

Instead Neri did what her father taught her as a child when facing unpleasantness. She visualized herself holding a box. Then carefully she placed into it all the love and anguish she felt for her daughter, and just before locking and storing the box deep down in her psyche, safe from prodding memories and painful recollections, Neri stopped and placed inside it her passion and dreams for Bill too.

"There," she sighed. "It's done."

Part III

They say there's a window
That opens from heart to heart;
If there are no walls,
There is no need for any window.

Mevlana Celaleddin Rumi

(Translated by Talat S. Halman, *Nightingales & Pleasure Gardens*)

50

Neri was sitting on her balcony, wrapped in a sweater and watching the Bosphorus slide by. She was content. All things considered, the last year had been a good one, passing quickly without too much drama. She was now working at her old school in charge of the newly-established alumnae office. She had two others working with her, contacting and updating the addresses of graduates and developing fund-raising projects. She liked her job. It was challenging, keeping her busy and purposeful.

Her life had fallen into a comfortable seamless routine. The tempo of her life had changed too. The last six years had been excruciatingly long, but now days, weeks, months were all blurring together. As her mother was fond of saying: "You sneeze and before you know it, it's spring again."

Her house was a gift from her parents. It had taken her father six months of successful evasions and cover-ups of his whereabouts to secretly buy a house near her old school and have it renovated. Then one nice sunny October morning, he'd taken them on a ride along the Bosphorus all the way to Arnavutköy and then up a narrow cobblestone street with old wooden houses close enough to touch across the street. They'd arrived at a sunny clearing where he'd stopped the car and pointed at a little white house with blue shutters standing all by itself on the hilltop. It had three stories with a small curved balcony on the second floor. A newly planted garden with two lilac trees graced the front garden behind a low stone fence and a blue wooden gate. A large grove of trees nestled against the house in the back. Neri thought it looked like a miniature version of a fairy tale castle—she could not believe it was hers.

During the next couple of months, Neri's parents started feeling relieved and more convinced that their daughter was going to be all right. They shopped for furniture together and helped her decorate the house, and before long Neri had become one of those steady, semi-if-not-fully-satisfied independent working women, no longer floundering between childhood and adulthood.

Neri glanced down. Tekir and Pamuk—her big twenty pound Persian cat—were curled around each other, fast asleep in their basket. As usual Tekir had all but disappeared under Pamuk. Tekir had taken to the larger cat the first moment he'd laid eyes on him. They'd sniffed, circled each other, arched and butted their backs, and started purring so loud that Neri and her parents could not contain their laughter.

The cats did everything together. And they shared Neri together. Once or twice they'd tried to fit on her lap together but soon gave up the idea. Now they were content to sleep cuddled up in the basket as long as Neri was nearby. At night, they took their positions beside her in bed, Tekir on the right and Pamuk on the left. It took Neri a while to get used to sleeping like a mummy for fear of rolling on top of her cats.

She loved watching the Bosphorus. Its dazzling color displays always fascinated her. Today against the deep blue of the sky, its colors were shifting capriciously from ultramarine to emerald to milky blue. The orange-red tiles of the houses sent a warm glow over the purple flowering Judas trees. The white faces of some of the newly-painted houses contrasted with the ox-blood red of others. It looked as if each color was competing, daring the others to be bolder and livelier. The enduring beauty of the

Bosphorus was a constant challenge, demanding the onlookers to be in awe, live fully and enjoy life.

Neri could not decide which Bosphorus she preferred: the richly colored, razor-sharp beauty of sunny days, or the quiet one creeping into your senses with its early morning fog that laps its shores, blurring all shapes into soft and indistinct hues of grays and lavender. She decided she loved every mood the Bosphorus revealed, including its stormy tantrums like the one two nights ago when the stars had disappeared and the sky had become a threatening blackish-blue. The waters of the Bosphorus had started churning with white caps, and squall after squall of thick heavy rain had shot horizontally down across the neighborhood, crushing trees and scattering blossoms. Then just as quickly as it had arrived, the storm had passed, leaving a clean sheen of fresh air in its wake.

Sometimes Neri felt that she could sit on her balcony and never move. Watching the Bosphorus was enough. It was life-giving, she thought. No, she corrected herself; it was simply the force of life itself. It was impossible not to feel part of its power or be challenged by its moods. The Bosphorus never failed to invigorate you with a shot of adrenaline. It was like an old lover, demanding sometimes but familiar and calmly satisfying. No wonder the elderly teachers on the hill always seemed so content with their lives!

She bolted straight up. She had been watching the two large ships absent-mindedly, but her eyes now focused on them with worry. A steel-gray Russian destroyer was coming from the Black Sea, hugging the European side of the Bosphorus. Meanwhile an empty north-bound oil tanker, riding high with the rusty-red paint of its hull showing, was on the Asian side, going the other way. There wasn't much space between them and they were both sounding their horns furiously at four tiny fishing boats in their way. There were hundreds of such boats in the Bosphorus at any time of day but hardly any foolish enough to stay in the path of big ships. As the two ships closed on each other, still sounding their horns, Neri shut her eyes tight. Her heart was pounding. She was sure the small boats were going to capsize, but a moment later she saw four tiny dots bobbing up and down in the heavy wake.

"See nothing happened," Neri said to the cats, waking them up. They gazed up at her with puzzlement, stood up, licked themselves, spun round and settled down again, exactly as they were. Neri started laughing. She felt good. She knew she was no longer standing still. All this past year, it had seemed she too was bobbing in the wake of unknown forces without any sense of direction, with each bob pushing her a tiny bit closer to that yet-to-be-determined goal.

Eventually, everything had fallen into place. She now had a job and her own home, plus two cats. She knew she was as happy as she could hope. Sometimes she suspected she was confusing the relief she felt at the absence of any more trauma in her life as happiness, because every time she started to count her blessings, an incredible sadness that the Turks call "*hüzün*" would creep up on her out of nowhere. The more she tried to ignore it, the more persistent it became, overpowering her and weakening her resolutions, forcing her to ask questions she would rather ignore.

Did she do the right thing by not keeping in touch with Bill? Could she have been happy with Stan?

Her friends had asked her the same questions again and again, but they had never been satisfied with her answers. They were always certain she was throwing her life away.

"You want to be a spinster at your age?" A frustrated Leyla shouted at her only recently. "Like those old teachers at school, self-satisfied but unhappy? Why are you giving up?"

She was not giving up—at least not on life—just on love. What was wrong with that?

51

A taxi was slowly coming up the cobblestone street. Neri and her parents looked at it with curiosity. They were having tea and they weren't expecting anyone else. The car finally came to a stop and Ayla got out. Neri ran downstairs, opened the door and embraced her with both arms. She had not seen Ayla since her stay in the hospital. The last time she was in Ankara, Ayla was still in jail.

"You're out! Why didn't you let me know? I'm so glad to see you." She was babbling like crazy.

Ayla smiled and kissed her on both cheeks. "Let me look at you. You look great, like your old self. I'm glad to see you Neri. I missed you, we all did." She kissed her again. She was relieved to see Neri looking so healthy and cheerful again.

"I'm dying to see your new home. Aren't you going to invite me in?"

"I'm so happy to see you, I forgot my manners. Welcome to my home, Ayla Hanım. Please come in. How are you?" She mimicked the traditional salutation. They both giggled and walked in. Ayla looked around and liked what she saw. Neri had divided the large room on the first floor into two sections. On one side low comfortable chairs were arranged around a large copper tray. The vibrant reds and oranges of the old *kilim* on the floor were repeated on pillows and in the rich colors of the oil paintings on the walls.

The other side of the room served as a dining area with a small round table and six elegant antique chairs. The only decoration was a large Kutahya bowl on the table and two still-life paintings on the walls. There was no rug on the floor and somehow the contrast between the austere dining room and the lively sitting room worked, like Neri herself, Ayla thought, both demure and exciting. Neri was proud too of her small but very modern and efficient kitchen.

After Ayla greeted her parents, Neri took her upstairs to show off her bedroom. It was very serene, all whites and blues. The back room was her study, lined with books. A large bathroom and linen closet occupied the rest of the third floor space.

"This house suits you, Neri," Ayla said. "It's warm and beautiful. I'm glad to see you settled down finally. So are you happy?"

"Not you too!" moaned Neri. "Why is everyone asking me that question?"

"Because we want you to be happy. You went through hard times. Besides, none of us understood your rejection of Stan." She smiled. "What was wrong with him anyway?"

"Nothing was wrong with him. But at the time we were both married, remember?"

"But now you are both free, so what's holding you up?"

"It's a long story Ayla; please don't ask me any more questions. My parents must be wondering what happened to us. Let's go down now. We were in the middle of having tea."

"I thought you loved him," insisted Ayla.

Neri grabbed her hand and led her downstairs. "I love many people but it seems I love my solitude more!" she whispered as they walked into the family room.

Ayla loved the sitting room with its comfortable chairs and uncluttered elegance but she was immediately drawn to the balcony.

"This view is beautiful," she muttered in awe, "*too* alluring, it could lull you into false sense of serenity. But Neri, life has a way of catching up with you."

"Maybe Neri needs a little more time," Nermin said who had just walked onto the balcony. "She is still vulnerable, although she tries very hard to conceal it."

"We better go in," Neri suggested, "the tea is getting cold."

They all settled down around a table laden with cakes and pastries. Neri wanted to know about everybody in Ankara.

"Have you heard from Professor Horowitz?" she asked. "He returned home a couple of months before I left Ankara," she explained to her parents.

"Yes, we have, actually," Ayla smiled. "Did you know he's dedicating his book to us?"

"What do you mean us?"

"Us, the Turkish women! Something about those courageous secular Turkish women who keep the flame of Atatürk's reforms alive...Cannot remember the exact words but the whole thing sounded very nice."

"You should all be very proud," commented Metin. "He must have admired you all."

"Wow! I'm impressed," Neri laughed. "Despite all that partying and boozing, he must have paid attention to us after all."

"Oh, indeed!" Ayla giggled. "And remember how!" They stared at each other and burst into laughter. Nermin and Metin looked bewildered. The two young women described their 'Professor pinching' escapades in hilarious detail. Although they were taking comedic license and exaggerating, it was clear that they both liked and respected the Professor.

"Clearly he needs to grow up a little," Neri added, and then thought of herself.

"Less alcohol consumption would speed up the process, don't you think?" Ayla said, still grinning. "By the way, have you heard that Tom and Christie are going back home too? It is rumored that Tom had gone native and lost his objectivity."

"But the Millers are staying, right?" Neri asked, anxiously.

"Yes, the Millers are staying, and so is Stan. His contract with the US military has been renewed. He'll be here for at least another four years but nowadays he is mostly in Diyarbakir." She looked at Neri meaningfully but Neri changed the subject again.

"When did you get out of prison? And how bad was it?"

"Nearly a month ago and it wasn't that bad at all."

"I read in the papers that the judge finally threw out the prosecutor's arguments," Metin said. "At least there are a few honest judges left."

"Honest and courageous," Ayla replied. "One by one any judge who goes against the government ends up being transferred to a forsaken little town in Eastern Turkey."

"And are you back to teaching?" asked Neri.

"Yes, and there's another thing you perhaps read in the papers. The Minister of Education ordered the president of the university to fire the three of us jailbirds. He would not. The minister threatened to fire the president. That led to student protests, including sit-ins at the ministry. A small group of students began fasting in protest. The papers were full of stories about starving students. Actually, one had to be hospitalized. The police reacted badly as usual. It was a public relations nightmare. So, in the end the minister caved in and all four of us got reinstated."

"I wonder if the poor minister realized that he was opening the floodgates," said Metin. They all looked at him questioningly.

"Well, it's probably one of the few examples of civic disobedience in Turkey that ended well. Don't you think this has given the students a taste of power? High time, too!"

"Dr. Horowitz would have been proud of them," said Neri.

"How come?" Metin asked, puzzled.

"He believed in political involvement. Political and civic complacency infuriated him. Remember how he used to goad us?" Neri asked Ayla.

"Yes, rightly so too." Ayla answered. "We, the so-called enlightened and Westernized Turks, we are good at talking and giving advice but when it comes to civic activism, we lack the necessary courage." She sighed apologetically and glanced at the Bosphorus.

"From this distance, it's hard to see how treacherous the Bosphorus can be with its two strong currents flowing in opposite directions. We Turks are like the Bosphorus: one current pushing us West, the other deep under the surface pulling us East. I hate to think what would happen if the two ever collide! We have an almost impossible task before us. The cultural divide in our country boggles the mind."

"What do you mean?" Nermin asked. Ayla looked at Neri's mother, still young-looking, smartly dressed, and comfortable with herself.

"Nermin Hanim, you live in İstanbul," Ayla said. "İstanbul is worlds apart from the rest of the country, as are some other cities like İzmir. I'm not just talking about the differences between rural and urban areas. Take Ankara, for instance, which on the surface looks like a modern city. We have government bureaucrats and academics, knowledgeable about Western culture and political history, quoting Voltaire or Oscar Wilde, depending which foreign-language school they graduated from, going to opera or jazz clubs, and living much like their European counterparts. They're concerned about human rights, equality before law, and improvement of our so-called 'democratic' style government."

"I get it," Nermin said. "Then there are others who are centuries behind both in mindset and lifestyles."

"Precisely! For example, the honor-killings are still part of life in Eastern Turkey. When a young girl is raped, it is she who is punished and even killed, not the rapist. Just recently a thirteen year old boy in Diyarbakir murdered his twenty-five year old sister because 'she dishonored the family name.' In some areas the village girls are still sold and bought as if they're property. But coming back to Ankara, I have met many people who look well-educated and modern on the outside but are trapped in a centuries-old mentality inside, narrow-minded and mean-spirited. They're authoritarian in their personal lives and autocratic when it comes to governing."

"I suppose it's hard to get rid of nearly seven-centuries of Ottoman traditions in one generation," Metin said.

"Yes, and our religion is no help: it abhors change, negates individuality and free thinking, and expects nothing but blind obedience to an inflexible religious community." Ayla stopped and took a sip from her tea. Her face was flushed. It's a good thing her husband is not here, Neri thought. It must be hard for Mete to try to discourage his wife from publicly attacking such increasingly sensitive topics while he agreed with her totally.

"We have such a task in front of us. How can we change our system of strong central government without changing our authoritarian culture which allows it to function without accountability or transparency? I'm doing my best to teach my students to become better citizens, more involved and more demanding, but it's an almost impossible task in a culture that values blind obedience to authority figures. I realize that we are still a new democracy but sometimes I fear we are going backwards!"

Metin was thoughtful. "At least your generation is raising the right questions," he commented.

"Amen," replied Nermin.

After the tea things were cleared, Ayla and Neri went and sat in the front garden, waiting for Ayla's taxi. They were still discussing the worsening political situation.

"You know, Ayla," Neri was saying, "maybe our expectations are too unrealistic. Don't laugh at what I'm going to say, but sometimes I see a parallel between the path my life has taken and the path our country is on now. I think we were both born from parents who were progressive and enlightened but with too high hopes for us. I hate to say this, but maybe Atatürk over-estimated our capacity to adapt to rapid modernization. Maybe what's happening now is a reaction to too rapid change, like a cultural, mental and moral recidivism. As my father said, it can't be easy giving up centuries-old conservative traditions. Besides, the old and familiar ways must be less threatening and more comforting, don't you think? For many Turks, Islam provides a familiar reassuring identity." Neri stared at the beautiful view. No solace there today.

"We all deal with threats to our identity in different ways. Look at me. I couldn't take Ismet and his family's parochial traditions. So what did I do? I ran back to the safe circle of my parents and friends. Turkey seems to be on a similar path, seeking solace in the old and the familiar. It takes courage to change. It requires civic maturity too. As democracies go, we are toddlers, not even teens. It's been just over some thirty years since we declared our republic and a democratic form of government. Maybe we need time to grow."

"You may be right," Ayla agreed. "We are a new and inexperienced democracy. My worry is that the way the government is squandering Atatürk's legacy, we may not get the time needed to mature. What also worries me is that most of the countries which have gone through the process of nation-building and modernization did so after episodes of serious civil conflict. I didn't want to say this in front of your parents, but things are not going well in Ankara. I think this government is sowing the seeds of future troubles that may lead to civic strife. There are factions in this country who have never accepted or understood Atatürk's social reforms. They are hostile to everything you and I take for granted and hold dear. Unfortunately the government insists on making matters worse by using religion as a political tool, increasing the conflict between the Muslims and non-Muslims, the secular and the non-secular, the educated and the uneducated. It cannot end well."

"I'm so sorry to hear that Ayla," said Neri. "I've been so self-absorbed lately with my own problems that I have not followed things too closely."

"Don't apologize. You had every right to be self-absorbed, as you call it. I'm happy to see you looking so well. We have all missed our old Neri. I know you're going to be completely happy one of these days. I wish I could say the same for Turkey. Some say that the military is running out of patience and that they will soon interfere to protect our secular constitution. I don't know if this will be a good thing or not. It may work for a little while but in the end, as they say, people deserve the government they get, don't they?"

"I wish I knew," Neri said sadly, just as they heard Ayla's taxi rattling up on the cobblestones.

Neri's parents quietly waved goodbye to Ayla. Afterwards they stood on the balcony watching the Bosphorus flowing calmly without a single ripple like a smooth shiny blue ribbon. Neri was home safe and sound; as far as they were concerned, all was right with the world.

52

"**N**eri settled? That's an oxymoron if I've ever heard one," Ceylan had once quipped. But that's the image Neri was trying very hard to project about herself: settled, happy, steady, hard working...like a respectful, dependable old aunt. It fooled only those people who didn't know her.

When she first started shopping at the food stores in Arnavutköy, Neri's youth and beauty had attracted attention, particularly when the rumors about her being the sole owner of the renovated white house turned out to be true. Why is a young woman like her living all alone? Why isn't she married? Some said she has a broken heart; she's been jilted. Others said she must be a widow. But why live alone? She should be with her family. Maybe she did something immoral and the family threw her out. But her parents come and see her every week, don't they? So why are they leaving her by herself? That's one thing everyone agreed on, namely that no young woman should be living alone. Women needed protection.

Eventually the old biddies living in the dark houses down her street lost interest and stop saying "poor girl" whenever they saw her speeding down the hill on her bicycle to Arnavutköy for shopping. She was quiet, polite and friendly. So one by one, the men working in the food stalls, young and old, adopted her and became her protector. They discouraged their regulars from talking about her and in time the rumors ebbed away. They started calling her "*Neri Abla*". The butcher kept his best lamb chops for her. The fresh fruit stall owner sent her his newly-arrived cantaloupes guaranteed to be as sweet as honey. If she bought more than she could carry in her bicycle basket, they sent along one of the youngsters in the shop to carry her purchases home. She soon became another invisible face among the village crowd. She felt she belonged and called herself "*Arnavutköylü,*" a native of Arnavutköy.

The baker found her a young cleaning woman who came to her house twice a week. Neri soon discovered that the girl was from Bolu, a town in the mountains half way to Ankara, famous for its chefs. Her brother owned a little fish restaurant further up the Bosphorus which Neri and her parents frequented. The girl had inherited her family's cooking genes. Soon little Emine took over the duties of cook as well, something Neri was more than happy to relinquish.

With Emine doing most of the cooking, Neri started giving little dinner parties for her family and friends. They came bearing gifts and were all impressed with her little house and the view. They discussed and agreed among themselves that Neri was finally over her problems and looked settled, at least physically. But they also suspected that she was still emotionally weakened inside.

Her friends took her out, introduced her to eligible bachelors. She remained uninterested, untouched. She went to parties, the theater, and concerts. It was all déjà vu, a repetition of what she had gone through after graduating from college. She started resenting the speeding tempo of her social life. It seemed to intensify her loneliness. She felt less lonely when she was alone, but she was grateful to her friends. She knew they had her best interests at heart, whatever they were!

She noticed that Leyla was the only non-matchmaker in the group. How long had this been going on? And why wasn't she pushing her like the others to be more sociable, more responsive to all the young men lining up for her? Leyla had something up her sleeve, but Neri had no idea what. And since when had Leyla acquired that funny I-know-something-that-you-don't-know smirk on her face? It was time for Neri to find out.

They were at a party at Selma's new flat. Her husband Feyzi had finished his military service and had opened a health care clinic with four other physician friends. The party was to celebrate its success.

It was a young crowd, bachelors and single girls still outnumbering the married couples. As usual Neri was attracting her share of attention which she found both flattering and annoying. Finally she was able to slip through the crowd and sit by Leyla who was pregnant again.

"I really like Sermet, Feyzi's partner. Do you know him?" Neri asked.

"No, I just met him."

"He's so handsome and so polite," Neri added.

"Yes, isn't he?"

"Selma says he comes from a very rich old family."

"That's nice."

"He also seems to like me."

"How wonderful!"

"Maybe I should go and dance with him?

"Suit yourself."

Neri exploded. "What's wrong with you? I thought you wanted me to get interested in men. Now you sound as if you couldn't care less. How come?"

"The last time we talked, you told me to butt out of your life, don't you remember? So this is me butting out."

"Since when do you ever listen to me? Come on, Leyla, what's going on?"

That odd smirk appeared on Leyla's face again. "Nothing's going on. Don't become paranoid!"

"What is it you're keeping from me? I know you too well. You're up to something. What is it?"

"That's for you to discover and me to hide!"

"Oh, God!" moaned Neri. "We're back to childish games again, aren't we?"

"Heh, heh," smiled Leyla, unresponsive as a sphinx.

53

In mid-August, Neri found out what Leyla was up to. It had been an unusually hot day but Neri's little house was exposed to breezes blowing from the Black Sea and stayed refreshingly cool. Now that the late afternoon sun had almost disappeared behind the hills, Neri could sense the approaching fall. The lilac trees on her lawn had lost their blossoms, but the rose bushes her father had planted were ablaze with flowers as if daring the fall to come. Overhead, storks were circling, testing their wings for their winter departure.

Neri was on her knees playing with the cats when the doorbell rang and surprised her. She hadn't heard a car arriving and very few of her friends ever walked up the steep hill. She ran downstairs and opened the door. Her hand went to her mouth to prevent her heart from jumping out of her body.

"Hello Neri," he said, beaming and caught her in his arms as she staggered. She could not focus her eyes and her head was spinning. Neri could not feel her feet either but she held onto his arms, his lips, his familiar breath...She opened her eyes and smiled. The painful emptiness, the hollowness inside her that she had endured for so long was gone. She was whole again.

He swooped her up and carried her upstairs. When she told him "one more flight," he groaned and laughed. She clung to him tight to make sure this was not a daydream. But it was not. It was real, more real, more intense, more immediate than she could ever have imagined. She gave herself willingly and lovingly with a passion she'd forgotten she was capable of feeling.

When Neri woke up, her bedroom was bathed by the full moon rising over the hills on the Asian side of the Bosphorus. She was lying on top of him, his arms holding her tight on his chest. She tried to slide down.

Bill opened his eyes and said "Don't you dare move." She laughed. She felt dizzy with happiness.

There was movement on the floor. He turned and looked down. The two cats stood still in the moonlight, their faces blank and eyes staring hard at him. Their tails whipped side to side in perfect sync.

"Hello," he said, "who are you?"

"They're Tekir and Pamuk. Tekir is what we call tiger-striped cats, and the white Persian is called Pamuk, meaning 'cotton,' for obvious reasons." The cats bobbed their heads in unison in response to her voice.

"Hello Tekir and Pamuk," Bill called the cats in his sweetest, friendliest voice. They growled and continued glaring at him without moving. "Oops. Am I going to have trouble with them?"

She assured him with a big kiss. "No, they love anyone...who I love."

"Maybe if I show them just how much I love you," Bill answered and started doing things that curled her toes again.

"Stop it," she giggled. "We need to talk."

"We do? Why?"

"Because I have tons of questions. Like what are you doing here? And how come you knew where I lived."

"It's a long story. You're sure you want to waste this wonderful romantic moonlit night, which by the way is as big as the one we wished upon years ago, remember? We can talk tomorrow morning, I'm not going anywhere."

"That's my point, isn't it?" Neri insisted. "Why aren't you going anywhere? How come you're even here?"

"Oh well, if you insist." He pulled her gently off his chest and cuddled her on his side, close to his body.

"Bill," she smiled. "I need to breathe and see your face." He grinned and rolled even closer as the two cats jumped up on the bed, trying to find their night-time spots. Neri patted and coaxed them to settle at the foot of the bed. They were not happy but they curled together, and after a cold penetrating look at Bill, started purring.

"You sleep with all that noise?" Bill said.

"It's strangely soothing. You'll get used to it. So... start talking. How come you knew where I lived?"

"Leyla told me."

"Leyla?" Neri nearly jumped out of bed.

Both cats hissed and spat at Bill. "Neri, don't make movements like that. I have a feeling they already want to kill me."

"Don't change the subject. What do you mean Leyla told you?"

"Leyla has been in touch with me ever since Oxford. I don't know what I'd have done without her. When you left without leaving me any real hope, I was devastated. Leyla kept me going. She made me believe that things could work out. She was certain you wouldn't get involved with anyone else and advised me to concentrate on my studies and get my degree as soon as possible. But when I heard about your accident and your long months of recuperation, I thought I'd lose my mind. My first impulse was to ditch everything and run to your side but Leyla said no and kept me relatively sane by keeping me informed about your recovery. Then I heard about your divorce and it became very hard to listen to Leyla, but again she was able to convince me that it was not a good idea, and that you needed time alone to go over the trauma of the last year before you could make any life-changing decisions."

"She did, did she?" said Neri, totally stunned.

"Leyla is really a wonderful person Neri. She loves you like a sister and wants the best for you. So does Bulent."

"Bulent?" Neri chocked. "You talked to Bulent too?"

"Yes," he laughed. "He was in England about six months ago, and we talked about the possibility of my getting a teaching job in Robert College."

"Teaching job in Robert College? Really?"

"Yes, Bulent helped me get an interview with their recruitment officer, and to make a long story short, in September I'll be teaching at the illustrious Robert College which used to supply you with all your boyfriends," he teased, kissing the tip of her nose.

She was white as a ghost—to the point where Bill was not sure she was still breathing.

"Neri, please take a deep breath. You look as though you're going to pass out."

"You'll be teaching at Robert College in September," she repeated, "for how long?"

"Right now it's a three-year contract but don't worry, I'll behave myself and do my very best to please them so they'll be willing to renew it."

Neri was stunned. This was just too much for her to take in. She gazed up at the moon. It was high now, and the Bosphorus was like a flow of silver lava. Her surrounding world looked much the same, but she couldn't believe Bill was real. This had to be a dream.

"Neri, look at me. I've waited all these long years. Will you marry me?"

"Yes," she said. "Yes, I will, I will!"

Bill wasn't sure what woke him. Maybe it was the cats who kept on jumping on the bed and trying to settle down. He stared at Neri whose still face looked like a delicate statue in the moonlight with her long eyelashes casting shadows on her cheekbones. He felt he could watch her forever and never tire. This incredibly powerful connection between them was nothing but a miracle. He had never been able to explain it. It had hit him like a transforming bolt of lightning when she'd first walked into her father's office and stared at him with those almond-shaped eyes, making him feel as though he'd lost and found himself at the same time.

Since then, every step Bill had taken and every hardship he'd endured had been for Neri and for this very moment. He smiled and relished the moment, leaning his head back on the pillow.

Even when he had given in to despair—Bill remembered— the connection had remained strong, giving him strength and pulling him through. Now every cell in his body was humming with renewed energy. He felt completely reborn. Neri was his sustaining fire...his new life.

As if hearing his thoughts, Neri opened her eyes and gazed at him, her eyes reflecting a thousand fragments of moonlight. She smiled sleepily and Bill bent down and started kissing her.

The sun was beginning to peek out beyond the hills on the Anatolian side of the Bosphorus when Neri woke up and quietly slipped out of bed without disturbing Bill. He was sleeping deeply, exhausted. No wonder, she smiled to herself. She ran downstairs and called Leyla.

"Where have you been?" Leyla said, sounding pleased with herself. "I've been waiting for your phone call since last night. Still making love?"

"Oh, be quiet Leyla" Neri laughed. "You've been arranging my life again, haven't you?"

"You don't need to thank me. I just did it so that all of us can at last have some peace and quiet. You don't realize what a heavy burden it is to be your friend, Neri!"

"I don't know how to thank you Leyla. You gave me my life back. But I still have my parents to deal with."

"No, you don't!" Leyla laughed. "Bulent and I have been talking to them. They've changed their opinion of Bill. Do you know what your father said? He said that after playing chess with Bill, he thought Bill was a nice man but lacked a killer's instinct. Now, he has to admit that he grossly underestimated Bill's determination. They are amazed at what Bill had accomplished with his life, all for the love of their own daughter, which makes it even sweeter for them, right? Did you know that he's been taking Turkish lessons for the past couple of years? Talk about dedication! He is sneaky though, isn't he? He never mentioned it. I bet he understood everything we were saying in Turkish in Oxford. Anyway, your parents were very impressed. Your mother shed tons of tears when she met him yesterday."

"What do you mean, yesterday? Bill was in İstanbul yesterday?" Neri was stammering like a child now.

"Yes, he arrived yesterday. We had official business to attend to, although it was really very hard persuading him to stay away from you; he was like a tiger in a cage, restless and impatient, but he calmed down eventually and behaved beautifully when he met your parents." Neri was speechless. It was all too much to take in.

"Your parents are happy, and they approve of Bill. You don't have to worry about them any longer. And, here comes the big news, we've got your marriage license all ready. Do you know that you're getting married in two days?"

"I am?" cried Neri, ready to faint. "How could you get the license without us?"

"My father pulled a lot of strings. By the way, he wishes you the best. And your friends from Ankara are coming to your wedding too."

"Who? What?" was all Neri could say.

"What do you mean who? The Millers, of course, and Ayla and Mete. I was told Tom and Christie had returned home. By the way, Maude was so happy to hear the news on the phone that she started crying and kept on muttering something about 'so that's why'. Do you know what she meant?"

"No, I don't. You can ask her when she's here but, Leyla, how am I ever going to thank you enough?"

"Don't get all soft and mushy on me. We still have a lot to do. Bulent and I will be there early afternoon, and so will the girls. Later your parents and other family members will be arriving."

"I am stunned! Does the whole world know what's going on? Am I the only one who's been kept in the dark?"

"Well, yes," Leyla said, matter-of-factly. "We didn't want any histrionics."

"Oh, Leyla, you're impossible but I love you."

"Keep your love for your husband-to-be. Oh, did I forget to tell you? Today is your engagement party!"

Neri ran upstairs and jumped into bed, waking Bill up. He smiled and opened his arms. Happier than she'd ever been, Neri wished with all her heart that every morning for the rest of her life she'd wake up feeling exactly like this. And so as not to tempt fate, she leaned over Bill's body and knocked on the bedside table three times, pulling her right ear after each knock. Bill erupted with laughter. He was back in Turkey, at last.

54

It was April again. There was a hint of lilacs in the air. Neri was on the balcony with the cats, waiting for Bill to come up the hill. She loved watching him. In bright days, when he stepped into the clearing out of the shadows of the dark houses, his blond hair shone like gold in the sun.

They'd been married nearly eight months now. Still getting to know each other, each step was bringing them closer. It was a marriage of body and mind. She no longer felt the need to hide her feelings, opinions, weaknesses and strengths. He loved Neri just the way she was, and she adored him, her love growing more intense each day.

The cats saw Bill before she did. They made little contented sounds and looked up at her. She waved. He beamed back, without waving. He was carrying a large macramé bag in each hand full of groceries. He loved shopping at the food stalls in Arnavutköy on his way home from work. The tradesmen there had taken an immediate liking to him, relieved that Neri, their favorite customer, did not have a shady past but a nice, albeit a foreign, husband. All the gossiping women who thought Neri lived alone because of this or that outrageous reason were now congratulating themselves for having predicted this outcome. And what was wrong with having a foreign husband? He obviously cared enough about their country to learn Turkish, didn't he? Everyone was now calling him *"Bill Abi"*, older brother, including Neri just to tease him now and then.

Today as usual Bill had stopped at his favorite patisserie and bought some cakes and savories. He had gotten used to the Turkish tradition of having salty goods with tea along with the sweets. Neri's parents were coming in the afternoon and he was looking forward to his chess game with Metin. It was still hard to beat Metin but he was getting better each time. He knew his deep undying love for Neri had secured a permanent place in their hearts and the unease he used to feel in their presence had long vanished. They treated him like a son, amazed at how easily he had assimilated into the Turkish culture and way of life.

On the other hand, not used to having things go so smoothly, Neri kept on having anxiety spells which she tried to quell by knocking on wood and whispering *"Maşallah"* many times a day whenever no one was looking.

They were both working in the kitchen arranging the cakes and the savories on plates when the doorbell rang. It was too early for her parents. Neri opened the door and gasped with delight. It was Stan, holding a beautifully wrapped package in his hand.

"Sorry I missed your wedding," he said, kissing her on both cheeks. He looked tanned and a little thinner.

"When did you come back from Diyarbakir?' Neri asked. Maude had more or less hinted that his staying in Diyarbakir was by choice and not a job requirement. The implication was clear. He needed to be as far away from Neri as possible.

"Two weeks ago," he smiled, looking at her. "You look great. Marriage agrees with you." He flushed and added: "This marriage, I mean."

"I know what you mean, Stan. Thank you." She turned and took the hand of her husband who was standing at the kitchen door, looking at them with interest.

"Bill, this is Stan, a friend from Ankara. Stan, this is Bill, my husband."

The two men shook hands. Standing across from each other, the same height, the same slim body, they could have been separated twins, except Bill was fair and Stan dark. A shadow of understanding passed Stan's face which Bill caught. They both turned and stared at Neri. She could feel herself blushing to the roots of her hair. "Tea anyone?" she asked and disappeared into the kitchen.

"Let's go upstairs," suggested Bill, leading the way.

"What an amazing view," Stan murmured, looking at the Bosphorus. "You could live here all your life without ever wanting to leave."

Bill suspected he was not talking about the scenery only. "You've known Neri how long?"

"Ever since she came to Ankara with her first husband," Stan replied. He glanced at Bill and felt compelled to respond to a question in his eyes: "Ismet was not a good husband. But even if he had been an ideal husband, I don't think it would have worked anyway. We all suspected her heart was elsewhere."

"But you still fell in love with her, didn't you?" It was not an accusation.

"Can you blame me?" Stan looked at him directly. They were silent for a minute.

"Look, I'm glad you two have worked it out. She's an incredible woman and you are the luckiest man in the world. And I can see that you know it too. I'm happy for both of you."

When Neri walked in carrying a tray of tea cups and plates of savories, she saw them shaking hands, her two favorite men. Somehow the image would stay with her forever.

Much to Neri's relief Bill never asked her about Stan except to say that he liked him. It was dark now. Her parents had come and gone. The stars were out and the lights on the opposite shore twinkled on the Bosphorus. It was quiet, as quiet as that moment when the curtain goes up on stage and the audience is hushed, waiting for the play, the drama, to suspend their disbelief.

"You know, Neri," Bill said all of a sudden, "we never had a honeymoon. As much as I love sitting here watching the Bosphorus flow by, we should tear ourselves away and go have a proper honeymoon someplace. How about Tekirdağ? Or better still England? My parents, my whole family, are eagerly waiting to see you."

"Not Tekirdağ, please! I don't want to activate that gossip mill ever again, but England is a great idea. How about going to Oxford for our honeymoon? Can we afford the Reynolds? I'd love to stay there." Her eyes were warm and alive with the memory.

"Then we'll go and meet your family, and you can show me your Newcastle."

"That's what I was hoping." He pulled her closer. "That would be wonderful, don't you think?"

"That'll be great, and *I am* eager to meet your family. How about after the schools close in June?"

"You're sure?"

"Yes," Neri replied, "we'll go in June."

"*İnşallah*," said Bill.

Celebrating last day of school in Bebek, Istanbul.

The inspiration for Leyla is on the far left and the author is on the far right.

Also by Parkgate Press (Dionysus Books)

www.parkgatepress.com
www.dionysusbooks.com

Tom Robertson

NAPOLEON Vs. THE TURK

A play based on the chess match of Napoleon Bonaparte and 'The Turk,' the famous 18th century chess automaton. Who will triumph, the master tactician or the technology? First performed at the Toronto Fringe Festival.

Thomas Laird

THE UNDERGROUND DETECTIVE

Danny Mangan of Chicago Homicide is on the trail of a serial killer...while his own life is falling apart. By the author of CUTTER, SEASON OF THE ASSASSIN and BLACK DOG, reviewed by *The Washington Post*, *The Chicago Sun-Times* and *The Independent on Sunday*.

Acknowledgements

I'm so thankful to all my friends, Lena Astin, Nafia Ülgen, Yüksel Şekili, Carol Holmstrom, Ayla Simon, Şehvar Cağlayan and Belma Baskett for their enthusiasm and support of my first draft and my Duke University friend Frank Gado whose sharp criticism and insightful comments spurred me on to another year of rewrites. I don't know how to thank my dear friend Tony Robson for coming to my rescue with his last-minute proof reading, but many, many thanks Tony. My thanks also go to Yüksel İnel who designed my book cover with Dionysus Books.

I'm very grateful to my editor and publisher Matt Fullerty who cleaned up my prose, getting rid of hundreds of unnecessary adjectives and other writing sins of a novice. And last but not least, my love and gratitude to my husband for his undying encouragement and patience and for never complaining about eating nothing but peanut butter sandwiches for nearly two years. My parents taught me to dream but it is my husband who let my dreams go wild.

Also by Parkgate Press (Dionysus Books)

www.mattfullerty.com

www.dionysusbooks.com
www.parkgateoriginals.com

THE KNIGHT OF NEW ORLEANS
The Pride and the Sorrow of Paul Morphy

A quiet boy is born in New Orleans with a
spellbinding gift: he can beat anyone at chess.
But what happens when love, desire and
ambition intervene?

THE MURDERESS AND THE HANGMAN

The story of female killer Kate Webster, the man
who hanged her and the missing head found 132
years later in Sir David Attenborough's garden.

Katharine E. Willers

WHAT TOOK ME OUT TO THE BALL GAME

The Determinants of Attendance of
Major League Baseball Games from 1989–1999
and the Implications of the 1994 Labor Strike

Jennifer M. Fullerty, PhD

LIFELONG LEARNING

Post-Compulsory Education and the
University for Industry: A Case Study

An analysis of UK LearnDirect educational policy

About the Author

Engin Inel Holmstrom was born and raised in Turkey. She graduated from the American College for Girls in Arnavutköy, İstanbul and received her masters and doctorate degrees in Sociology from Duke University, Durham, North Carolina.

Engin has over fifty professional publications, mostly dealing with higher education and public policy. She has lectured widely in the United States on issues concerning Turkish women, gender equality and Atatürk's reforms.

Her hobby is painting. Retired now, she lives in Leesburg, Virginia with her husband and two cats.

Loveswept is her first novel.

www.ingramcontent.com/pod-product-compliance
Lightning Source LLC
Chambersburg PA
CBHW070548130626
46556CB00001B/63